God and Uncle Dale

God and Uncle Dale

By Lester Bauman

Rod and Staff Publishers, Inc.
P.O. Box 3, Hwy. 172
Crockett, Kentucky 41413
Telephone: (606) 522-4348

Printed in U.S.A

ISBN 978-07399-2362-7

Catalog no. 2246

4 5 6 7 8 — 26 25 24 23 22 21 20 19 18 17

Contents

Author's Introduction

My parents joined a conservative Mennonite church a few years after the time pictured in the setting of this book. I was barely a teenager at the time, and I had no idea what heartache and trauma the founding families of our group had faced just a few short years before. Since then, however, I have talked with many people about those times.

I have been especially interested in the feelings and experiences of the young people who were caught in the vortex of the dying Mennonite conferences as they went down into apostasy. Some years ago, I had the privilege to become more closely acquainted with several people who were in their teens during this time. Many of the stories and situations in this account are based on their memories, though they have been adapted to fit the situation pictured here. Some of the happenings are filler, of course, but are true to life.

I tried to make sure that the setting of this account is realistic. However, for various reasons, I have watered down or omitted the details of some situations typically faced by godly youth caught in those settings. For instance, I only hinted at the extent of the immorality that existed within the Mennonite Church in some communities during those times.

This is more than a story—Dale and Sheila symbolize dozens of youth in many different times and places. Thank God for those who stood the test. Let your heart be broken for the ones who did not. There have been some of the first and many of the second.

During the writing of this book, I was tempted to twist reality and give this book the happy ending that many readers would expect. But I could not change the ending and retain the symbolism. You see, for most of the youth of those times, *there was no happy ending*. For whatever reasons, they made wrong or unwise choices and had to suffer the consequences. Almost all of them felt that the way back was too hard, and today many of their children and grandchildren are lost.

Most of those who read this book will find the setting hard to understand. Those who have been raised within secure families in a conservative setting have never faced what Dale and Sheila faced. *May God grant that you never need to.* Yet, all of us face times when we need to stand for truth alone. The tragedy of this story has been repeated over and over far too often, in some form or other. Unless we continue to appreciate and embrace Biblically conservative positions, such will be replayed in our churches today.

I firmly believe that even if we are part of a Scriptural church, we still need genuine commitment to God and help from Him to succeed spiritually. We have among us too many nice people who want to do what is right, but who are not quite committed enough to pass the crucial tests of life.

In the end, wanting to do what is right will not be good enough.

—Lester Bauman
Tilley, Alberta

Prelude

A Visit With Uncle Dale

"And further, by these, my son, be admonished: of making many books there is no end."
—Ecclesiastes 12:12

I have always wanted to write a book. You see, people love to read, and it is a marvel the way a good writer can take a person to a different world by putting words on paper. Writing seems a little like a miracle. So maybe it's no wonder that I finally decided that I would like to try writing this book.

It is also no wonder that I decided to write about Uncle Dale, but I might have to explain a bit so that you understand what I mean. Uncle Dale is one of those unique individuals that you really have to meet in order to understand. He has gone through many tough times in life, and some people will tell you that he's a bit cynical. But he isn't, really. It is just that he has seen so much that he has learned to read people. He can tell a hypocrite a hundred feet away, all the way across the yard from his old wicker rocking chair, which sits on the back porch of his old farmhouse.

There are many so-called religious people in the world nowadays. But so many of them are hypocrites, it seems. They talk a lot about trusting the Lord and doing His will and about how good God is to them, when all along they are living for self, grumbling at their high credit card bills, and trusting in their insurance policies. I guess Uncle Dale is a bit old-fashioned in the eyes of such people. But he believes in living out the Bible in everyday life. He does not have a lot of patience with artificial people and hypocrites, but if you really want to serve the Lord and do what's right, he's one of the finest people you'll ever meet.

Uncle Dale and I have been friends ever since I was old enough to totter from my mother's arms to his knee. He led me to the Lord when I was fourteen, and it was his advice that kept me from leaving our little church in town for a liberal Mennonite church when I was twenty. And when I was twenty-two, it was his advice that gave me the courage to strike up a friendship with the girl I married several years later.

In fact, going to Uncle Dale for advice became a habit for me, and we became close friends in the process. Through the years, he has told me so many stories about his younger years that I almost feel as if I had lived through a lot of those times with him.

But my favorite story is how Uncle Dale had to decide whether to stick with the church he had been brought up in or to follow his Christian convictions. Even back then, when he was in his early twenties, Uncle Dale had strong convictions about following the teachings of the Bible literally. But his church didn't, and many of the young folks scoffed at his feelings and called him a goody-goody.

He had told me this story a few times, but a while ago when I went to see Uncle Dale, I told him that I wanted to hear the story again. He chuckled at this because he knew that I knew it almost as well as he did. But I wanted something a bit different this time. I wanted to know how he felt about what happened and why he did what he did.

Uncle Dale sobered down in a hurry when I put it to him that way. That was quite personal. I knew that, but then, I had shared my personal feelings with Uncle Dale many times, and he knew that too.

He leaned back in his old rocker, with his eyes fastened on a little cloud in the distance, and I could tell that his mind was going back through the years. When he finally spoke, his voice was quiet. I can remember his words yet. "That's a story that I've never really told anyone," he said. "But we've been friends for a long time, and maybe the story will do you some good. It was not easy, son, and I almost didn't make it. But God helped me through it."

He hesitated for a bit, which was unusual for him. He is usually a spontaneous talker, and you often can't get a word in edgewise. But he finally continued. "In order for you to really understand what I went through, I first have to tell you about a girl called Sheila Lawrence. . . ."

1

Who Is Sheila Lawrence?

"For man also knoweth not his time:
as the fishes that are taken in an evil net,
and as the birds that are caught in the snare;
so are the sons of men snared in an evil time,
when it falleth suddenly upon them."
—Ecclesiastes 9:12

It was 1960!

From the perspective of the common man of the world, 1960 was the best of times. It was a time of change and revolution—politically, socially, financially, and spiritually. From the Christian perspective, however, it was a time of catastrophe—so many people were losing their faith and their convictions. The world and the church were traveling away from God at a breathtaking pace. But the world was so fascinating that few worried about the Christian perspective.

It was 1960, the year that Quaker-influenced Richard Nixon lost his first bid to become president of the United States by 112,800 votes. John F. Kennedy—rich, flamboyant, and Catholic—was elected instead. He was later assassinated, but in 1960 that was still future, and the aura was positive and progressive. Things were good, and could only get better, in the minds of many Americans.

It was 1960, the year that Elvis Presley, the musical phenomenon of the fifties, was released from the army and had started to rebuild his career, skyrocketing to almost overnight fame for the second time, even if the traditionalist status quo hated him. Building on his fame, the rock music revolution that climaxed in Woodstock less than a decade later was just around the corner. Already, in England, a group of young musicians was sharpening its musical skills in preparation for becoming the world's most famous singing group. They became so famous, in fact, that before the end of the decade one of the band members would boast truthfully that they were "more popular than God." The Beatles went on to become the gurus of a "counterculture of hedonism and uninhibited experimentation"—the idols of a whole generation of youth going wrong.

It was 1960. The second of the world's wars to end all wars had been fought and mostly forgotten, but the Vietnam War with its draft dodgers and free-loving hippie generation was just around the corner. Postwar prosperity was booming, and the American dream of "a chicken for every pot and a car in every garage" had become a reality for many. The stock market was climbing, and the bull ruled. The Dirty Thirties were a memory only to the older generation, and people were getting rich on borrowed money once again. Optimism ruled, and nothing could go wrong!

It was 1960, and the technology of the twentieth century had transformed the face of North America in less than fifty short years. Already Alan Shepard and NASA were working on the space program that saw him become the first American in outer space, and which would climax in another historic first—the first manned flight to the moon. The man of the streets expected that the new technology would shortly turn his life into a heaven on earth, and some even talked about personal helicopters and automobiles that guided themselves down superhighways to fantastic destinations. It is true (though few would admit it) that some still remembered Hiroshima and lay awake in the wee hours of the night, worrying about a future nuclear holocaust, but most reassured themselves that western civilization was supreme and man undefeatable—the master of his own destiny.

It was 1960, but to twenty-two-year-old Dale Eberly, most of this seemed distant. He was a serious-minded young man and an active member of a denomination known for its conservatism. He lived in Alberta, the most traditional province of a conservative nation—Canada. In fact, Dale seemed almost totally unaffected by most of the dreams and events that made 1960 unique. As an isolated Canadian farm boy, he knew little, and cared less, about the inner workings of American politics and finance.

The vastly varied worlds of religion, music, and technology—headed on a direct collision course—were curiosities but not really part of his everyday life. In fact, to Dale, 1960 was merely another year, good because life is good when you are young and healthy and love the Lord. Unknown to him, however, these mysterious forces and others were rapidly changing his world—had already changed it, in fact, even though he didn't realize it. Neither his world nor his church would ever be the same again as they had been just a few short years before.

It was 1960. Revolution and catastrophe were in the air, and spiritual storm clouds were just around the corner. But all of this was far from Dale's mind as he opened the back door of the family farmhouse and strode across the back yard to his car. Tall and athletic, he was the picture of health and youth. He had slung a jacket over his one shoulder because even in September, the Alberta evenings became chilly. He was bareheaded, and his hair was cropped in late-fifties style—unaffected as yet by the long, Beatles-inspired hairstyles, which would sweep North America in the next five or six years. Before jumping into his car to leave for the Saturday evening MYF[1] gathering, he tossed his jacket into the passenger seat. Then he turned and waved to his parents, Richard

---

1 MYF was an abbreviation for Mennonite Youth Fellowship. Youth groups gathered weekly for various activities—sometimes games, sometimes work bees, and sometimes Bible studies. The initial purpose of MYF was to revive the church through its youth, but by 1960, it had deteriorated in many congregations to merely providing entertainment.

and Carrie, who stood together at the window, watching him.

Richard sighed and turned from the window as Dale's car, a '54 Chevrolet, half skidded and half lurched out the muddy, rutted lane, the engine roaring in low gear. "I'm glad our children have friends, and I'm glad Dale is interested in church activities," he said wistfully to his wife. He passed his fingers through his graying hair, and the worry marks in his forehead deepened. "I just wish I could be sure that his friends and the church are doing the right thing for him."

Several hours later, the evening's activities were pretty well finished, and the young people were having some refreshments and were socializing in the church basement. Dale was relaxing with some friends when he noticed her. A new face wasn't that abnormal, but this girl had an aura about her that attracted his attention. That in itself was somewhat unusual, since Dale was normally quite unaffected by girls, whether pretty or otherwise. In fact, his friends periodically made somewhat snide remarks about his bachelor tendencies and despaired of ever getting him interested in the fairer side of the house. So it made a bit of a sensation when Dale suddenly sat up straighter and asked the boy beside him, "Say, Allister, who's the new girl over there?"

Allister McLelland, Dale's best friend, was a black-haired, cheerful-looking boy of about twenty. He looked surprised. "Dale, I didn't expect it of you. That's a *girl* you're looking at."

Dale grinned and took the teasing with his usual good nature. "I'm not blind," he pointed out. "But I haven't seen her around before."

One of the other boys in the circle popped to his feet. "Say, we'd better follow up on this before he loses interest again," he said dramatically. "I'll tell her you want to take her home tonight, Dale. Then you can find out all you want about her."

The laughter from the circle of boys drowned out Dale's protests, and his self-appointed Good Samaritan—a boy called George—was gone before he could stop him. Casual dates after youth activities were common enough, and most young folks and their parents didn't think twice about them. Dale's parents, however, frowned on them, and Dale himself wasn't really very interested. He was friends with lots of the girls, and was even well liked by most of them. It was nothing new for him to chat with one or the other of the local girls after an MYF evening or after church. But he looked at dating and courtship more seriously than most, and hadn't gotten involved in the dating game.

This time, however, he was stuck. The new girl—whose name he still hadn't managed to find out—was assured by George, and by the girls who were with her when he came with his message, that Dale was the safest and most eligible boy in the crowd. Not knowing that it was a joke, she glanced over at Dale, smiled, and then accepted the invitation graciously. Since he didn't want to embarrass her in front of everyone, he went along with the joke. And of course his friends escorted them to his car to make sure that he had no chance of backing out.

Several minutes later, Dale and the new girl were alone in his car, and he was maneuvering it out of the church parking lot. They grinned at each other, but both were a bit shy, due to the sudden turn of events. She was a pleasant and talkative girl in her own right, but she had caught on by now that something a little unusual was in the wind, so she waited for Dale to start the conversation.

Dale was both genial and outgoing, and seldom had a problem getting to know someone, so starting a conversation was normally no hardship for him. But this situation was a little outside his frame of reference, and he wasn't quite sure how to handle it properly. He figured that he had better say *something,* however, before the silence became too embarrassing. So he said the first thing that came to his mind. "Who are you, anyway?"

Then he gulped, realizing how silly it must have sounded to her. But the new girl's laughter tinkled through the car. "You mean you really don't know?" she asked incredulously. "I guess I haven't left much of an impression. This was the third MYF that I've been to, and we've been to all the church services here in the last several weeks."

Dale gulped again. Then he laughed too. "I wasn't at the meeting a week ago," he said. "And the one before that was a joint one with Carstairs, so there were lots of strange faces. I thought tonight was the first you were around."

"So is it normal for you to welcome new girls into the group in this way?" she asked him curiously.

Dale's ears got a trifle pink, and he knew he would need to do some careful explaining to bail himself out of this situation. He pulled up to the stop sign at the edge of town and turned left, while he was trying to get his thoughts together.

The new girl laughed again. "You're not bashful by any chance?" she asked cheerily. "And by the way, we live south of town, not north. Or are you taking the long way around so we have more time to talk?"

This time Dale's ears turned totally red, and he slowed down, looking for a farmer's lane where he could turn around. "Sorry about that," he said. "I honestly don't know who you are or where you live. I'm a bit befuddled, I guess."

He managed to turn the car around and head in the right direction before continuing. "And no, I don't usually ask a new girl for a date to welcome her to the group. Actually, I don't normally date at all. My parents prefer that I not get involved in casual dating."

She sensed his embarrassment and looked at him more seriously. "So what is going on then?" she asked. "I take it that you decided to bend the rules for once, but not because you were so impressed by me."

Dale sensed that she was trying to make it easier for him, and he relaxed a little. "I didn't intend to take you home at all," he admitted. "That was George's idea of a joke."

She looked startled. "I'm sorry," she said. "I didn't mean to put you on the spot by telling him I'd go home with you. We were used to casual dating where I came from. I didn't realize that it wasn't the thing to do here."

"Oh, it's common enough here too," he assured her. "But our family doesn't usually get involved. My parents feel that dating should be left until a person is ready to find God's will for marriage, and that casual dating cheapens a person's view of marriage. Dating and courtship are too serious to be turned into a game, in my mind. I could have said something, but I didn't want to embarrass you in front of everyone by turning you down. I figured it would be better to take you home and explain what happened. My parents will understand."

She was quiet a bit before replying. "Thanks," she said sincerely. "It would have been awkward."

Dale was opening his mouth to reply, when she quickly put her hand to her mouth. "Oh," she gasped, "the next lane is ours. I forgot to tell you which farm we live on!"

Dale jammed on the brakes and just barely managed to negotiate the corner safely. He pulled to a stop beside the house with a sigh of relief. "Well, it's been an adventurous evening anyway," he said with a chuckle. "Though your father might ask some questions about my driving, the way we took that corner."

She smiled. "Would you like to come in and meet my family?" she asked. "I have a feeling we're going to be friends, even if we don't date. After an introduction like this, how could we help it?"

Dale smiled too. "You're probably right," he admitted. "But I'd better get home. I'm later than usual already, and tomorrow is church. Maybe I can meet your family then."

She nodded and opened the car door. "By the way," he added, a little desperately, "what *is* your name? I still don't know who you are!"

Her infectious laugh was genuine. "I'm Sheila Lawrence," she replied. "I'm nineteen, and we moved in from Ontario three weeks ago. My parents are Donald and Martha, and I have two younger brothers. I'll introduce you tomorrow." She closed the door behind her and was gone.

For some reason, Dale had a hard time sleeping that evening.

Uncle Dale rocked quietly for a moment, and then he looked at me as if wondering if I wanted him to continue. I did, and he closed his eyes and took a deep breath. . . .

Dale's parents did understand, though his father looked troubled when he told them the next morning what had happened. However, he didn't comment, other than to say, "I met the Lawrences last Sunday. I was hoping they would be a help to the situation here. But my impression so far is that they are even more liberal-minded than is normal in our setting here."

The look on his father's face startled Dale. He had noticed that troubled expression quite a bit the last while, and he wondered what his father was thinking of. And Sheila's family, liberal? That was a new thought. When he stopped to think of it though, he had to admit that Sheila had looked rather borderline last evening, wearing a shimmery, knee-length, variegated blue dress with a white leather belt and no cape. And she had worn her blond hair piled on her head in a rather realistic imitation of a haystack, as his father had remarked several times recently about some other girls. Of course she had a covering on top of it, but he had to admit it was pretty small. True, some of the girls dressed worse than that—a few were starting to regularly appear in a skirt and blouse. But still, Sheila's appearance put her into the liberal side of the crowd.

He was still pondering this as he drove to church. *Why didn't I notice before? She does fit into the more liberal crowd, somewhat. And liberal girls don't usually appeal to me like Sheila did. What was there about her that made me overlook that?*

Sheila met him in the lobby shortly after church. "Good morning," she greeted him pleasantly. "Have we met before?"

Dale grinned. "It seems to me we have—rather dramatically, actually," he replied. "Are your parents here this morning?"

"Yes, they are," she said. "They would like to meet you. My father thought our situation was pretty interesting. I'll try to find them if you want to wait here for a minute."

Forgetting for the moment his uneasy thoughts of that morning, Dale watched her slip away through the crowd.

Donald Lawrence was a large man, with an obviously

sanguine personality and a booming voice. It was easy to see from his mannerisms that he either was or had been a successful salesman. He reached out to shake Dale's hand with a genial smile when Sheila introduced Dale. "Well, well," he said, his voice warm. "So you're the young man who tried to take the corner of our lane on two wheels last night!"

Dale blushed a little as people looked in their direction, and he wished Donald would speak more quietly.

Sheila almost blushed as well. "Don't mind him," she told Dale, giving her father an affectionate glance. "He knows what happened." She looked across the crowd in the foyer. "There's my mother—I'll try to catch her too."

Donald smiled and clapped Dale on the back. "That's right," he said, speaking in a lower tone. "Sheila was quite impressed with you, I must say, for the short time that you spent together. Next time, come on in for some coffee. We like to meet our children's friends."

Dale felt a little overwhelmed by Donald's boisterous friendliness, and he was rather glad when Sheila returned with her mother. Martha could have been a carbon copy of Sheila, except for her age and slightly graying hair. Later, when Dale had a chance to think things over, he remembered that her appearance, including her hairstyle, matched Sheila's almost exactly. But he had little time for that now.

Martha greeted him cordially, taking his hand with both of hers. "I'm really pleased to meet you," she said, graciously acknowledging Sheila's introduction. "I almost felt as if I knew you already, after Sheila described your evening together. Thank you for looking after her so well. We're glad that our children are making good friends out here."

Dale smiled. "Well, I hope you folks like it here in Alberta," he said. "We'll probably see more of you."

"Say," Sheila's father said, "why don't you join us for lunch? We were thinking of going out to Knox's Steak House for one of their steak dinners."

Dale hesitated a little. He knew what his parents thought of eating out at a restaurant and especially on Sundays. Even though it was becoming increasingly common in the congregation, they had always avoided it.

Sheila noticed his hesitation and came to his rescue. "We don't want to make your plans for you," she said. "Maybe you had other plans for today."

He hesitated a bit more before answering circumspectly. "Actually, I know that my parents were planning to invite company today, and they like it when we're all home when we have company."

Sheila's mother nodded her head understandingly. "It's nice to have the family together like that," she said. "We like that too. But you must plan to come over sometime soon. Bring your whole family. We want to get to know the church people better."

"That's right," Donald boomed. "My job is out here now, and it looks like it will be permanent, so we'll see more of you and your family."

Dale's head spun a little as he drove home. *They treat*

me almost as if I were Sheila's boyfriend. They are a friendly family, but that does seem to be going a bit far. . . .

Then he remembered his earlier thoughts, and reviewed what he now knew about the Lawrence family. Sheila's mother, nice as she seemed, did not seem to have any more conviction for the traditional form of dress than Sheila did. It was true that not nearly all the women at church wore cape dresses anymore, but many of the ones Martha's age still did, at least for church. Martha, however, not only didn't wear a cape, but her dress, even to his inexperienced eye, had seemed to be tailored just a little too well for what he had been taught was modest.

And Sheila's father? It was hard to place him, but his professional suit-and-tie image and his boisterous mannerisms put him with the part of the congregation that Dale's family tended not to have much in common with.

In fact, Dale could hardly help but contrast Donald and Martha with his parents. Really, his parents had little in common with the Lawrences, from their effusive mannerisms to their meticulous appearance. He couldn't imagine his parents looking like the Lawrences. Nor, for that matter, could he imagine them greeting Sheila the way the Lawrences had greeted him. Certainly, his parents would have been friendly, but not so over-whelming.

Still, the Lawrences seemed to be a nice family. Maybe it didn't matter. He had noticed that in the last years outward appearances didn't seem to matter as much in the church as he thought they had when he was younger.

Hmm. I haven't thought about that very much before.

I guess things are changing. I wonder if it matters. I should ask my father what he thinks. Maybe that's why he seems so troubled the last while.

Sheila sure seems to be a nice girl though. I wonder if she could be the girl God wants for me. Maybe I ought to talk to my parents about that too. I'll have to introduce Sheila to them and see what they think.

2

Dale Talks to His Parents

"Dear Lord, take up the tangled strands,
Where we have wrought in vain."
—Mrs. F. G. Burroughs

Dale's parents had noticed his encounter with the Lawrences at church. Dale's father was especially concerned, since he had met Donald and knew what kind of personality he had. Several days later, when they were alone in the house, Richard and Carrie talked about it.

"The Lawrences are a very outgoing family," Richard told Carrie. "If we're not careful, they'll sweep Dale right off his feet. He's not used to such attention from people like that."

"I noticed that he was talking with them after church on Sunday," Carrie said. "What was going on? Donald seemed to have a lot to say to him."

"I think they look at him as an eligible suitor for

Sheila," Richard said. "Donald is a salesman for El-Tago, and he is apparently about as good as they come. He was his company's top salesman in Ontario, and they moved him out here to kick-start their western branch. What he doesn't know about manipulating people isn't worth knowing. Dale will be like putty in his hands if he decides he wants him for a son-in-law."

Carrie looked quite concerned. "But surely they won't do that," she said. "Sheila will surely want to have some say in what happens."

"I would have thought so," Richard said, seating himself at the kitchen table. "But some parents can be pretty pushy. I wish I knew what kind of girl Sheila really is." He hesitated and looked across the living room at his wife. "If only there was some way that we could get to know her better, without her parents around."

"I met her in town this morning," Carrie said, pulling out a chair across from Richard. "Actually, I was impressed with her. She was very friendly and went out of her way to talk to me. She seems spiritually-minded, compared with some of the girls at church. Maybe she just hasn't been taught some spiritual truths. Her parents certainly don't seem to be the kind who promote conservative values."

Richard nodded. "I know. I thought the same," he said. "However, we might just be fooling ourselves. I would really hate to see Dale get interested in a liberal girl. But I must admit, there are hardly any girls at church who would fit my ideal for him. Most of them really are not much different from Sheila. In fact, a number are definitely more borderline than she is. We have drifted so rapidly the last few years that it is hard to know what to recommend to our children. I dread to see what the future holds for our congregations in Alberta."

He bowed his head for a moment, and Carrie could see by his stooped shoulders how seriously he was taking the situation. When he looked up, there were tears in his eyes. "I'll be honest with you," he said huskily. "I am horribly afraid for our family sometimes. What future can there be for our grandchildren, the way the church is going?"

Carrie looked troubled. "Is there really nothing we can do? Could we move somewhere else before it's too late?"

Richard got to his feet and looked out the kitchen window, across the fields of his farm. "I'd give everything I owned for a chance to be part of a Scriptural church setting going the right direction," he said. "But I don't know of anywhere that it's really much better. In fact, the Alberta churches tend to be more conservative than most. We are in the middle of a wholesale departure from the faith in North America. There might be some churches in places like Pennsylvania that are a few years behind us, but they're all going the same direction, as far as I can tell. So there is little use in moving."

He walked to the refrigerator and poured himself a glass of milk. Carrie noticed that his hands were shaking. He returned to the table with the milk and set it untouched beside him. Finally he looked at Carrie again.

"Has Dale said any more about Sheila at all? Do you think he is genuinely interested in her?"

"He hasn't said anything outright," Carrie said. "But he's been very quiet ever since Sunday. I can tell he's thinking about something. I'm almost sure that he's thinking about her."

"Well, maybe I should talk to him about it," Richard said. "But let's start thinking of a way to get to know her better. We can't really give him good advice until then. Years ago, you could tell a person's character by the way he reacted to the church's teaching. But today that doesn't mean much. About the only thing we can do is get to know her better and see what spirit she seems to have."

He took a drink of milk before going on. "And most of all, we need to pray. Surely God will honor our prayers. Dale seems to want to do what is right. God won't let him or us down. Surely He will show us the way to go."

Uncle Dale paused. I could tell that he had almost forgotten that I was listening.

Carrie was right. Dale was thinking about Sheila. And his thoughts were running parallel to those of his parents. *How can I know if she is the girl God wants for me? I don't want to make a mistake. Yet I don't want to lose this chance if it really is one.*

Sometimes he was almost sure that she was the girl for him. *I have never been impressed like this by a girl before. She's attractive, courteous, and friendly. Yet she isn't a flirt. She's just—nice. Surely that is one way that God is directing me. Surely her convictions would grow if I gave her some help.*

But the next minute, he struggled with doubts. *But what if I'm wrong? What if her friendliness is just a front? What if she actually is a liberal at heart who will lead me astray? Maybe she wouldn't be happy with someone who had stronger convictions than she has. Besides, she might not even be interested in me for a husband. Maybe she just wants to be friends.*

Finally, after battling with such thoughts for several days, he came to the same conclusion that his parents had reached. *I'll have to take more time and get to know her better, first. I really don't want a wife who would lead me away from God and the church. I had better hold off for a while and pray about it. If she's the girl God wants for me, He'll surely keep her for me. And if she isn't, then I don't want her either.*

But I'd better talk with my parents about it. I know they are concerned. I can tell it in the way they are watching me . . .

On Friday evening, when his sister Jane went off to bed, Dale stayed sitting at the kitchen table. His father sat down across from him, and his mother brought each of them a mug of steaming tea and sat down as well.

After a moment, Richard broke the companionable silence. "You have been sort of quiet this week, son," he said. "Do you have something on your mind?"

Dale set down his mug and sat back in his chair. "Rather," he said slowly. "Though I think I've settled it for now. I've been trying to decide whether to pursue a closer relationship with Sheila."

Richard looked at him closely. "So what have you decided?"

"I'm going to put it on hold until I know her better," Dale replied. "First of all, I'm not sure if she wants me for a special friend or if she only wants a casual friendship. But more important, I don't really know what kind of girl she is. I like her, and she seems to be decent, but I have no idea what she thinks about a lot of important things."

He stopped and grinned at his parents. "Furthermore, I don't know what my parents think of her," he said. "And I'd hardly consider a relationship with a girl without knowing how you feel about it."

Richard relaxed visibly. "That sounds like good thinking to me," he said. "I was a bit afraid that she had swept you off your feet. Or maybe I should say I was afraid her parents had swept you off your feet."

Dale picked up his mug and took another sip. "I'll admit I rather fell for her. The events of last Saturday evening helped see to that. She did carry her part well, and I appreciated her response. But her father didn't particularly impress me on Sunday morning, though he was friendly enough, I suppose. If I decide to ask Sheila for a special friendship, it sure won't be because her father has talked me into it!"

Carrie had simply listened to the conversation so far,

but now she injected a question. "How did you feel about her mother?" she asked. "Was she like her husband?"

Dale considered this for a moment. "No, I don't think so," he said finally. "I felt she was genuinely friendly—more like Sheila. That's probably where Sheila gets it."

Carrie nodded. "I thought I would invite Sheila and her mother over for tea some afternoon and get to know them better."

"What do *you* think of Sheila?" Dale asked. "Am I completely on the wrong track?"

His father took his time in answering. "It's a bit hard to say," he said slowly. "Just going by appearances, I would hesitate. She fits into the more liberal part of the church, and she comes from a liberal family. That's a bad sign."

Dale nodded. He already knew that.

"On the other hand," his father continued, "that doesn't say everything nowadays. Even ten years ago, I would have given you a flat no and asked you to look elsewhere. But things have changed so much that a person hardly knows anymore. Is she what she is because of the desires of her heart? Or just because she doesn't know better?"

Richard absently swirled the tea in his mug. "I understand that the Lawrences were members of a liberal General Conference Mennonite congregation back in Ontario," he said. "Either Sheila has changed, or she was fairly conservative in that setting."

Dale looked surprised. "Really?" he said. "What kind of church did they go to anyway? And how do you know about it?"

His father smiled. "An old friend of mine goes to church there—or did anyway. I called him about six months ago, wondering about conservative congregations in Ontario. He told me that they actually have girls Sheila's age attending church regularly who cut and curl their hair and never wear a covering."

Dale gasped a little. "Are they members?" he asked dubiously.

"Not all of them, though most of their parents are members. I think the ones who are members all wear small coverings to church, even if they cut their hair, but elsewhere they leave them off," Richard answered. "And of course they have some members who look more like Sheila and her mother. But when I heard where the Lawrences came from, I did change my mind a little about Sheila. If she was among the more conservative ones in their last congregation, maybe she will be interested in holding back here too if she receives the right kind of encouragement."

Carrie spoke up again. "I met her in town this week," she said. "I must admit I was impressed. But you can't go on just one chance meeting."

Richard nodded. "There is another side to it though, which does trouble me some," he said. "Sheila comes from a very liberal background. Her family is among the liberal families in the church here. With that frame of reference, there is a lot of potential for trouble. I am glad for your decision to wait until you know her better. We will try to get to know her as well. And we'll all pray that the Lord would reveal His will to us. There are enough pressures trying to lead us astray right now, without looking for more."

Dale nodded and drained his mug before setting it back on the table. Then he leaned back in his chair and clasped his hands behind his head. "You know," he said thoughtfully, "I hadn't really thought much about what was going on at church until recently. But when I think back five or six years, I see quite a change. What's happening, anyway?"

Richard and Carrie exchanged glances. Then Richard asked, "What kind of things are you thinking of?"

Dale scratched his chin contemplatively. "Well, I suppose the women's dress is one of the more obvious ones," he said. "If I remember correctly, when I was thirteen or fourteen, most of the married women looked a lot like you do." He looked at his mother. "Now, you look different from most of the others, especially the girls. I mean, the way you comb your hair and the size of your covering. And your cape dress and dark stockings. And—and—just your general appearance, I guess. "

He glanced over at his father. "And none of us boys wear plain suits. In fact, most of the men are switching to ordinary suits and wearing ties."

He stopped and scratched his chin again. "And it isn't just appearance. A whole host of little things seem to be changing. Like youth activities. We hardly ever have Bible studies or singing at our Saturday evening MYF meetings anymore. Instead, we play games almost all the time. And I don't remember that there was much dating after MYF meetings when I first started going. Now some of the young folks have dates almost every week."

His father nodded soberly. "I know," he said. "I have been concerned about all of those things, as well as lots of other things that you might not notice. For instance, we have a lot more young sisters working at public places in town. And many of our people are wearing gold or silver watchbands. When I look at the general appearance of our people, I wonder how long it will be until we have sisters cutting their hair and wearing jewelry. Already in some Mennonite congregations, they are accepting wedding rings. How soon will we be tested that way?"

"Hmm—I almost bought a watch with a gold band last week," Dale said. "That's different from a wedding ring, isn't it?"

"I know people seem to think so," his father said slowly. "But I'm not really sure why—though they are worn for a different purpose. The Bible says that godly women are not to wear gold. It doesn't specifically mention rings, but it does seem to refer to jewelry and ornamentation in general. I don't see why a gold watchband is any less a violation of that command than a gold wedding ring, or why the principle would be any different for men than for women."

Dale was taken aback. "I never thought of it in that sense," he said. "But I suppose you're right. I should study some of those concepts more so that I have a better idea what is right and wrong."

His father nodded. "I'm afraid the time is coming that that will be the only way to learn the truth. You cannot depend on the example of the church anymore. We tried to teach you truth and to be a good example for you, but you will not be able to depend on your mother and me forever. If you learn it from the Bible, however, truth will be yours as long as you are determined to follow God's will."

Dale looked at him seriously. "I would have bought that gold watch and never thought twice. I wonder what else is in the Bible that I never thought of. What else did the church teach that we don't practice anymore?"

"I have lots of old doctrinal books in my library," his father said. "Books, such as *Doctrines of the Bible*, that were once considered a standard guide for our people. You're welcome to read them. But don't just read them—study the passages that these teachings are based on. You can argue with a writer, but you can't argue against God's Word—not if you're a genuine Christian."

"I'll do that," said Dale. "We're not that busy anymore on the farm. I'll have lots of time in the evenings." He stood up. "Well, I guess I'll head for bed."

Richard and Carrie sat for a few moments in silence after Dale went downstairs. "I wonder sometimes if we haven't drifted further ourselves than we realize," Richard said. "I know it's a constant battle to keep from drifting with the tide. Maybe I should read some of those books again myself."

He stood up and walked to the kitchen window, where

he stared out into the darkness for a few minutes. "You know," he said slowly, "I've often wondered what it will take to bring all this to a head. We are drifting slowly along, closer and closer to the brink. It's happened in other places, and it will happen to us. Today our young folks practice casual dating—tomorrow it will be mixed bathing. Today our girls wear flesh-colored stockings and dresses without capes—tomorrow it will be skirts and blouses, or worse. Today those same girls wear their hair piled on top of their heads, with small coverings on top—tomorrow they will cut and curl their hair and go without coverings. Today we have gold watchbands—tomorrow it will be wedding rings. Today our young folks play partner games—tomorrow they will go to dances. And when it has come to all that, the parents and the leaders of the church will still claim that we are following God and doing His will."

He turned to Carrie and spoke directly to her. "How long can we stay with a sinking ship without drowning?" he asked, almost fiercely. "We're only fooling ourselves if we think our children and grandchildren won't go along with the rest. Surely we're not the only ones who see that. Surely—somewhere—there are other people who feel the same as we do. If only we could get together and start over."

Several hours later, all was dark and everyone else was sleeping, but Richard Eberly still tossed and turned in his bed. In his mind's eye, he kept seeing his children, then the grandchildren and great-grandchildren that might follow. It seemed to him that they were marching past him in a long line, one by one, over a cliff. And as they went over the edge, they looked back at him for help, with pleading eyes. It was more than he could take. *They all depend on me. There has to be a way—surely God hasn't left us without an answer. If only I could find that answer. I have to find that answer before it's too late. Dale is teachable and wants to be faithful. But can he hold out? And what about our grandchildren? What will happen to them—and to us—if we can't find that answer?*

Finally his anguish drove him from his bed, and he knelt beside it. Weeping bitter tears, he brought his burden to his Father, who understood, as only He can.

A while later, his peace restored in a measure, he got to his feet and sat at his desk. Switching on the little desk light, he picked up his Bible and turned the pages, looking for the verse that had come to his mind while he was praying. There it was—"Yet I have left me seven thousand in Israel, all the knees which have not bowed unto Baal, and every mouth which hath not kissed him" (1 Kings 19:18).

3

Sheila's Struggles

"Touch, Lord, the sad, discordant keys
Of my poor troubled breast,
And change to peaceful harmonies,
My sighing of unrest."
—Mrs. F. G. Burroughs (adapted)

It was another Saturday evening, a few weeks later. Once again, the young people had gathered in the church basement for refreshments before going home. Dale picked up a sandwich and some punch and then looked around for someone to visit with. Allister was occupied elsewhere, but he noticed Sheila sitting by herself across the room. She looked up and smiled, so he walked across and sat beside her.

"I hate to see someone looking lonely," he said, grinning at her. "Or were you saving this chair for someone else?"

Sheila blushed a little. "Actually," she said, returning his smile a little shyly, "I was saving it for you if you want it. We haven't had a chance to talk for a while."

Dale nodded. "I guess I haven't gotten to MYF since our famous evening. I have been doing some work around home, and some studying. Somehow, I didn't feel like coming—the games the committee has been planning the last while seem so childish."

Sheila nodded. "I know what you mean," she said softly. "You go home feeling like you've wasted your whole evening." She looked across the group of young folks thoughtfully. "Everyone seems so—so giddy."

"That word sure fits," Dale said. "We have some good, serious-minded young folks, but they seem to be more and more in the minority. Of course, some stay home, like I have the last while."

Sheila grinned at him. "Does that mean that you are one of the good, serious young folks?" she asked.

Dale looked a bit sheepish. "That wasn't exactly what I meant," he said. "But actually, that is the kind of person I want to be."

Sheila nodded. "I noticed," she said.

Dale leaned back in his chair and changed the subject. "So I suppose you've been having lots of dates with young fellows who want to get to know you better?"

Sheila's face clouded over. "No, I haven't," she said slowly. "Well, actually, I had a date with George the week after you took me home, but I didn't enjoy it. I kept thinking about what you said about dating being a preparation for marriage and about it being too serious to just turn into a game. I don't think George had a serious thought all evening. I didn't enjoy it at all, and I haven't had a date since."

Dale glanced at her out of the corner of his eye and saw the look on her face. "Sorry about that," he said apologetically. "I didn't mean to make you feel bad."

Sheila turned and smiled, the clouds vanishing from her face. "My father was a bit cross with me after George left," she said. "He wondered why I wasted my time with such a shallow-minded boy. He also wondered why you've never been back, and I told him it was because you *aren't* shallow-minded." She lapsed into silence for a moment and then added, almost as an afterthought, "You've been praying for me, haven't you." She said it as a statement rather than a question, as if she was sure it was true.

Dale looked stunned. "Well—yes, I have," he said slowly. "But what makes you think that?"

For the first time since Dale had known her, Sheila seemed embarrassed and would not look at him. "I—I just thought maybe. You seem different from any other boy I have ever known. I have been having some struggles the last while and I just had a feeling that someone was praying for me. I knew no one else here would care enough to do that."

Looking at her, Dale was surprised to see her in tears.

However, before he could think of anything to say, she changed the subject. "My parents really liked the talk you gave the other Sunday evening at church," she said. "I did too. You must do a lot of reading and thinking."

"I like to read," he said. "I don't know if I do more thinking than anyone else, but I do think life is serious. I get tired of all this silliness." And he looked across the crowd of youth toward a group of boys who were bent over with laughter at some joke.

Sheila nodded. "You said you were doing some studying. What are you working on?" She half turned toward him and put her arm on the back of her chair so that she could see his face more clearly. "Are you thinking of going back to school?"

Dale shook his head. "No, I've been studying the Bible," he said seriously. "I feel that I need to know more about the things the Bible teaches. It seems that the more I read and study the Bible, the more I see that I need to grow."

Sheila's face mirrored his seriousness as she opened her mouth to reply, but he never learned what she intended to say. At that moment the youth leader called for everyone's attention. "There have been a few who are tired of playing games all the time at MYF," he said, grinning at the moans and groans from some of the younger boys. "We thought we would have something a bit different next week. We're asking Anne Carter to give a talk on what she thinks makes a man an ideal husband, and we're going to ask Dale Eberly to talk about what kind of girl he thinks would make an ideal wife. Then we'll follow up with an open discussion." There were a few cheers as well as some catcalls, but he held up his hand for silence. "We want this to be a serious evening," he said. "So come with your questions and ideas."

Sheila looked at Dale and smiled. "*This* should be interesting," she said softly; then she added quickly, "Who is Anne Carter?"

A few moments later, the group broke up and people started leaving, many of them coupling up amid sundry giggles, coy looks, and smart remarks. Sheila and Dale got up as well. Sheila looked up at him soberly. "Thanks for the chat," she said. "By the way, my mother was going to call your folks this evening and invite them over for supper tomorrow evening. We don't have church, and she thought it would be a good time for our families to get to know each other." Then she turned and was gone, leaving Dale standing there alone.

His dreams that night were happy ones.

Uncle Dale paused and looked at me soberly. "That evening I was pretty sure that Sheila Lawrence was the girl God wanted for me," he said. I opened my mouth to ask a question, but he shook his head. "We'll get to that," he said, as if he had read my mind.

Dale spent Sunday afternoon in his bedroom, reading. He had picked up a few books at the church library and was reading them as he had spare time. His book was interesting, but his mind kept wandering back to the evening before. By now, he had regained his equilibrium and was better able to evaluate the evening than he had been the night before. *I wonder what's troubling Sheila. She does have a serious side to her. She doesn't seem to care for silliness any more than I do. And she took my ideas about casual dating seriously enough to quit dating. But I still don't know how she feels about some of the other things the Bible teaches.*

He thought back over the things he had been studying, and he realized how big a change it would be for her to measure up to such a standard. *She knows what my mother looks like. I wonder what she thinks of that. Is it really fair for me to expect that she would change that much? Is it really necessary?*

He laid down his book and picked up his Bible. *But really, I don't dress like my father either. So why should I expect her to dress like my mother when even my sister doesn't? Maybe I should make some changes myself first and see how she reacts. But is it really necessary? If we both stayed looking like we do now, wouldn't that be good enough? After all, she doesn't look like her friends back in Ontario apparently do.*

Dale paced back and forth in the narrow room, hands clasped behind his back, deep in thought. *How can I know for sure what is right? After all, times do change. Is it right for me to expect her to return to the standards of twenty years ago, when hardly anyone else seems to think it is necessary?*

He glanced at his watch and saw that it was time to

leave for the Lawrences. In fact, he could hear doors banging as the rest of the family prepared to leave. *I'd better go too. It will look funny if I'm a lot later than the others.*

He thought again about the differences between his father and Sheila's father. *I wonder how this visit will go. My father and hers are about as opposite as they can be. But Donald is enough of a salesman and diplomat to know that he has to be a bit careful. And my father is never the kind to pick a fight, though he won't back down on what he knows is right.*

A knock on the door interrupted his thoughts. It was his seventeen-year-old sister, Jane. "Are you awake?" she called. "It's time to go!"

"I'm coming," he said, laying his Bible back on his nightstand. "Did you want to ride over with me?"

It was an interesting evening from several perspectives. Donald met them at the door, and Dale and his father followed him into the living room to wait until supper was ready to be served. Dale's mother and sister went to the kitchen to help Sheila and her mother finish their preparations.

It was a cozy, comfortable living room, and a quick look at the furnishings would have showed even a disinterested onlooker that the Lawrences were well to do. However, a closer examination revealed that their tastes matched their budget. In fact, Dale had never seen anything quite like it. From the Persian carpet on the floor to the deeply stuffed, floral couch and easy chairs, the room breathed quality and dollar signs.

Donald, however, didn't seem to see anything unusual about it. "Find yourself a place to sit," he invited. "It's nice it suited you to come over. We've wanted to get acquainted."

Dale sat gingerly on the couch while his father chose one of the large easy chairs. Donald dropped himself into another chair and crossed his legs. "So, I guess you two are farmers, are you?" he asked. "I grew up on a farm, but I never got into farming myself."

Richard nodded. "That's right," he replied. "I like the lifestyle. It hasn't made us rich, but it's a nice way to raise a family."

"It might make you rich yet," Donald said. "Anyway, if you own your land. Real estate values have been creeping up, and economists are predicting that properties are going to be the most volatile commodity on the market in the next several decades. I know people think I'm funny when I say it, but I think property will increase in value faster than the money you have invested in it. That's why I bought this farm, even though I don't intend to farm it myself. I paid $25,000 for it. In twenty to twenty-five years, I expect it to be worth at least three or four times that. That's almost a six percent return on my money, at the very least. You won't get that kind of return anywhere else.

"In your case, you're making your living off your farm too," he added. "You had to invest a bit more to buy equipment; but still, in the long run, your returns will beat anything you could have made working in town."

Richard nodded. "That's probably true," he said. "The Lord has been good to us. Though all of that could change pretty quickly. If we were hit by a depression like we were in the thirties, all of that could be different overnight."

"That's right," Donald agreed. "And that's another reason I bought a farm. Real estate usually survives a depression with better value than anything else."

This conversation set the tone for the evening. Dale was surprised to discover that his father knew almost as much about the intricacies of investment and finance as Donald did. But he could also see that his father didn't get the same enjoyment out of the discussion that Donald did.

In the meantime, Sheila and Jane were setting the table for supper. Since the dining area was separated from the living room by only an archway, Dale had a clear view of them. His attention soon wandered from the conversation in the living room to the two girls in the dining room. *Jane and Sheila sure seem to have clicked. They're chattering like old-time chums.*

He smiled to himself at the sight, but he couldn't help contrasting the two girls. Even though Jane didn't wear a cape dress as her mother did, she still left an impression of godliness and modesty. Sheila, on the other hand, was dressed in her normal, catchy manner, in a carefully tailored dress. The effect left Dale with an uneasy feeling, though he could hardly have explained why, since her dress did not strike him as being altogether immodest. He pondered this for a moment, but before he could put his finger on what was troubling him, Sheila's mother came to the living room and invited them to come for supper.

It was a candlelight supper, and it went to a full four courses. It started with soup and salad. This was followed by baked potatoes, ham, and dressing; and then a fruit cocktail. The fourth course consisted of scrumptious apple pie piled with whipped cream. Finally, when Dale felt that it would hardly be possible to eat anything more, Martha served coffee brewed from fresh Egyptian coffee beans, which she had ground herself while Sheila served the second course.

The whole meal had been quite formal, especially by Alberta standards, and Dale had felt a little on edge the whole time, lest he make a serious error in protocol. But the atmosphere changed with the coffee. His father was the first to comment. "This is good coffee," he said. "I'm not sure when I last had genuine brewed coffee. I must say it beats the instant coffee we usually use."

Sheila's mother seemed a little surprised. "Why, we normally grind and brew our own coffee," she said. "We do often have instant coffee during the week, since it's more convenient; but I really prefer this, especially when we have company."

Dale's mother nodded. "It's good," she said. "But I think you'll find that not many people here are used to serving it. We tend to be more laid-back and relaxed, even with our meals."

Martha smiled. "I've noticed that," she replied. "I suppose the meal tonight probably seemed rather formal to you. This is what we were used to, back East. But maybe we'll have to change some of that. We don't want to appear ostentatious. I hope you don't feel that we were trying to appear better than you, or anything like that."

After the supper was cleared away and the dishes washed, the young folks gathered around the fireplace in the family room downstairs to sing, relax, and play a few games. A little later, the rest decided to play shuffleboard, which left Dale and Sheila alone.

Dale seated himself comfortably on the couch beside Sheila, near the fireplace. In silence, they watched the flames together for a few moments. Then Sheila turned to him. "Does it seem to you that our family is putting on airs?" she asked soberly. "I never thought of how it might look to others. My mother likes formal meals and candlelight suppers. But I sure don't want you to think we're—what was that big word she used? Ostentatious? What does that mean anyway?"

Dale grinned. "It means something like showy or artificial, I guess. Maybe even putting on airs and thinking yourself better than others."

Sheila made a face. "I never could get past all those

big words. But anyway, do we seem like that to you?"

Dale pondered her question for a moment. "Well," he answered judiciously, "I was a bit afraid a few times that I might make a big blunder—like eating my soup with my fork."

Sheila's laughter tinkled across the room. "Now you're making fun of me," she said. "I'm sure you aren't quite *that* dense!"

Dale grinned back at her. "Well, I was a bit unsure of myself a time or two," he said candidly. "But it sure was a good supper. Though if I'd known how much there was going to be, I'd have eaten a little less ham and dressing!"

Sheila smiled. "My father likes good food. He gets a little huffy sometimes about the fuss, as he calls it, but he sure likes my mother's cooking." She looked a little wistful. "I hope your parents don't feel inferior to us though. I would love to have a meal at your place, and I know my parents would too. I am sure your mother is a terrific cook, and I hope she does not think she needs to try to prepare a fancy meal if we come. I was impressed the time my mother and I had tea with your mother. She served us some really good cinnamon rolls. My mother still talks about them."

They sat in companionable silence for a few minutes; then Dale turned and looked at Sheila. "You said last night that you were having a few struggles the last while," he said quietly. "Would you care to tell me about them? Or would you rather not talk about it?"

Sheila didn't answer for a moment. When she finally turned toward him, he was surprised at the depth of emotion he saw mirrored in her face. "Do you ever wonder what is right and what is wrong?" she asked. "I have often wished that God would speak to us and tell us exactly what He thinks."

Dale nodded. "I know. I've had some thoughts like that the last while too."

Sheila turned her face back toward the fire before continuing. "My parents don't quite agree on some things, so they end up leaving me to decide for myself; and it's so hard to know what to do sometimes."

She turned to him again. "Do you know what our last church was like?" she asked. When he nodded, she continued. "Well, my father felt pretty much at home there. And when we moved out here, he thought of going to a church in town, since he thought your church was too conservative. But my mother felt more comfortable with your church, and finally my father agreed to come here. However, he wouldn't care at all if I took off my covering and cut my hair. He thinks the traditional Mennonite positions are just culture."

Dale sat up a little straighter. "What do you think?" he asked.

"I don't know," she said hopelessly, and Dale could see by her face how serious the question was to her. "I don't want to be a rebel. I want to do what is right—what God wants me to. But even my mother tells me that I will need to decide for myself what that is. I try to read my Bible and pray, but everything seems so confusing that it only makes me more discouraged."

She stopped and wiped a tear from her cheek. "Back East almost all of my friends cut and curled their hair. Most of them didn't wear coverings. I was the odd man out, I guess, but somehow I couldn't make myself go to a hairdresser. It just didn't seem right, no matter how my father felt."

She turned to Dale again. "I—I hope you didn't think I was bold by talking like I did last night." Her voice shook as she spoke. "But I feel like I need someone like you to talk to. You seem so much above me spiritually, and I don't know where else to go. I hope you understand."

Dale groped for the right words. If only his parents were there. But he knew that Sheila needed help right then that probably even his parents could not give her. In his heart, he breathed a prayer before replying. "I think I do understand," he said quietly. "I've faced enough struggles like that to know how real they can be. It seems that nothing is secure in the church anymore. We hear messages on psychology and current events and interpersonal relationships, but no one ever tells us what is right and wrong or how to find God's will for our everyday life. But I'm sure the Bible has answers. That is why I have been studying it so much the last while.

"My parents have been a big help too, but they seem pretty depressed about church life and don't always say much," he continued. "Though I know that they will support me to the hilt in doing what is right. But I wish our ministers would really teach us the Bible as it is."

He paused a moment; then he suggested hesitantly, "Why don't we pray about it? I'm sure God cares and wants us to go right."

Her eyes brimmed over at this. "You go ahead and pray," she whispered. "I—I just can't, right now . . . "

Later that evening Dale shared his conversation with Sheila with his parents as they sat around the kitchen table. Richard shook his head. "The poor girl. What she told you fits almost exactly with my conclusions about her parents. It isn't *right* to leave a young girl in such a position."

Carrie looked at him in concern. "But what can we do?" she asked. "We're almost in the same position. We hardly know anymore what is right either."

Richard buried his head in his hands. "God help us," he whispered. "And only God can help Sheila."

4

A Friendship Bears Fruit

"I know not . . . the way of a man with a maid."
—Proverbs 30:18, 19

It was Thursday evening when Dale settled down to his desk to start getting together his topic for MYF. As he tried to think what characteristics he really did consider as an ideal for a wife, his thoughts naturally turned to Sheila. *Poor girl, she seemed so blue on Sunday evening. I think I had a few questions answered during that discussion. Even my parents are coming to the point of thinking that she might be the girl God has for me. Though it might partly be sympathy for her situation.*

He leaned back in his chair and stared at the ceiling, trying to get his thoughts together. *Sheila sure has a lot of the characteristics I would like to see in my wife. I could write those down, I guess.* He bent over his desk and started to jot down a few ideas. A few minutes later, he paused, chewing on the end of his pencil. *I guess she doesn't have them all though. I had better add a few more.* Somewhat reluctantly, he started to write again.

Dale didn't normally get nervous addressing a crowd. But that Saturday evening, he was. He knew that his topic, as he had written it, was pretty revealing of his thoughts. Not only would the youth group get a glimpse into his heart, but Sheila would too. *I wonder if she'll like what I'm going to say. This could be make-or-break, I suppose. Though on Sunday evening she sure seemed open to learning what God wanted of her.*

However, Dale had a sister, and he was astute enough to know that girls sometimes changed their opinions, depending on their feelings at the moment. *She might feel different by now about the things we discussed.*

He thought about this while he drove to the church. *Maybe I could tone down that part of my topic a bit. But that might disappoint her too. Anyway, would it be right? Especially if I do it just to impress her?*

He parked his car and crawled out, his notes clutched in one hand. He squared his shoulders in sudden decision and headed toward the church building. *I guess I'll say it as the Lord gave it to me. That's the only right way. It might be another means of finding out if she really is the girl God wants for me. But she won't be the only one who might question what I am going to say. I have a feeling the open discussion might get pretty warm.*

The youth committee had asked the congregation's assistant pastor, a young man in his early thirties, to be in charge, and he opened the meeting with a short prayer. Anne Carter's talk was first and generated a boisterous interest. She was a charismatic speaker, and she filled her talk with body language and human-interest stories. When she finished, everyone clapped enthusiastically.

Then it was Dale's turn. The first part of his talk went well, though he was a more serious speaker than Anne. He saw the warmth on Sheila's face as he went down over the description of the wife of his dreams—much of which bore a striking similarity to her character. Everyone smiled when he said he would like a girl who admired him. And the older boys nodded in agreement to his list of personality traits such as being kind, tenderhearted, respectful, and enjoyable to be with. But when he started to describe the spiritual traits of his ideal wife, the room gradually went silent. Even the least astute of the young boys realized that they were getting an unusual glimpse into Dale's heart.

He first noticed Sheila's tears while he was describing the personal relationship that he wanted his wife to have with Christ.

"I think this is perhaps the most important of all the traits I have described tonight," he told the group soberly. "I know that there is no such thing as a perfect girl, and I hope I haven't discouraged any of you this evening. But even if I can't find a girl with all those other traits I mentioned, I do want my wife to have a close relationship with Christ. I want her to have Jesus as her best friend and to know that He is with her at every moment. I want this relationship to be so real to her that she would give me up rather than Jesus, if she needed to choose between us."

He looked over the sober group of youth for a moment. "I think that a girl like that will also be doing some other things," he continued finally. "I think she will be concerned about modesty and about separation from the world. I think you will be able to see in her actions, in her talk, and in her appearance that she is a close friend of Christ's, and that Christ is more important to her than the world is."

He saw Sheila wipe a tear from her cheek, and his voice softened. "Again, I'm not asking for perfection, because I'm not perfect either. I have a lot of growing to do in this. But I want a wife who will be willing to grow with me and who will encourage me to grow closer to God, rather than trying to draw me away from Him."

When he sat down, the room was deathly still. Then the pastor got to his feet. "Well," he said, "you've heard what Dale had to say. Any comments or questions?"

George—Dale's Good Samaritan of several months before—spoke first. "Well, I guess we know now why Dale is a bachelor," he said, snorting. "Girls like he described are found only in storybooks or in Dale's imagination."

This wisecrack broke the tension of the meeting, and several other boys made smart remarks. But the pastor held up a warning hand. "Hold on, boys," he said. "Let's not get out of hand. Maybe Dale's expectations are a bit unrealistic, especially in the area of appearance, but he said a lot of good things."

An older boy in the back stood up. "I suppose many of us have longed at times for the days when life was simple and you could recognize a Mennonite girl half a mile away. But we have to remember that those things have changed, and we can't go back. I think the church is gradually coming to the realization that it's the inner life that's important, rather than outward appearance. Anyone can wear an old-fashioned dress, but that doesn't change the heart."

The pastor nodded. "We probably all agree with you on that. Notice, though, that Dale did center on the need for a personal relationship with Christ."

Anne Carter, who had given the first topic, stood up. "I noticed that too," she said, "and I agree with that part of it. But I don't like Dale's insinuation that there is a connection between that relationship and our outward appearance. The time is fast coming that the girls in our congregation will not look any different from the world around us. That will not reflect on the reality of our relationship with Christ. In fact, I think it will show that our relationship is doing what it should—that we no longer need to look different in order to make us feel spiritual."

There was a murmur of assent from various parts of the group when she sat down. The pastor looked a little nonplussed at the course the discussion had taken. He adjusted his glasses and smoothed back his hair before answering. "I suppose there are variations of opinion on some of that," he said uneasily. "We don't want to forget our traditional values entirely, or we might as well attend one of the community churches.

Yet there is truth in what you are saying, and I suppose the younger generation sees that more clearly than some of us older ones do."

The discussion was not entirely one-sided. Dale's friend Allister spoke up several times in his defense, as did one or two others. Several of the older girls tried to cast some oil on the troubled waters as well. But on the whole, the discussion went against him. Dale sat quietly off to one side and listened. He was not particularly surprised at the heat of the discussion that surrounded his statements about his ideal girl's appearance. *That is about what I expected. I knew Anne felt that way. In fact, I think she's been trimming her hair for quite a while already, and she wore a skirt and blouse to give her talk tonight. But I wonder what Sheila thought, or what she's thinking by now. Oh well, I should soon be able to tell, if I get a chance to talk to her. Maybe I should ask to take her home tonight so we can talk. I wonder if she's feeling better than she did Sunday evening. But she knows how I feel about dates, and she might read too much into it.*

All of a sudden, Dale sensed that the room was quiet. He looked up and saw that everyone was looking at him. The pastor saw his blank look and repeated his question with a slight smile. "I was just wondering if you had anything more to say about the discussion, Dale?" he asked. "We've been pretty tough on that last part of your talk."

Dale leaned back in his chair for a moment. "Oh, I'm

not sure," he said. "I think I pretty well made it clear what I think. There are many passages in the Bible that verify what I was saying, in my mind. And up until about five or ten years ago, our own ministers said the same thing."

The pastor nodded. "I suppose you're right," he said. "I wasn't here then. It is true, these issues are being debated across the nation, even at the ministers' meetings. But I think most of our leaders are slowly coming to the conclusion that we were a bit radical in our interpretations in the past."

Anne Carter jumped to her feet, her eyes flashing. "I know one thing," she snapped. "I wouldn't stay long with a church that tried to make me look like a museum figure." She stopped and then grinned a little. "So, anyway, I guess that counts me out as Dale's ideal girl!" She sat down abruptly, and the room echoed with laughter and a few whistles.

Dale's question about talking to Sheila was answered for him. By the time the meeting was over, she had vanished, and he couldn't find her anywhere. Dale was more troubled by this than he was by the general response to his topic. *I wonder if she didn't want to face me after what I said. She did take it pretty hard. I wonder if this will finish our friendship?* The idea troubled him more than he liked to admit even to himself.

The next morning Sheila wasn't at church. But Dale bumped into her father on his way out after the service.

Donald clapped him on the back, with his usual boisterous greeting. Then he got serious and shook his finger in Dale's face. "Say, young man," he said, for once speaking quietly, even though his tones were forceful, "I've been wanting to have a word with you. How long is it going to take you to decide whether Sheila is the girl you want? Or am I wrong in assuming that you are at least considering her?"

Dale was so flummoxed at Donald's abrupt approach, that he stuttered his reply. "Well—ah—well—I guess that's right," he said. "I—I've been praying about it a lot the last while. But I wasn't sure whether she was really interested in me either."

Donald softened his approach a little at Dale's response. "I know," he said. "It isn't always easy to know these things. But you aren't signing your life away just to court for a while. That might help you decide."

He looked at Dale earnestly. "Listen," he said. "Sheila's eating her heart out, wondering if you're really interested in her and whether she's good enough for you. You've got to let her know one way or the other soon."

Dale looked at the floor, gathering up courage to reply. "How do you feel about it?" he asked finally. "Do you feel we would be compatible in our convictions?"

Donald looked at him keenly. "Young man," he said slowly, "Sheila has all the convictions anyone could ever use. You surely know by now that she takes her Christian life seriously. In fact, she has more convictions on some things than her mother and I do.

"I know that you come from a pretty conservative family, and all that. I don't understand the need for some things like your parents do, though I respect them. But I don't think that Sheila will make any problems for you that way. Nor will her mother and I, if that's what's troubling you."

Dale hesitated a little. "Is she sick this morning?" he asked. "Or could I stop by and talk to her this afternoon sometime?"

"She's not ill," Donald said. "She's just heartsick. She'd be glad to talk to you. I'll tell her you're coming."

He started to walk away; then he turned back and added, "Your talk last night must have been a real sizzler. Sheila came home early, crying. Scared the wits out of us. She told us that she just didn't see how she could ever measure up to your ideal in a girl."

He placed his hand on Dale's shoulder and added gruffly, "Don't be too hard on her, boy. She's our only daughter, and she means a lot to us. She's taken quite a liking to you, and I don't want to see her hurt."

Dale sat down with his parents right after lunch and told them about his conversation with Donald. "I guess Sheila's been taking this pretty seriously," he concluded. "Maybe I haven't been fair to her. I thought we could just be friends for now, but I guess we've gotten a little too close. Anyway, I promised Donald I'd drop in this afternoon and talk to her."

His father sighed. "I was a bit afraid of this after what

happened last Sunday evening," he said soberly. "She would hardly have opened up to you like she did unless she had a deeper feeling for you than mere friendship. A girl doesn't share her heart that easily with a boy."

Dale's mother looked at him affectionately. "Dale," she said, "you don't understand girls very well. I didn't realize your friendship with her was getting this deep. We should have warned you."

Dale looked a little unhappy. "I didn't mean to hurt her," he said. "I thought that being friends was the only way I would really get the answers to my questions about her. I'm friends with lots of the girls, but I know that my friendship with Sheila is different from those relationships."

He stared at the table for a moment. "But what should I do now?" he asked.

His father looked at him contemplatively. "How do you feel about her?" he asked.

"Like I always did," Dale replied. "I'd ask her to be my steady[1] girl today if I did what I felt like. Do you think that would be all right? I've prayed about it a lot."

Richard rubbed his chin and sighed again. "Well," he said slowly, "I suppose that is the only way you'll know for sure. As far as I can tell, she is a spiritually-minded girl, who wants to do what's right and who will probably grow spiritually with the right guidance. If circumstances at church were different, I might hesitate, but we

---

1 *Going steady* was the common term used to designate a courting couple in the sixties. It has vanished from our teminology, due to our elimination of casual dating.

no longer live in normal times, it seems. But go slow and seek the Lord's direction every step of the way. I am sure if you truly want God's will, He will keep you from doing the wrong thing."[2]

It was about 3:00 when Dale got to the Lawrences. Sheila met him at the door and invited him in, somewhat self-consciously. Her parents were not in sight, though apparently they were home—at least Donald's late-model Cadillac was parked in the driveway. Dale could tell by Sheila's pale mien and the dark circles around her eyes, that she had been through an emotional trauma of some sort, and for a minute, he fought the temptation to run away.

Without speaking, Sheila led the way to the family room, where they had talked the week before. In front of the crackling fireplace lay an open Bible, a notebook and pen, and a crumpled handkerchief, mute evidence of what she had been doing when Dale arrived.

Dale spoke first, after they found seats—Dale on the leather couch and Sheila across from him on a matching easy chair. "I'm sorry," he said simply. "I shouldn't have let this drag on as long as it did. I should have realized how you were feeling, especially after last Sunday."

Sheila gave a shaky laugh. "I feel so foolish," she

---

2 You may question this advice coming from a godly father. But keep in mind the circumstances and the lack of teaching at the time. We have almost no concept of what it was like to face such questions without the security of a sound congregation and spiritual leaders to look to for advice.

said huskily. "I understood why you were taking your time and why you wanted to just be friends for now. But it seemed that things just kept piling up until I almost couldn't handle it. Our talk last Sunday really helped me, but I let my heart get away on me, I guess."

She stopped and wiped away a tear. "Then when you gave your talk last night at MYF, I just couldn't take it anymore. I felt that I was so far from your ideal that there was no way that I could ever be good enough for you. And then, on top of that, they had that *horrible* open discussion. I couldn't *believe* how some of them talked, and that the pastor let it go on. I don't know if I'll ever be able to face that Anne Carter again."

In spite of himself, Dale chuckled a little. "I am not in the least bothered by what Anne Carter thinks of me," he said. "I have no interest at all in her stripe of a girl. I can't understand why so many boys flock after her—as shallow-minded as she is."

Then he paused and looked Sheila straight in the face. She met his look directly, but she waited quietly for him to continue. He hesitated a moment as he noticed the depth of the feelings mirrored on her face.

"We've known each other as friends for a while," he said soberly, changing the subject abruptly. "Would you be ready to be my steady girl now?"

Sheila's face glowed for a moment, but then clouded over. "I really did appreciate your talk last night," she said softly, momentarily evading his question. "What you said is what I aspire to be. But I know that I am far from it. I am afraid I can never reach that kind of spiritual ideal. Are you sure I can be good enough for you? I don't want to disappoint you."

A slight fear gripped his heart. Had he said too much after all?

"I suppose I feel a lot the same way," he answered slowly. "I have a lot of growing to do before I'm ready to be a Christian husband and father. But I think God takes us up His ladder a step at a time, helping us to grow as we face the issues in life where we need that growth. Actually, I've been impressed by your spiritual desires. That's all I ask in a girl, that she wants to do what's right and that she does God's will as He reveals it."

Sheila looked at her lap for a moment and clasped her hands. Then she looked up again. "In that case," she whispered, "yes—I'm ready. But please pray for me."

A little later, they went up the steps to look for Sheila's parents. She wanted Dale to be along when she told them what had taken place. Her mother heard them coming and met them at the top of the steps. Seeing the glow on Sheila's face, she held out her arms, and Sheila met her with a sob, hiding her face on her mother's shoulder. Dale, unused to such emotion, was somewhat abashed and held back. But then Donald was there as well, pumping his hand vigorously. "Well, so you came through," he said in his booming voice. His smile matched his voice. "I knew you wouldn't let her sit now. I was sure we could depend on you."

By now, Sheila and her mother were laughing together. Then her mother turned to Dale. For a moment, he was afraid she would embrace him too, but she simply took both his hands in hers. "Thank you so much for what you have done for Sheila," she said, and he could tell that she meant it. "You are welcome in our home anytime."

The four chatted for a few minutes, and then Sheila glanced shyly at Dale. "We'd like to go over to Dale's parents now and tell them too," she told her parents. "They know the whole story, and they will be wondering too."

A few minutes later, they were on their way. Dale's shoulder still smarted a little from the vigorous welcome Donald had given him, but he was smiling. So was Sheila.

"I'm looking forward to getting to know your parents better," she confided. "They seem so nice, I can hardly wait. Yet I'm a bit scared too. I hope I can live up to their expectations."

Dale smiled at her. "I'm not scared at all. They will be just as happy about it as your parents were."

Dale was right. Now with the die cast, both Richard and Carrie sincerely welcomed their son's friend, determined to do what they could to make the relationship a successful one.

Uncle Dale stopped and looked at me. "That's enough for tonight," he said gruffly. "It's my bedtime. Come back next week, and I'll tell you some more."

I could tell that the story was stirring up some emotions in Uncle Dale that I had never seen in him before. I went home with many questions.

5

Sheila's Questions

"Ye shall . . . find me,
when ye shall search for me with all your heart."
— Jeremiah 29:13

A month or so later, Dale crawled out of bed one morning and stre-e-e-e-tched until his back crackled. It would have been easy to see, had anyone been there to see it, that he was feeling good that morning. The expression on his face and the bounce in his step testified to it as he came up the steps from his bedroom. In fact, as Dale and Richard headed out into the frosty early morning to feed the cattle, it seemed to Richard that Dale carried a constant aura of happiness and anticipation.

Richard was glad that Dale was happy, but he didn't share Dale's anticipation of the future. *I want to trust that God is still in control, but I sure wonder what kind of future my children and grandchildren really have. Dale is so happy with Sheila now; I hope he doesn't forget his convictions and go along with the crowd at church. It is so easy to do.*

But Richard's thoughts did brighten a little at the thought of Sheila. *I think she's an answer to prayer, even though I had some qualms at first. She really is trying to fit in well.*

That afternoon Dale and Richard took a load of cattle to the sale barn. Carrie had just finished the dishes when she heard a car drive in. *I wonder who that is. Dale and Richard will be gone for the afternoon, so it can't be them.*

Before Carrie got to the window to see who was there, she heard a tap at the door, so she went to open it. At the door, looking a little self-conscious, stood Sheila.

"Well, this is a surprise," Carrie said. "Come right in."

Sheila stepped inside and closed the door behind her. "I hope I'm not interrupting you from something important," she said somewhat shyly. "I was going by on an errand, and I thought I would stop in for a few minutes."

Carrie shook her head. "No, I'm all alone this afternoon. Dale and his father took some cattle to the sale, and Jane is helping her grandmother do some cleaning. Come in and have a cup of coffee. I just baked some cinnamon rolls this morning."

"Ooh, that sounds good," Sheila said. "I still remember the rolls you served us when my mother and I were here several months ago."

They soon sat at the kitchen table, chatting like old friends. Carrie was keen enough to see that Sheila had something on her mind, but she let the conversation take its natural course. Sure enough, a little later, after a moment of silence, Sheila changed the subject.

"I was wondering if you could give me some sewing tips," she said hesitantly. "I was looking at Jane's dress last Sunday, and I thought maybe her pattern would fit me. Somehow, my dresses seem a little showy beside hers."

Carrie looked a little surprised, but she quickly passed it off. "Certainly, I'd be happy to help you. Would you like to try on one of Jane's dresses? I'm sure she wouldn't mind."

"Could I?" asked Sheila eagerly. "I'm sure it would fit me."

Soon Sheila reappeared, wearing Jane's dress. Carrie opened her sewing closet door so that Sheila could see herself in the mirror attached to the back of the door. Sheila looked herself over carefully, even turning backward and using a hand mirror to see her reflection from that perspective. Carrie watched the expressions on her face curiously, wondering what she was thinking.

Finally Sheila sighed and turned to Carrie. "What do you think?" she asked wistfully. "Do you like how it fits?"

"I do," Carrie said gently. "How do you feel about it?"

"It—it feels a little strange," Sheila admitted. "It's looser and longer than I'm used to. Does it look too big?"

"Well, it depends on what you are used to, I guess," Carrie said carefully. "I think it looks really good on you, but it is a bit looser and longer than what you've been wearing."

Sheila blushed a little. "That's what I was after anyway, I guess," she said sheepishly. "When I compared my dresses with yours and Jane's, I felt a little funny about them. Do you think my dresses are modest enough?"

Carrie sat down at the table again, and Sheila sat across from her, still wearing Jane's best Sunday dress. "I asked my mother, and she thought I should ask you about it," Sheila said. "She and my father promised Dale that they wouldn't interfere with his convictions, even though they might not agree with them. I had never thought of my dresses as being immodest, but I know that Jane looks different from the way I look."

She paused for a moment, looking uncomfortable. "Why do you wear a cape dress?" The question almost burst from her. "My parents don't like cape dresses at all; they think they are just a traditional leftover from the past. But I was sure you had a better reason than that for wearing them."

Carrie's eyes filled with tears. "I know that many people feel as your parents do," she admitted. "Because of that, we haven't insisted that Jane wear them. I have tried to help her make dresses that aren't formfitting, but I still hope that she will decide on her own to wear a cape someday."

"So is that why you wear a cape?" Sheila asked. "To hide your form?"

Carrie nodded. "That's right. I don't want to be a temptation to anyone, and the Bible teaches women to be modest. But it's a conviction that is fast being lost in our congregations."

Sheila looked a little nonplussed. "I don't want to be

immodest," she said. "And I surely don't want to be a stumbling block for Dale or any other boy. But I'm not sure what my parents would say if I started to wear a cape dress. Nor am I sure I'm quite ready for a big change like that. Would it help if I started to make my dresses like Jane does?"

Carrie smiled. "I'm sure that would be a big step in the right direction," she said. "You want to respect your parents wherever you can. But you mind the Lord, and I'm sure you will come out at the right place."

A few minutes later, Sheila left, taking Jane's dress pattern and a dress along. She turned to Carrie as she went out the door and gave her a spontaneous smile. "I'm so glad for your help and concern," she whispered. "Please pray for me so that I can learn to be the kind of girl that Dale deserves." Then she was gone.

When Carrie told Richard about Sheila's visit that evening, he looked relieved. "Good," he said. "That shows that our influence is doing the right thing. We'll have to keep praying for her."

Carrie nodded. "She seems really open to talk about things. It will take some time, but if she stays this open to the Lord's direction, she will make a good wife for Dale."

Richard scratched his head. "I just wish we could find a better environment for all of us. Sheila is going to face a lot of pressure. She is going against the tide, and she will get very little sympathy from the church or her parents. Except for us and a few other families, she will be on her own. I hope she is doing this from genuine conviction, not just from a desire to please us or Dale. She will never make it without God's help."

Carrie smiled at him affectionately. "You're a bit of a pessimist," she said. "I think she means business."

Richard smiled back a bit sheepishly. "Maybe I am," he admitted. "But Dale's future—and Sheila's—is at stake. Neither of them has any idea of the kind of pressures they will face if they keep on following this path."

The following Sunday was singing Sunday for the youth, so Sheila went along home with Dale after the morning service. They met in the lobby, but it wasn't until they were walking to his car that Dale noticed Sheila's new dress. He saved his comments until he had maneuvered his way out of the church parking lot.

Sheila had noticed his sudden silence. "A penny for your thoughts!" she said, her laugh tinkling through the car. "Or are they worth more than that?"

Dale grinned. "They're priceless," he replied. "That means that for most people they are way out of reach. But for you, it means they're free."

He negotiated a turn onto Main Street before continuing. "Actually, I noticed you had a new dress on. At least I don't remember seeing it before."

Sheila blushed. "It's new," she said. "Do you like it?" She looked at him anxiously as he glanced at her again.

He grinned at her. "I sure do," he assured her. "It looks good on you." He paused a moment before asking cautiously, "Did you use a different pattern?"

Sheila's blush deepened, but she looked pleased that he had noticed. "I—I borrowed your sister's pattern," she said shyly. "I thought maybe you would like it better if I dressed more like your family."

Dale's smile got broader. "Well, I sure like it," he assured her again. "How do your parents feel about it?"

Sheila's face clouded over. "My mother didn't say much, but I think it bothered her a bit," she said. "I overheard my father talking to her about it. He told her that he promised you that they would not interfere with your convictions. He has taken quite a liking to you. He told my mother that you are worth it."

Dale pondered this before answering. "I hope it doesn't drive a wedge between you and your parents," he said. "I would hate to see that. But I do think that you look more consistent this way. You really surprised me."

They drove in comfortable silence the rest of the way home. Then as they turned into the Eberlys' driveway, Sheila spoke again. "I hope the other young people don't think I'm trying to put on a holier-than-thou appearance," she said anxiously. "I guess I feel a little self-conscious about going to the singing."

Dale looked a little startled. "Oh, they probably won't think of it that way," he assured her. "I don't see how anyone could feel that way about you."

But Dale was wrong. When they were finished singing at the hospital, the group of young people spent some time chatting in the parking lot before heading out again. Dale was chatting with one of the other boys when he saw Anne Carter heading across the parking lot toward Sheila, with a determined look on her face.

He overheard the conversation clearly.

"Well, Sheila," Anne said sarcastically. "So you've allowed Dale to turn you into a grandmother."

Sheila blushed furiously but didn't reply, so Anne continued. "I knew it would happen when you started going steady with Dale. I thought you were going to be a good sport, but now you're turning into a goody-goody. All for a boy."

Anne looked around and saw Dale listening. Her next comments included them both. "I know why you're doing this. You want him to admire you," she said scathingly. "You aren't doing it because you really want to. No one in his right mind would make a change like that because he wanted to."

She looked at Sheila challengingly, as if daring her to deny it, but Sheila didn't know what to say. Instead, she looked imploringly at Dale. He saw the tears starting to trickle down her cheeks, so he stepped over to her. "Come; let's go," he said gently. "Just ignore her." But neither he nor Sheila missed the triumphant grin on Anne's face as she watched them go.

Sheila wiped some tears from her cheeks as they pulled away from the hospital. She didn't look at Dale; she stared out the window instead, as if she were wishing she could just vanish. Dale could see her shoulders shaking; but he didn't know what to say, so he said nothing. *I wish I could comfort her. That Anne! I hope she wasn't right though—I hope Sheila isn't changing her dresses just for me.*

Then Sheila squared her shoulders and blew her nose rather emphatically. Dale looked over at her. "Feeling better?" he asked gently.

Slowly she nodded, but he was shocked at the look of discouragement on her face. "How could she be so mean?" she asked, almost bitterly. "Right in front of everyone."

"I don't know either," Dale said slowly. "Something must really be eating her. I suppose she is dead set against anything that could cramp her freedom to do as she pleases. She probably took your change as a personal threat."

Sheila sighed. "I wish I knew more about the Bible," she said wistfully—changing the subject abruptly. "Sometimes I feel like my relationship with God is so shallow. You know, I thought I was doing the right thing by changing my dress pattern. Now I wonder if I did it all for the wrong reason. Somehow, Anne's attack has taken all the joy out of what I did."

Dale looked at her compassionately. "This kind of thing can be hard to take, I know," he said. "But don't get discouraged. The same thing has happened to me, different times. It seems that the young folks here can be pretty unkind if they feel that their liberties are being threatened. But we can't let it get to us. How can we ever help someone like Anne see her problem if we let her criticism get to us?"

Sheila was quiet for a moment. Again, Dale was impressed with the depth of her feeling. *She is really troubled by this. I have to help her somehow . . .* He turned his eyes back to the road and quickly brought his car back across the centerline to his side of the road.

"Oops!" he chuckled softly. "I'd better watch where I'm driving." Sheila smiled wanly but still didn't say anything.

They were driving in silence when all of a sudden Sheila gasped and covered her mouth with her hand. "Oh, no," she moaned. "I forgot my jacket and songbook. I left them by the coat-rack in the hospital."

Dale slowed down immediately. "We'll have to go back and get them," he said. "Hard telling what'll happen to them if we leave them there."

Sheila made a face. "This is so foolish," she said huskily. "I was going to go back in and get them, but then I forgot all about them. I hope the others are gone when we get there. I—I'm not sure I can face Anne Carter again right now."

Dale smiled grimly. "I have a few things I would like to say to her," he said soberly. "But I doubt she would be very happy to hear them. It might be best if she is gone. I'll go in and get your things. You can just wait in the car, and you won't have to meet anyone."

Anne had not left yet. She was in the middle of a group of boys, entertaining them with wild tales of a trip to the mountains that she and some friends had recently taken.

As Dale walked past the group to get Sheila's coat, he overheard part of the story—just enough to know that this was no place for him or Sheila. The group was in stitches—some of the boys literally bent over laughing—and no one even noticed him.

He looked so disgusted when he got back to the car that Sheila asked curiously, "What is going on over there? It doesn't look very edifying."

Dale grimaced. "Edifying?" he said. "Anne Carter doesn't even know what that word means." He revved up his engine almost savagely before letting out the clutch. The car lurched ahead with a jerk, and Sheila gasped. Dale shifted into second gear a little more carefully and grinned at her crookedly. "Sorry about that. I guess I got a bit upset. But that gets my dander up. Anne Carter can talk so spiritual when she wants to, but it doesn't mean a thing."

Dale drove in silence for a few minutes. "I didn't know that any of the young folks were as far gone as Anne's story sounded," he said slowly. "Though I know that Andrew and George and maybe a few others often go cruising the streets of town, looking for girls they went to high school with."

Sheila looked at him seriously. "Oh, I hope it isn't too serious," she said. "That kind of conduct can make such a mess in a youth group. Surely your church wouldn't go for that."

Dale lifted his shoulders dubiously and let them fall again. "I'm not sure," he said. "It seems that the ministers would rather look the other way when things come up. I know they wouldn't like it, but I'm not sure they would do anything about it, other than hope it goes away."

Sheila looked disturbed. "But—but then, the church here soon won't be much different from the one we went to back East," she said. "And that was terrible. You wouldn't believe some of the stories I could tell you."

She watched the barren prairie landscape for a moment before continuing. "I don't want to take that route," she said, almost hopelessly. "But how is a person to know what's right and what's wrong? You have your parents to help you, but I don't even have that. And anyway, how do we know that your parents aren't just radicals?"

Dale nodded. "I know what you mean," he said. "But I think that God will tell us what is right and what is wrong, if we really, honestly want to know."

When she turned to look at him, her seriousness struck him. *She is sincere all right. She really does want to know.*

"But how?" she asked almost desperately. "I mean, He doesn't actually *speak* to you in a voice, does He?"

Dale shook his head and smiled. "No, that would be a bit scary," he said. "But I really believe that the Bible has the answers to all of these questions. I know that we are responsible to apply what it says, but the answers are there, if we look for them."

They turned into the lane leading to Dale's home, and Sheila waited until Dale had parked. Then she turned to him again. "Are you still studying?" she asked. "You told me months ago that you were studying the Bible."

He nodded. "Yes, I am," he said. "I've worked myself

most of the way through my father's *Doctrines of the Bible*. It sure has a lot of interesting thoughts. I look up all the Bible passages listed in the book. I never had any idea that the Bible taught some of those things."

Sheila looked at him wistfully. "Could we study together sometimes?" she wondered. "I feel like I know so little. And I don't know much about studying the Bible."

"Why, sure," Dale said. "That would be a good thing to do when we're together. I was afraid you'd rather do other things when we're together. Is there anything in particular you'd like to study?"

Sheila hesitated a moment; then she made a face. "I wish I could study modesty with someone," she said. "Anne Carter kind of got under my skin, but I really don't know why I'm changing my dress pattern. I mean, I wouldn't have been able to give her a reason from the Bible—though I would never have admitted it to her."

"My mother would probably be glad to study that with you," Dale said hesitantly.

Sheila's face brightened immediately. "Do you think she would mind?" she asked. "I'd love that. Could you—could you ask her for me?"

"Sure," Dale said. "I'd be glad to. Maybe Jane would be interested too. The three of you could have a nice Bible study group together. I'll talk to my parents about it tonight yet and get back with you about it."

6

Eastern Visitors

"The Bible knows nothing of salvation apart from obedience."

—*A. W. Tozer*[1]

Dale stood for a few moments on the back porch, enjoying the balmy breeze blowing out of the southwest. Spring was back! Another long, hard Alberta winter had been laid to rest in the archives.

It had been an eventful winter, a winter that Dale thought at the time was one of the happiest he had known. Most of his memories centered around Sheila—sledding with Sheila, skating with Sheila, discussing the Bible with Sheila, playing checkers with Sheila's father, and taking Sheila to church and MYF.[2] Even now, as he took

1 *Paths to Power* (Camp Hill, Pa.: Christian Publications, Inc.), p. 24.

2 In this setting it was taken for granted that a steady couple went everywhere together. They spent much more time together than we are accustomed to, or consider proper, today.

deep breaths of fresh May air, he was thinking of Sheila—and the future. He was beginning to think a lot about the future—a future that centered around Sheila. It would be a great day when he could walk in the back door of his own house, and Sheila would be there to greet him with her cheerful smile.

The thought was so enthralling that he forgot for the moment that supper was waiting and that there was a special MYF meeting that evening. But his reverie was shattered abruptly.

"Dale!" Jane opened the back door and stuck out her head. "Supper's ready! We have to hurry, or we'll be late for MYF. Aren't you picking up Sheila tonight?"

Dale came back to earth with a thud and turned to grin at his younger sister. "I'm coming," he said. "I'll be there as soon as I wash up."

The Eberly family was soon gathered around the table, enjoying their supper. Richard filled his plate and then looked at Dale. "So you're going to MYF tonight, by the sounds of it?" he asked.

"Yes, we thought we'd go," Dale said. "A Gospel team from Pennsylvania is around for the weekend, and they're going to be there tonight as well. Sheila knows one of the girls somewhat, so we thought we'd go."

Richard nodded. "They're going to be in charge of the morning service tomorrow as well," he said. "The main speaker is a graduate student from Eastern Mennonite College. It should be interesting."

Dale swallowed his spoonful of potatoes before

answering. "I'm looking forward to it. I thought probably a group from Pennsylvania would be more conservative than what we are used to, but Sheila seems a little dubious about it. So I'm not sure what they will be like. But I hope they will give us some good direction."

They got to MYF in good time, and Dale helped set up chairs. They were almost finished when the visitors trooped in the back door of the church basement, so Dale had a good chance to look them over. *Hmm. I guess Sheila was right. They don't look very conservative. Far from it, in fact. I wonder who invited them to come.*

The newcomers soon surrounded the local young folks, and Dale saw little more of them. But he had seen enough. The girls were all wearing frilly blouses and matching plaid skirts. One of them obviously had trimmed her hair. And the leader was a tall, dark-haired, handsome boy with an Elvis Presley hairstyle—longish, swooped up without a part, and glistening with hair cream.

It was soon evident that the demeanor of the visitors matched their appearance. They had the whole group in stitches over their antics, even before the events of the evening got under way.

The main event was a slide show of a mission trip one of the visitors had taken to Mexico. It would have been interesting had not some of the younger boys kept cutting up and disturbing the meeting. As it was, Dale was about on the verge of leaving and taking Sheila and Jane home. However, Sheila hadn't had a chance to talk with the girl she knew, so they decided to stay.

During the refreshments, things grew even worse. Henry, the boy who was in charge of the visiting group, had brought his guitar and started to entertain the group. He and his girlfriend, the girl with the trimmed hair, started singing Western cowboy songs, and next they introduced a song by Elvis Presley.

"Sing with us!" Henry called. "Come on, don't be bashful."

Dale and Sheila and a few other young people stood by themselves at the other side of the room and watched the carrying-on. Finally Dale turned to Sheila. "I'm not sure how much more of this I can handle," he said grimly. "This sure wasn't what I expected."

Sheila looked up at him. "Let's just go," she said. "I can meet Amy tomorrow. Anyway, I'm not even sure I care to meet her after this. I knew that they would be a pretty borderline group, but I didn't realize they were this bad."

Blake Martens, an older boy standing close by, overheard the exchange. "Good idea," he said. "This evening reminded me again why I don't bother coming to MYF anymore. I knew it was bad, but this is even worse than I expected. And that fellow singing those Elvis Presley songs will probably give a talk in church tomorrow morning. It's totally disgusting!"

Sheila was very quiet on the way home. But before she got out of the car, she turned to Dale. "You know," she said thoughtfully, "that's the kind of party we used to have back in Ontario. It's hard to believe that I actually enjoyed them at one point. But you know, it won't be long until it's common here too, at the rate things are going."

Dale looked serious. "I know," he said. "I'm beginning to understand why my father is so troubled about our church life. It just doesn't seem right."

Richard and Carrie were still up when Dale and Jane got home. Jane went off to bed, but Dale poured himself a cup of tea and sat down at the table with his parents. Everything was quiet for a little; then Richard asked, "Something wrong?"

Dale looked a little startled; then he sighed. "I've never seen anything like it," he admitted heavily. "We'd never have gone if I'd known what a party we would have. I really wish Jane had stayed home. She got pretty carried away."

Richard put down his mug and looked at Dale with concern on his face. "What was going on?" he asked. "Was it a lot worse than usual?"

"Yes, it was," Dale said. "Of course, we haven't gone much the last while, but I am sure it was worse than usual. Those visitors got everyone all keyed up. They had a guitar along, and one of their girls played the piano. They played country songs. Everyone was singing along and clapping the time. It was like a real concert."

Richard bit his lip. "That doesn't sound good," he said. "Our church never used to allow that kind of songs, let alone singing them at MYF."

Dale sighed again. "Actually, that wasn't the worst," he said. "Henry, the fellow who played the guitar, is an Elvis Presley fan, and he got going on some Elvis songs. Not everyone knew them, but they were having a real hootenanny when we left. I couldn't believe it. Some of those rock songs are even suggestive. We finally left. For all I know, they're still at it."

The three sat silently for a little, and gloom settled around them like a poisonous fog. Richard buried his head in his hands and whispered, "Lord, how long?"

The Pennsylvania group left a better impression in church the next morning. The songs they sang were in good taste, and the talks they gave were inspirational. In fact, had Dale not seen and heard the events of the evening before, he would hardly have believed it possible. Henry, the EMC graduate student with the Elvis Presley hairstyle, presented a scholarly and thoughtful treatise on the subject of Christian influence that impressed even Richard and Carrie.

When dinner was over, Richard and Carrie visited with Dale and Sheila for a while in the living room. "It's hard to believe that that was the same group you were describing last night," Richard said to Dale.

Dale looked perplexed. "I know," he said. "I didn't even feel like going this morning, after what took place last night. But the program was interesting and worthwhile. It doesn't make sense to me."

Sheila was sitting beside Dale on the couch. She looked up at him and then across at Richard. "That's exactly what church life was like back East," she said. "Some of the wildest fellows in the group could give the most spiritual talks in church if they had to. We never saw anything inconsistent in that. It was just life. Saturday evening had nothing to do with Sunday morning. I'm sure Henry would be shocked to learn that someone thought his actions last night didn't line up with his talk today."

Richard nodded. "That is saying it exactly as it is," he said. "That's the problem of the Mennonite Church in a nutshell. The sermons we hear are good enough, even though they leave out some important things. But our people no longer make a connection between the sermons and everyday life. The sermons belong to Sunday, and our everyday life isn't part of it. Even our ministers too often feel that way. Like Henry, they can say one thing over the pulpit and take a totally different stand on issues the rest of the time."

"But surely there are some people who see the problem," Dale said, looking perplexed. "Isn't anyone concerned about it?"

"A few," Richard replied. "There are several other families in church who feel like we do, but we don't have any support from the leaders. I talked to our bishop a few weeks ago, and he tried very hard to be supportive without committing himself to anything. He told me that times are changing and that our young people really want the same thing we do, except they are approaching it from another perspective. He said he doesn't want to discourage them and drive them away."

Dale shook his head. "I wonder what he would have said if he had heard Anne Carter last winter at the hospital."

"I don't know," Richard said wearily. "I am sure he wouldn't have liked it. I thought of talking to him about it, but I knew it would be useless anyway. A person finally gets to the point where he almost gives up."

Sheila's eyes widened with concern. "Please don't give up," she pleaded. "What would Dale and I have left if you gave up? We need your help."

Richard looked a little sheepish. "I'm sorry," he said. "I don't want to give up, but sometimes it seems so hopeless." He looked at Carrie and smiled affectionately. "You always did call me a pessimist, I guess. Maybe you're right."

Carrie smiled back. "A little," she admitted candidly. Then she sobered. "But I am sure our church situation is enough to turn anyone into a pessimist. Surely the Lord doesn't expect us to simply go on like this."

Sheila looked thoughtful. "There was a small group of ministers in Ontario who left the Ontario Conference to start up something new, just before we moved out here," she said. "But they seemed pretty radical. At least that's what my parents thought. Our congregation was part of General Conference, and they were part of the Ontario Conference, so we didn't know them very well."

Richard pricked up his ears. "Really?" he said. "I hadn't heard about anything like that. I wonder who they were. At least they had some ministers who saw the need.

That's what we need here. If only we had someone to lead out, I think there would still be some support for a more Scriptural congregation."

Sheila looked troubled. "Would you actually start another congregation?" she asked. "My parents are really against anything like that. You see, they think that everyone in the church should have the right to make his own choices. So my father doesn't have anything against your position as long as you don't try to pressure him to do like you do. That's why he hasn't stopped me from making some changes. He says I will have to make up my own mind on these issues. But he would never let me leave the church for a more conservative group."

"Well, at this point it doesn't seem too likely to happen," Richard said. "Though I don't really see any other answer. I don't want to leave the old church either. No one has ever done that except to become more liberal, and it would really ruin a person's reputation to instigate something like that. But there are some things that I won't be able to do if they come along. For instance, I don't see how I could take Communion with someone who was wearing a wedding ring. That's in plain violation of the New Testament."

"We had people with wedding rings back in our old congregation," Sheila said. "I don't remember when it started. In fact, my father wanted to get a set of rings for him and my mother, but my mother refused. She said my grandparents wouldn't understand, and she didn't want to offend them."

Dale had listened to this exchange without comment, but now he spoke up. "I was reading 2 Corinthians 6 recently, and I was impressed with the last verses in the chapter. They say that we are to 'come out from among them, and be . . . separate.' It must be right to separate from evil sometimes."

Richard nodded. "I have read those verses many times," he admitted. "I have looked at the context over and over, trying to figure out how bad things need to get before we are required to separate ourselves. The context is talking about paganism and unbelievers. I'm not sure if we should apply those verses to our situation or not. Separation could be the easy way out. I know that the church in Corinth was in really bad shape, and Paul never suggested that a remnant should separate from the rest of the church. Yet, how long can we stay with a sinking ship and not be drowned?"

Sheila said no more, and the subject changed to a more pleasant one. But she was strangely quiet that afternoon. When it came time to go singing at the hospital, she begged Dale not to go. "I don't know if I can face that crowd this afternoon," she said. "They'll still be all wound up from last night, and I don't feel up to it. I'd rather just stay here and have a quiet time together. Or you could drop me off at home if you want to go."

Dale looked a little concerned, but she brushed it aside. "I'm all right," she assured him. "I just don't feel like facing that crowd."

Later, on the way to church, she came back to the

subject of the afternoon. "Do you think your parents would actually leave the church if they had the chance?" she asked.

Dale noticed the troubled look on her face. "I'm sure they would if they felt that God wanted them to," he said slowly. "Would you have a problem with that?"

Sheila was quiet for a moment. "I don't know what to say," she said finally. "I always thought that leaving the church was really radical. Our minister back East always said that church divisions tear apart the body of Christ and that it was better to stay with a setting that had some weaknesses than to do that."

"I suppose that's right, to a degree," Dale said. "As long as it's just weaknesses that we're talking about. But I would think that outright sin would be different. Can the body of Christ contain known sin? If we leave a church because of evil, then we would be trying to *find* the body of Christ, not dividing it."

Sheila looked even more perturbed. "I just hope it doesn't come to that," she said. "I don't know if I could ever do that."

Dale and Sheila sat together in church that evening, as the practice was. Dale sensed that Sheila was deeply troubled. Her voice shook as she sang, and her hands were unsteady as she shared a songbook with Dale.

The Gospel team had moved on to another congregation that afternoon, and the local pastor and bishop, Samuel Martens, had the evening message. Before the message, he made an announcement. "Some of you were a little disturbed about what all took place at MYF last night. I talked to Henry a little bit about it, and he admitted that the group got a bit carried away. He said they forgot that the congregation here was more conservative than they were accustomed to, and he wanted me to apologize to you for being an offense. So I would encourage you to accept that and remember that not everyone views these things the same. We don't encourage Elvis Presley's music or the lifestyle he represents. But neither do we want to be judgmental of others who don't see it exactly as we do."

He went on with the message, but Dale's mind stayed on the announcement for a while longer. *Now what was he really saying? It's nice of Henry to make an apology. But really, he didn't admit that what he had done was wrong—he was just sorry he offended some of us. And Pastor Martens didn't say it was wrong either, just that we don't encourage it and that we shouldn't judge others who see it differently.*

Sheila, however, seemed more relaxed after the announcement. On the way home, she spoke about it. "I'm glad Pastor Martens said what he did. I just hope your father will accept it too, and not do anything radical."

Dale cocked his head at her a little questioningly, but he kept his doubts about the announcement to himself. "I don't think my parents are ready to do anything, really," he said. "They don't have a lot of options. Not unless they want to do something like move to Ontario to join the group you mentioned."

Sheila shuddered. "Oh, I hope they don't think of something like that," she whispered. "Surely we can stay true to the Lord here."

Dale didn't pursue the subject, since he sensed her strong feelings about it. "I sure hope this puts a stop to such antics at MYF," he said. "You surely wouldn't want that to continue, would you?"

Sheila shook her head emphatically. "No, I don't," she said. "I didn't like that any better than you did." She looked at him and smiled. "Let's not let this get between us," she added. "At least we'll always have each other, no matter what happens."

Dale's heart warmed as he returned her smile.

However, that evening, as he prepared for the night, Dale couldn't help but think back over the events of the weekend and Sheila's reactions. *She sure reacted pretty strongly to the idea of leaving the church. I guess she's had a lot of teaching about that being wrong. I wonder what would happen if I felt that I had to go somewhere else or if someone actually started a more conservative church here. What if she decided to choose the church instead of me? What would I do then?*

He picked up his Bible and turned to 2 Corinthians 6 again and reread the closing verses of the chapter. *I wonder what all would fall into the category of evil. And it uses some pretty strong language. I wouldn't want to say that Henry is an unbeliever, though I still can't understand how he can be so inconsistent. Nor would I call him an infidel or an idol worshiper. Yet I can't see how a spiritual person could act like he did on Saturday night and then turn around and give such a talk on Sunday morning. A lot of what he said could have applied directly to the way he acted the night before. . . .*

Perplexed, he closed his Bible and knelt to pray. On his knees, he brought his perplexities to God. His church, his girlfriend, his family—all of them tugged at his heart; but most of all he wanted to be faithful.

God, help me to know Your will and to be true to it, no matter what. It was the essence of his prayer and also his last conscious thought as he drifted off into a restless sleep.

Several days after the MYF episode, the Eberly family was eating breakfast together. Richard glanced at his watch and then walked over to the radio sitting on the kitchen counter. "It's almost time for the news," he said, turning a dial. "I wonder what's happening in Ottawa these days."

The set crackled at first, but as the tubes warmed up, the static turned to music. Richard and Dale were discussing the day's work and paid little attention, but Jane sat up straight in her chair and exclaimed, "That's Elvis Presley! That's one of the songs that Henry sang on Saturday evening."

The whole family's attention turned to the radio in time to hear Elvis's tenor voice crooning a love song. Then the music faded off, and the announcer came on. "We'll be back with some more favorites by Jerry Lee Lewis, Carl Perkins, Buddy Holly, and *Elvis Presley,* right after the news."

There was nothing exciting on the news, and Richard soon walked over to the radio to switch it off. Jane protested. "Why don't you leave it on for a while?" she asked. "I'd like to hear the music. We never listen to anything fun—just the news or some preacher."

Richard looked at her thoughtfully. "I wouldn't consider Jerry Lee Lewis or Elvis Presley to be a worthwhile kind of fun," he said. "I don't want you listening to that kind of program."

Jane made a face. "Really," she said, "everyone else listens to the music programs. I felt silly on Saturday evening. I hardly knew any of the songs they were singing."

Richard looked stern. "Jane," he said, "I'm glad that was the case. And I want it to stay that way. I wonder sometimes whether the radio isn't more trouble than it's worth. The church certainly hasn't done very well in controlling it."

Dale looked up from his breakfast. "You know," he said thoughtfully, "I was wondering how come our people know so many of the hit songs so well. I never even thought of the radio.[3] That's where a lot of this comes from."

He sat back in his chair and picked up his mug. "By the way," he added, "Sheila's father has been talking

---

3 Many of our people do not remember the time when the radio was so common in some churches that no one gave it a second thought. However, that was the case in the early sixties, even in some conservative congregations that had stepped out of the apostate settings.

about buying a television set. Sheila's mother wasn't too impressed with that. She put her foot down. But he feels he needs it to stay up with the programs his clients are talking about. Her brothers were pretty excited about it."

Richard looked perturbed. "What did Sheila think of that?" he asked.

Dale shook his head. "She didn't like it at all. She thinks it would just make a lot of trouble in their home with her brothers. But her father thinks it's harmless."

His father bit his lip. "That would make trouble. Those boys have little interest in the church, the way it is. But a television set would make matters even worse. I didn't think we had any television sets in church."

Dale shook his head. "We don't, as far as I know," he said. "But that would hardly stop Donald. Nor would he let Martha's concerns bother him. But it turned out that our area is still too far away from the transmission towers to get decent reception. They have good service in the big cities, but we're too far away. So he left it for now."

"Well, that's one advantage of living so far from an urban area," Richard said. "But I suppose it will come soon enough."[4]

Dale nodded. "Sheila said that her father checked into it. Within a year or two, we will have transmission towers right here in this area."

---

4 In the East, where the population was denser and TV coverage better, the TV made inroads into the church sooner than it did in the West.

Richard frowned. “I wonder how long it will be after that until our people start getting them,” he said. “That will be just one more step down.”

7

Sheila's Commitment

"Let God do with me what He will, anything He will; and, whatever it be, it will be either heaven itself, or some beginning of it."

—Mountford

Several weeks later, Richard and Dale delivered a trailer load of hay right after breakfast. It was a three-hour trip one way, and normally Dale would have delivered it by himself. However, since the rancher who had bought the hay was short on help for unloading, Richard went along to help. This gave them the chance to discuss some things that had been on Dale's mind.

"You know," Dale said, "I've wondered about being a missionary. Would that be a way to get away from these liberal church settings?"

Richard leaned back in his seat before answering. "Hmm. I'm not sure. Actually, from what I've read in the church papers, it almost seems as if some of the liberal pressures are coming from the missions. The church in Argentina, for instance, has been more liberal than most of our congregations from the very start. And the mission in Africa has had real problems too."[1]

Dale was astonished. "Why?" he asked in consternation. "I guess I just took it for granted that anyone out there trying to win souls for Christ would be a conservative."

"It would seem like it should be that way," his father acknowledged. "But it seems that too often the missionaries are ashamed to take our church standards along with them. They separate Christ from our practice, almost as if our practice was merely a culture. Then they pick up the local culture and think that it is just as good as our traditional practices. Also, they mostly fellowship with Protestant missionaries on the field and are influenced by them. Then they come home, and our young people can't understand why we have separate fellowship lines and practices at home if they aren't needed on the mission field."

"I can see that," Dale said. "But aren't there any conservative missions?"

"I don't know," his father said. "But how would Sheila feel about being a missionary?"

Dale made a bit of a face. "I'm not sure," he admitted. "She does seem to have a fear of anything that seems radical. Other people's opinions mean more to her than

1 See *Gospel Versus Gospel* and *African Safari* for documentation of these two statements.

they do to me. She struggled some with our discussion on Sunday afternoon about starting a more conservative congregation."

Richard was silent for a moment as he digested this. "Hmm," he said. "I guess that shouldn't surprise me, but somehow it does. I didn't think such things bothered her."

"Oh, they do," said Dale. "At least to a degree. That's why we didn't go to the singing on Sunday afternoon. She was afraid of how the group would act. She gets a bit tired of our needing to stand alone so often. I guess I never told you what happened when she changed her dress pattern."

His father turned toward him. "No, I don't think so," he said. "What happened?"

"Anne Carter really gave her a lacing about her new dress," Dale said. "She was rather crude about it, and Sheila was pretty unhappy. She was nervous about wearing it to start with, and Anne attacked her right in front of everyone. She cried that time."

Richard shook his head sympathetically. "Poor girl," he said. "That must have been tough on her. Girls find that kind of peer pressure hard to take. Besides that, she doesn't get any encouragement from her parents to take her stand. You'll have to be sure to do what you can to stand by her and make it easier for her."

"I do try to," Dale said. "But I know it would be really hard on her if the time came to actually leave this church. She was concerned that we don't fight over it, and she seemed sure that we would always stand by each other."

"Well, she has certainly grown spiritually since we first got to know her," Richard said. "I think that she has the desire to do what is right. As long as she allows God to lead her, she will come through it. But we'll have to remember to pray for her. Your mother is really pleased with the Bible studies they have been having. Sheila shows keen interest, and she has good ideas. She's been a good influence on Jane too. Jane thinks the world of Sheila."

Dale nodded. "I know," he said. "Earlier, I was a bit scared that she was just doing things to please me and you. That was why I was glad that she wanted to study the Bible like that."

They rode in silence for a few more miles, and then Richard spoke again. "How is your relationship going otherwise?" he asked. "Do you still feel that she's the girl for you?"

Dale smiled. "It's going great," he said. "I don't have any doubts, really. I'd be happy to marry her tomorrow."

He paused before continuing. "Actually, I've been thinking of talking with you about that," he said. "We've been courting for nearly six months now. Isn't it about time for us to start thinking of getting married?"

Richard looked sober. "I've been wondering if you were thinking along that line," he said. "I know that most of our young people don't court very long before they are engaged. I don't know that I want to make that decision for you. I don't think, though, that there's any rush.

I guess you'll soon be twenty-three, but Sheila only turned twenty a month or so ago."

Dale nodded. "I know it's a pretty important decision," he agreed. "But sometimes it's hard to wait. I'd love to have a little place of my own, with Sheila for my wife. It would seem a bit like heaven."

Richard chuckled. "I suppose it would," he said. "Just remember that Sheila is still human. Married life isn't always heaven."

Dale grinned. "I suppose," he said. "But I can't think of anything better on earth." Then his face sobered. "That is, it would be like heaven on earth if we didn't have all these troubles at church. I still wish we could do something about that. So you don't think the missionary idea is a good one?"

"I'm not against anyone being a missionary," Richard answered. "In fact, I think it would be good for the congregation here if we would put a lot more effort into reaching out to the world. But I don't think you should become a missionary just to get away from our church problems. Mission work has its own set of problems, and if you aren't truly called of God to be a missionary, you will soon be home again."

He hesitated for a minute while Dale negotiated a turn onto a side road. "Besides," he added, "our missions normally don't accept people without special training. You'd have to go back to school and get a college or university degree. And I'm not sure that I can recommend that."

Dale was shocked. "Why do they require that?" he

asked. "Does it take a college degree to tell people about the Lord?"

His father rubbed his chin and then grabbed the door handle for support as they hit a pothole in the road. "No," he said, "I never thought so. But our missions are basically copies of the Fundamentalist missions. And the Fundamentalists make a big deal of the importance of education. So we do too.

"It's true," he continued, "that a certain amount of education is useful. A missionary needs study skills and probably an understanding of language structures. But unfortunately, by the time our young people get through Eastern Mennonite College or Goshen College or the Mennonite seminary at Goshen, they no longer have a basic appreciation for conservative values."[2]

"In other words," Dale said, "they become people like Henry, with lots of knowledge but little conviction."

His father nodded. "That's right," he said. "It's happened over and over again. I don't know what they are doing in those church colleges, but they are not producing people with conviction. I am sure that the people who started them had good intentions, but it just hasn't turned out right."

Dale was silent for a moment. "Well," he said, "I guess that kills that idea. I'm not keen on going back to school. I have grade twelve, but it would take another four years

---

2 The same would have been true for Hesston College, even though Richard didn't mention it.

to get a college degree. I'm sure Sheila wouldn't be happy with waiting that long to get married."

That was where the matter was left, but Dale continued to pray for direction as far as the time for taking the next step in his courtship. Several months later, Dale and Sheila went to Sheila's home for Sunday afternoon and evening. After the dinner dishes were finished, Dale and Sheila settled down in the living room, and her parents joined them for a few minutes. Donald was at his flamboyant best. Like usual, he did not beat around the bush.

"Say there, Dale," he said in his booming voice as soon as he had settled himself in an overstuffed chair across from Dale and Sheila, "have you been giving any thought to the future? Seems to me that you and Sheila have some planning to do."

Sheila blushed furiously. "Father," she protested, "are you trying to push me out of the nest?"

Donald smiled at her affectionately. "Sheila," he said, "you will always be welcome in our home, and you may stay as long as you care to. But I'm sure Dale hasn't been coming here just because he doesn't know what else to do on Sunday afternoons."

Dale answered slowly. "No, I've got more in mind than that," he said. "But I want to be sure that we are following God's timing. I also want to be sure I can look after her, before we take any big steps."

Donald nodded. "Well, no one can accuse you of leaping before you look," he said. "That's a trait I like, actually, though I haven't often lived up to it. I can usually find some way to make something work after I've jumped into it. But caution can be good, I suppose. Just don't overdo it.

"You know," he continued, "we could use someone in our city branch. If you're interested, I could get you in there. You'd have to move closer to the city, of course."

Dale looked startled. "I guess I never thought of getting into sales," he said. "I'm just a farmer and a truck driver. I don't know how I'd do in something like that."

"Well, there's nothing wrong with farming, if that's what you prefer," Donald said. "I could put up some cash for you to get started on something of your own. I suppose your father will do something to help you get started too."

Dale scratched his head. "We've talked about that some. There's enough work for both of us on his land, with the hay sales we've had the last few years. We've talked about a partnership of some sort."

Donald nodded. "Your father's a good farmer. That would probably be a good opportunity. But you should invest some money in some land of your own rather than just riding along on his assets. It might make you tight for now, but down the road you'll be a lot better off."

Dale looked thoughtful. "Our neighbor is going to sell his half section[3] and his buildings," he said. "He was over the other day and said he would give us first chance at it. It's a pretty nice farm, and my father would like it;

3 In the West, land was surveyed into sections, with every section being 640 acres. Farm lots were often sold as quarter sections, or 160-acre parcels.

but he wasn't sure he wanted to go that deeply into debt. But we did talk a bit about the possibility of splitting it up. I could buy the quarter section with the house and corrals, and my father could have the other quarter."

"That sounds good," Donald said. "That way you'd be close enough to work together and share equipment. That would be a real advantage for you. Then down the road, you could buy the other quarter from your father and maybe eventually take over the whole operation."

He grinned at the look on Dale's face. "You've got to be ambitious these days, son," he boomed. "Dive into it while you're young; and when you're older, you'll reap the benefits. Land will never be cheaper than now. The more you can get your hands on, the better off you'll be down the road. That's my philosophy. Go take a look at the property, and if you like it, come and talk to me. I'm sure that between your father and me we can work something out."

Later, Donald and Martha went to take an afternoon nap, and Dale and Sheila moved downstairs to the family room. Sheila lit a fire in the fireplace and then curled up on an easy chair facing the fire. Dale stood beside her, hands clasped behind his back, staring into the fire. He was so absorbed in his thoughts that he didn't notice Sheila pick up her Bible from the stand beside the chair or hear her slowly turning the pages as if she were looking for something.

Finally, however, he remembered that she was there,

and turned. To his surprise, she was sitting there quietly with her Bible on her lap, watching him.

He reached down and pulled a stool over beside her chair and sat down. His feelings at that moment and her obvious interest in the Scriptures convinced Dale that she was for him.

Somehow, the moment seemed too sacred for words, and words weren't needed. Dale had read all he needed to know in Sheila's expression, and his silence answered her.

A little later—he could never remember how long they sat watching the flames—he looked at her again. "Do you feel like talking about our future?" he asked quietly. "Or would you rather wait a few more months?"

She didn't answer him directly. Instead, her eyes turned to the fire. "You know, sometimes I think I can see pictures in the fire," she said. "And then I wonder if they symbolize our future. Yet when I try to see them closer, they're gone."

She paused before continuing. "You know, the future scares me," she whispered, shuddering. "What if I should make some wrong choices, or what if somehow things didn't work out for us? We're so happy together now. I hope the future doesn't change that." Her voice broke. "I don't think I could bear it."

She was quiet for a moment before returning to his question. "I've given the timing of our courtship over to the Lord," she said. "I'm willing to leave it up to you."

She was quiet, and Dale could see that she was

waiting for him to continue. Now that the moment had finally arrived, he found it strangely difficult to ask the question that had been burning on his mind for weeks. Finally he took a deep breath and broke the silence. "I know I can't make you any promises about the future, but I know that God controls it, and I'm willing to leave it in His hands." He asked quietly, "Would you consider marrying me on that basis?"

He wasn't sure at first if she had even heard him. But finally she turned and looked directly at him. Softly she quoted the lovely, age-old passage from Ruth, which has been used to seal so many intimate covenants: " 'Whither thou goest, I will go; and where thou lodgest, I will lodge: thy people shall be my people, and thy God my God: where thou diest, will I die, and there will I be buried.' " She paused and then finished in a whisper, " 'The LORD do so to me, and more also, if ought but death part thee and me.' "

She wiped a tear from her cheek.

It was a holy moment, and they both sensed it. "Why don't we pray together," Dale suggested. "We want God's blessing on our life together."

She nodded, and they bowed their heads and poured out their hearts to God. Sheila prayed first, and her prayer revealed her heart to Dale as never before. She prayed for God's blessing on Dale; she prayed that God would bless them with genuine love for each other and that they would never disappoint each other. She prayed that God would reveal His will to them continually and help them to follow Him. And finally she almost faltered as in a whisper she asked God to help her overcome the doubts in her life.

It was a prayer Dale would never forget.

A little later, they went quietly upstairs again. Donald was in the kitchen, helping Martha prepare a light supper. He turned around, intending to make some kind of boisterous remark when Dale and Sheila entered, but the words died on his lips when he saw Sheila's face.

Dale stepped forward and addressed Donald. "Sheila has done me the honor of promising to be my wife," he said quietly. "Would you be willing to add your blessing to that?"

The kitchen was deathly silent for a moment; then Martha held out her arms to Sheila. Donald—speechless for one of the few times in his life—reached out and wrung Dale's hand.

Uncle Dale was silent. I sensed that the climax of his story still hadn't been reached. But he was so quiet that I left him sitting there, and went home without disturbing him further. I don't think he even caught on that I left.

8

A Trip to Oregon

"Break up your fallow ground:
for it is time to seek the LORD*."*
—Hosea 10:12

Dale never did find out who had sent him the notice, or why. But when he and Richard came in for lunch, his mother told him that he had received a letter in the mail that morning.

"It's from Oregon somewhere, according to the postmark," Carrie said. "But it doesn't have a return address. I put it on the china cabinet."

Mail for Dale was a bit rare, so he opened it before they ate. "Hmm," he said, looking down over the single sheet of paper. "This looks interesting. It's a program for a Bible conference at a Mennonite church in Oregon. I wonder what church that is."

Richard pricked up his ears. "Oregon?" he said. "I

know of several independent congregations there. They have never been part of the conference, as far as I know. I don't know much about them, except that they have a reputation for being fairly conservative."

Dale had been scanning the paper while his father was talking. "Say, this *would* be interesting," he exclaimed, getting more excited by the minute. "Look, here's a message on 'The Biblical Doctrine of Nonconformity.' And on Saturday evening, they have a message on 'The Necessity of Purity in Courtship.' "

Richard jumped to his feet and looked over Dale's shoulder. "Who are the speakers?" he asked. "Do we know any of them?"

Carrie smiled at the excitement but reminded them, "The food is getting cold. Maybe we should eat first, and you could look at that afterward."

Richard looked a little sheepish. "I guess we could," he said as he went to his chair at the head of the table. "But I do want to take a closer look at that program. I haven't seen anything like that for years."

Lunch began, but the conversation continued. "We used to have programs with titles like those, years ago," Richard said. "But now, we tend to get away from the practical doctrines. Oh, we still have messages on discipleship and so forth, but they don't uphold the same standards that they used to. Discipleship means something different today."

Dale looked puzzled. "What do you mean?" he asked.

"Well," his father said, "it used to mean obedience—following the teachings of Christ and the Bible in everyday life. Today, it means things like supporting the Mennonite Central Committee[1] or helping the Mennonite Disaster Service.[2] During the Second World War, it even meant supporting the Mennonite Peace Committee."[3]

Dale was amazed. "I always thought MCC and MDS were doing a lot of good," he said. "Do you think what they're doing is wrong?"

Richard shook his head. "No, I didn't mean to say that," he answered. "I simply said that supporting them isn't the same as discipleship. They do a lot of good, I suppose, though I think they sidestep the main purpose of the church and place physical needs ahead of spiritual ones. But discipleship goes far beyond that. Discipleship is following Christ in everyday life. It is being obedient to the Bible."

Dale nodded. "I can see what you are saying," he agreed thoughtfully. "We don't hear that emphasis very much." He picked up the program again, which he had laid beside his plate. "But this does seem to be different," he added. "It touches practical and doctrinal subjects that we hardly ever hear across the pulpit."

"That's right," Richard said. "Of course, it depends how they're handled. That's why I wondered who the speakers were. But I didn't recognize any of them."

1 The MCC gives social and humanitarian aid to downtrodden and suffering people, especially on an international level.
2 MDS gives help after natural disasters.
3 The MPC lobbied the government and used other pacifist means to try to promote peace on an international level.

Dale continued to look at the paper and eat at the same time until he accidentally knocked over his water glass. Then he laid it aside. But when they finished, he opened the subject again. "Would you care if we went?" he asked. "I should call Sheila and see if she would like to go. We could probably find someone to go with us."

His father picked up a toothpick. "I don't see why not," he said slowly. "I'd enjoy going myself, but someone has to look after the chores. You can give us a report of the meetings when you come back."

Dale called Sheila before he went back out to work. When he rejoined his father, his face looked pensive.

Richard looked at him curiously. "So, are you going?" he asked. "How did she react to it?"

Dale pursed his lips. "I'm not sure," he said, answering the second question first. "She tried to be excited about it, but it seemed a bit artificial—almost as if she were a bit reluctant." His face looked troubled. "I guess we'll go," he added. "But I wish I knew what was troubling her about it."

Richard scratched his head thoughtfully. "I wonder if she isn't a bit afraid," he said. "She's made a lot of changes, and she might be afraid of what the Lord will ask of her next. Or she might be afraid that you will go to an extreme. The area where she grew up had a lot of radicalism, and I'm guessing she has been taught to detest that. Naturally, it would be a struggle for her if she was afraid you might ask something like that of her."

He walked over to a large tractor parked in the back yard. But he stopped before mounting the steps to the seat and turned to Dale again. "I know Sheila loves you a lot," he said. "I'm almost sure that she's afraid that a meeting like this will drive a wedge between the two of you. You'll have to be careful to give her the time she needs to keep up with you in your spiritual journey."

Allister McLelland and his sister accompanied Dale and Sheila on their trip to Oregon. Allister had long been one of Dale's best friends. Even though Dale's courtship took up most of his spare time, Dale and Allister had kept in touch with each other. Allister was a little younger than Dale, and easygoing. Normally somewhat easily swayed, his ongoing friendship with Dale and Sheila had kept him from drifting with the crowd.

Sheila still seemed somewhat uneasy about going, but the four of them had an enjoyable trip together. The sessions started on Saturday and lasted until Sunday evening. Since all the meals were served at the church, they had lots of time to fellowship with other youth who had gathered from several Western states for the meetings.

Dale and Sheila found the sessions enjoyable and, due to their outgoing personalities, made a number of friends. Dale, especially, found the fellowship to be a real breath of fresh air.

They discussed the meeting on their way to their lodgings on Saturday evening. "This is sure different from our MYF gatherings, isn't it," Dale commented.

Sheila nodded. "It certainly is," she said. "The attitudes of the young folks impress me. There's no one fooling around and acting ridiculous and trying to make the group laugh."

"I know," Dale said. "And the young folks were actually standing around discussing the messages. I have never seen anything like it. And they dress a lot more decently than we are used to. I think half the young folks must be wearing plain suits and cape dresses. I sure wish we could be part of a group like this."

Out of the corner of his eye, he noticed her hands tighten involuntarily on her Bible when he mentioned plain suits and cape dresses. She quickly looked out the side window, but he had caught a glimpse of the troubled look that crossed her face. He immediately remembered what his father had said. *Oh, oh, maybe that wasn't a good thing to say. I'll have to be more careful.*

He changed the subject, pretending that he hadn't noticed her agitation. "That was an interesting message on courtship," he said. "I don't think I've ever heard one like it."

He could almost see her relaxing. She turned to him with a smile. "I liked it too," she said softly. "I'm glad our courtship has mostly been what was preached."

Dale looked at her. "I have always thought that it was respectful to a girl to maintain a hands-off policy during courtship," he said. "Even though we're engaged, you don't really belong to me. It wouldn't be right for me to take advantage of your love to suggest anything but a hands-off policy."

They fell silent then. But Dale's thoughts stayed with the girl riding beside him. *I wonder what she is really thinking about the meetings. I would surely feel at home with a group like this, but probably she sees things a bit differently.*

He continued to ponder this after he had dropped her off. *It seems that her convictions are a lot like mine in most things. But she still has this strange fear of looking a lot different from normal. She tries to hide it, but it keeps slipping out once in a while.*

The second message the next morning was on the Christian home. The speaker emphasized the importance of the home and the responsibilities of both the husband and the wife. When Dale and Sheila met for lunch, they both felt a little subdued. Sheila was the first to speak of it. "I knew marriage was serious," she said soberly, "but I never thought of it quite from that perspective. I'm afraid I have a lot of growing to do before I'm ready to be your wife."

Dale nodded. "I guess I never expected marriage to be all fun and games," he said. "But the speaker certainly gave us something to think about." He flashed her a quick smile. "I'm sure that *you'll* do fine. It's *me* that I'm worried about. He dumped quite a load on the men."

They returned their plates and went outside for some

fresh air. While they walked, Dale pulled his program out of his pocket. "Hmm," he said cautiously. "That subject on nonconformity is this afternoon. I wonder what the speaker will have to say about that."

Sheila didn't answer him, and once again he wondered what she was thinking. But when she spoke, her voice was light—almost deliberately so. "What other subjects do they have yet?" she asked. "I'm looking forward to the one about personal evangelism. That's an area I really need to grow in."

Then it was time for the nonconformity message. From where he sat, Dale could see Sheila clearly, and he noticed how tense she was as the speaker, a younger man from Pennsylvania, started into his subject. He also noted when it sank home to her that the speaker thought any girl or woman who wasn't wearing a cape dress was an apostate. His heart sank. Had he really done the right thing by bringing Sheila here? Was she ready to hear such a message?

When the speaker got into the main part of the message, he gave them some solid, Scriptural reasons for wearing distinctive attire. He pointed out the value of Christians dressing differently from the world. He read Numbers 15:38–40 and noted the reasons why God asked the Israelites to add distinctive fringes to the borders of their garments.

"Notice," he said, "that God wasn't concerned that the Canaanites would see how they were dressed. Their distinctive dress was a reminder to the Israelites themselves that they were God's people. In this way, it protected them and helped them to remember that they were responsible to God."

He looked over the audience, his eyes sharp. "How many times have you been tempted to buy a book or a magazine that you knew God would not be pleased with? If you are wearing distinctive attire at such a time, you will be ashamed to go to the counter to pay for it, and in that way your attire will be a help to you."

He flipped the pages of his Bible to 1 Peter 2:9 for another point. He read it: " 'But ye are a chosen generation, a royal priesthood, an holy nation, a peculiar people; that ye should shew forth the praises of him who hath called you out of darkness into his marvellous light.' " Then he looked at the audience again. "The word *peculiar* in this verse means 'special,' " he said. "In God's eyes, Christians are special, and He has chosen us to be His children. It is only right for us to show His praise to the world. One way for us to do this is to make sure that the world can see—in our speech, our actions, *and in our dress*—that we are His children."

By this time Dale had forgotten the speaker's remarks during the introduction, and he was following closely in his Bible. The next reference was Romans 12:2: " 'And be not conformed to this world: but be ye transformed by the renewing of your mind, that ye may prove what is that good, and acceptable, and perfect, will of God.' "

The speaker paused and allowed the words to sink in. "If we are truly transformed," he said, "then we will not be ashamed to show the world that we are God's children by dressing in a distinctive attire."

He turned to the matter of the plain suit.[4] "For many years, the plain suit has been worn by our brethren as a sign of unity and distinction. Many reasons are given today for dropping it. But even the world recognizes that the plain suit has religious significance. They expect you to be different from the world around you when they see you wearing it. Because of that, the plain coat will do for you what the blue fringe did for the Israelites."

Then he discussed the cape dress.[5] "The cape dress and plain suit go hand in hand. Our sisters do not wear the cape dress for modesty alone, though that is certainly an important part of the reason. Since I came here, I have seen a number of sisters wearing dresses without capes. However, such dresses—even though they may be modest to a degree—do not leave the same impression that a cape dress does."

He paused for a moment. "Perhaps I was a little sharp in my introduction, when I assumed that anyone here who wasn't wearing a cape dress was deliberately going against better knowledge," he added. "But in my time, I have seen where such laxness can take us. A dress without a

---

4 For those not acquainted with the traditional Mennonite practice, a plain suit has no lapels and is closed to the neck, with no room for a necktie. It somewhat resembles the traditional clerical collar.

5 A cape dress has a separate piece of cloth over the bodice, from the shoulders to the waist, to hide the form of the upper part of the body.

cape can very quickly become immodest if it shrinks, even if it was made loosely. And more and more people among us don't seem to mind immodest dresses. We need to draw the line at a safe place."

Dale thought of a dress he had seen Anne Carter wearing in town a few weeks before, and he winced. *I wonder what Sheila is thinking. She must be feeling a little embarrassed, sitting here dressed like she is.* He wondered again if he had really been wise to bring her to this meeting.

His question was partly answered at suppertime. He noticed her despondency right away but had no chance to talk to her about it. Another young couple, Robert and Janet, had invited them to eat supper with them. They came along just as Dale caught up with Sheila.

Dale had met Robert and Janet earlier, so he introduced them to Sheila. They were a friendly, attractive couple, but Dale noted that Sheila's eyes went to Janet's cape dress immediately.

They found a quiet place to sit together to eat. Dale and Robert were soon visiting. Janet tried gently to draw Sheila into a conversation as well, but she soon noticed that she did not feel up to visiting. In fact, Sheila seemed to be having a hard time eating, as if she had a lump in her throat. When Janet saw her blinking back a tear, she refrained from further conversation.

Dale had been watching Sheila too. As soon as he politely could, he excused themselves from the table. "Well, thanks for inviting us to eat with you," he said to

Robert. "Sorry to run off, but I think we had better go. Church will start soon and . . ." He didn't finish the sentence, but he didn't need to. Impulsively, Janet reached across the table and squeezed Sheila's hand.

Dale and Sheila wandered silently into the graveyard at the rear of the church property. They stopped in front of a large gravestone, but neither read the inscription. Instead, Dale looked down at her and said hesitantly, "You seem troubled. Is something wrong? Aren't you enjoying the meetings?"

Sheila looked at the ground and stirred a few pebbles around with the toe of her shoe. "I—I don't know," she said. "Everyone is friendly and nice, but I just don't feel at home here. I've struggled with it all weekend, but that message this afternoon was more than I could take."

She looked up at him, and her eyes begged him to understand. "I just don't seem to fit into this group," she whispered. "You do, but I don't. I wish I'd stayed home."

Dale felt his heart turn cold. He had been delighted with the chance for some good fellowship, and he had hoped that Sheila would feel like he did. He remembered his father's caution again. Was he pushing her too hard, too fast?

Dale saw panic rising in her, and his heart longed to help her. "Did you want to go back to where you're staying?" he asked. "We don't have to stay for the evening service if you'd rather not."

He hesitated and then added, "I'm sorry. I didn't consider the pressure this might put on you. I—I guess I was a bit selfish. I was enjoying everything so much that I didn't think of your feelings."

Sheila took a deep breath. "I don't know what to say," she said. "It wouldn't look right for the two of us to sit over there alone. Let's just stay for the service and then leave soon afterward."

The service that evening was inspirational again. Even Sheila found herself absorbing the messages, especially the one on personal evangelism. By the time the service was over, she felt a little better and was glad that she had stayed.

Dale had a more difficult time. He kept thinking of Sheila's depression. How could it be that the very meetings that were clinching his desire to maintain Biblical truths had so discouraged Sheila? Why did she feel that she didn't fit in? This was so out of character for Sheila that it baffled him. Normally she made friends wherever she went. He was going to have to ask her about it. Surely this wasn't going to drive a wedge between them. He remembered again the feeling of inferiority that Sheila expressed so often. Did that have anything to do with this?

After church, Dale tried to get to the back and find Sheila as soon as possible. But he had made many new friends that weekend, and it seemed that all of them wanted to say good-bye or exchange addresses with him. Every time he managed to get away, someone else stopped him. Normally, he would have enjoyed every minute of it, but tonight his concern for Sheila was eating away at him. Afterward, he could hardly remember whom he had met or what they said.

When he finally reached the back of the church, Sheila was nowhere to be seen. More worried than ever, he went into the basement to look for her. But she wasn't there either, so he went outside to the parking lot. Here, close to his car, he finally found her. To his relief, he saw that she was visiting with Robert and Janet.

Sheila heard the crunch of his footsteps on the gravel and turned to greet him. "I'm sorry I was late," he said. "I hope you haven't been waiting long. It seemed that every time I turned around, I met someone who wanted to talk."

Sheila smiled, though rather self-consciously. "Well, at least I got a chance to get to know Janet better this way," she said shyly. "I felt so foolish about the way I acted at suppertime."

Janet smiled and squeezed Sheila's arm in an affectionate gesture of camaraderie. "Don't worry about it," she reassured Sheila. "We all have our times when life seems to collapse around us. I'm glad we could still get to know each other."

The trip home was anticlimactic. Sheila was tired and slept part of the way. The rest of the time, she was friendly but subdued, and much of the time they drove in silence.

For Dale, the weekend seemed bittersweet. He had enjoyed the fellowship and had gained many new ideas to think about. He had considered himself a conservative, but now he realized that in spite of his studies in the past year, he still had a lot of growing to do.

That was the sweet part. The bitter part was Sheila's reaction. He realized now that she hadn't been as ready for the exposure as he had thought she was. That troubled him, because he had thought that they were in agreement on their convictions. Now he wondered if they were further apart than he had thought.

It was late when they got home. Dale carried Sheila's luggage to the house and said a quiet good-bye at the door. "I'll come by on Saturday evening," he said. "We can talk more then."

Sheila just nodded, as if not trusting herself to speak. The expression on her face seemed to be trying to convey a message to him. She opened her mouth as if to speak, but then thought better of it. He noticed, however, that she stayed inside the door and watched him drive out.

Tired as he was, he spent a long time on his knees beside his bed before crawling in. His last memory before sleep finally overtook him was the look on Sheila's face. What had she been trying to tell him?

His rest was a troubled one.

9

"Please, Give Me Time"

"Cause me to know the way
wherein I should walk."
—Psalm 143:8

Dale's parents listened eagerly to the report he gave them the next morning. But his father was very concerned when Dale told him about Sheila's reaction. "I'm not sure you should wait until Saturday evening," he told Dale. "I think she needs to talk to you now."

Dale hesitated. "I thought maybe she needed some time to sort things out," he said. "I don't want to push her."

Richard shook his head. "I don't mean for you to push her," he said. "But you need to be there. Let her tell you how she feels, and show that you are trying to understand. Otherwise, you might lose everything you have gained."

Sheila wasn't available when Dale called at lunchtime. But her mother sounded relieved when he asked if she thought it would work for him to come over that evening. "I'm sure she will be glad to have you come," she said. "I'll tell her you called and that you're coming over. She can call you back if it doesn't work for some reason."

Sheila met him at the door when he arrived after supper. He was startled when he saw her. Her demeanor and the haunted look on her face reminded him of the first time he had come to see her. She took his jacket but didn't speak. Instead, she led the way to the family room, where someone had lit a fire earlier.

It was a room that held many memories for Dale. Here it was that Sheila had first talked to him about her struggles. Here it was that they had prayed together that same night. Here too it was that he had asked her to be his special friend, and here it was that she had finally promised to be his wife. In between those two memorable occasions, they had spent many other evenings here, reading the Bible, praying together, and discussing the many things that a young couple needed to talk about.

All of this went through his mind as he paused for a moment at the door. He couldn't help but wonder what memories would be added to the list tonight.

He settled into the large, leather-covered easy chair by the fire, and Sheila sat on the floral couch close to the hearth. Both were silent. Both sensed that they had reached a crisis in their relationship, and both were hesitant to take the first step in a process that might either mend it or break it entirely.

Sheila stared into the fire, lost in thought. Dale was hesitant to break into her reverie. Instead, he watched her face, hoping to get a glimpse of what she was thinking. She brushed a strand of hair from her face, and Dale noticed with a start that she was wearing one of her old dresses—in fact, it was the dress she had worn the first time he had seen her.

He was still digesting this and wondering what it meant, when suddenly she turned and looked up at him for the first time that evening. Then, unexpectedly, she smiled. "Do I look as serious as you do?" she asked lightly. But her smile quickly faded, to be replaced with a pensive expression. "I'm glad you came," she added shyly. "I was feeling pretty blue today. My mother thought I should call you, but I didn't want to look like a baby."

Dale looked down at her and smiled affectionately. "I don't consider you a baby," he said. "You're the most important person in my life."

He leaned forward in his chair. "Want to tell me what was troubling you?" he asked. "Did I do something that's bothering you?"

Sheila shook her head emphatically. "It's not *you* that bothers me," she said. "It's *me*." She looked back into the fire, as if gathering strength to continue. "Actually, it's silly. I don't know why, but I can't get that sermon out of my mind."

She swung around and looked up at him earnestly. "Are you thinking of starting to wear a plain suit?" she asked.

Dale hesitated. "I've thought of it," he admitted cautiously. "Would that bother you?"

Her face took on a brooding expression. "It shouldn't, I guess," she said. "But I know it would. I keep getting this horrible picture in my mind of me wearing a cape dress and Anne Carter laughing at me." She shuddered.[1]

Dale looked at her soberly. "I've never said anything about asking you to wear a cape dress," he said.

"I know," she said, "but even I know that the cape dress and plain suit fit together. I would never let you face that stigma alone."

They sat in silence for a while. "Why does the idea of wearing a cape dress bother you so much?" he asked finally. "You've made other changes."

She pondered his question for a moment. "I don't know," she said wearily. "Unless it's because I've always been taught to look down on it. Somehow, I'm horrified at the idea."

She looked up at him again, and her face carried a plea for understanding. "I've been so scared that this would happen," she said, "that you would reach a spiritual plateau where I couldn't follow. Or that you would ask something

1 Some readers will find Sheila's struggle hard to understand, especially if they have worn a cape dress themselves all their adult life. But her struggles were very real to her, and they are very real to some who come into the church today from other settings.

of me that I wasn't strong enough to fulfill."

Dale was startled. "But I'm not asking anything of you," he protested. "I didn't ask you to make any changes."

"I know," she said wearily. "But I also know that my conscience will bother me dreadfully if you start wearing a plain suit. Yet, I just can't face Anne Carter and her friends in a cape dress. I just *can't.*"

They fell silent again, watching the fire. Then Dale sighed. "But I don't even know for sure if I'm ever going to wear a plain suit," he said. "I want to pray about it for a while. I don't want to make a sudden, drastic move."

She turned to him again. "But you will," she said. "I know what kind of person you are, and I know that you will wear one sooner or later."

After a pause she continued, "I talked to my mother about it. She doesn't think that the cape dress or the plain suit is necessary. But you know what else she said?" She paused, and when he shook his head, she said, "She told me to be glad that you have a tendency in that direction rather than in the other one, like my father has.

"I know why she said that," she finished, "but I just haven't been able to accept the idea." Her shoulders sagged.

She looked up one last time, beseechingly. "Please," she whispered, "please give me some more time. Put it off for a while."

He nodded, somewhat reluctantly. "Let's both pray

about it," he said. "But I think we should be together on this before we get married. We don't want to have something like this driving a wedge between us right after."

He saw the fear flash across her face. "Let's *not* let this drive a wedge between us, *ever*," she said emphatically. "Surely it's not important enough to do that."

He looked at the fire soberly. "If it's God's will, it's important," he said softly. "I can't let anyone, not even you, get between me and God."

A few minutes later, Dale prepared to leave. Sheila went to the door with him to say good-bye. He turned to her and asked, "Shall we get together Saturday evening?" It had been a while since he had bothered asking. Normally, they took it for granted.

Sheila hesitated, examining her fingernails. When she finally did look up at him, her eyes somehow refused to meet his. "I don't know," she whispered. "I—I need some time to think. Let's just skip our dates this weekend."

A cold fear shot through Dale's heart as he stood there. "Are you—are you—calling our courtship off?" he asked miserably.

She only waited a minute before answering, but it seemed like an hour to him. "No," she said finally, "but I have to have some time to sort out my life and face up to myself. I should have done it long ago."

This time she did look at him. "Dale," she whispered, "I love you. Please don't ever doubt it. But I need some time to think and pray. Please—please forgive me."

She turned and fled down the steps, leaving him

standing at the door. He thought of following her, but decided not to.

It was a long trip home that evening.

Dale's parents were still up when he got home. His father took one look at Dale's face and pulled out a chair for him at the table. "So it didn't go so well?" he asked.

Dale shook his head wearily. "She's really troubled," he said. "She doesn't want me to come back until she gets her thoughts sorted out—for sure not this weekend."

His father's shoulders sagged, and his mother sank into a chair across the table from him. "Why?" asked his father. "What's wrong?"

"It's—it's the cape dress," Dale said miserably. "She's horrified at the idea of wearing a cape dress. She's been taught that it carries a stigma, and—and she just can't bear the idea of wearing one."

He laid his face on his arms on the table for a moment and then lifted it again. "She keeps talking about facing Anne Carter," he added. "Though I don't know why she's so worried about her."

"Anne is the kingpin of the peer pressure here among the young people," his father said slowly. "But why is Sheila talking about the cape dress so much? Did you ask her to wear one?"

Dale shook his head. "I think God is asking her to, and she's resisting it," he said softly. "I didn't say a word about wanting her to wear it. But she knows that I am considering wearing a plain coat, and she has the idea that if I do that, she will have to wear a cape dress to fit with me. She also says she won't let me bear that stigma alone. But she can't reconcile herself to wearing a cape dress."

Dale's mother wiped her eyes. "Poor girl," she whispered. "She's under terrible pressure. Are her parents turning her against it?"

"No, they aren't," Dale said. "At least I don't think so. In fact, her mother told her that she should be glad that I have a tendency in that direction rather than the other one. And her father promised me long ago that he wouldn't interfere with our convictions. But neither are they really encouraging her, since they don't have convictions for plainer dress."

He stopped and rubbed his eyes. He was still tired from getting to bed late the evening before. "She begged me just to wait awhile," he said dully. "But I told her that we need to somehow settle it before we get married. She doesn't think that it's important enough that it should drive a wedge between us."

He looked at the tablecloth and traced the flowery design with his index finger. "I told her that God's will is important and that I couldn't let even her get between me and God."

He looked up at his parents and noted the sympathy in their eyes. "I won't let that happen," he said. "I'll stay single forever rather than lose my relationship with God." He paused before whispering, "But it would be hard to give her up now—terribly hard."

Uncle Dale grabbed his cane and pulled himself to his feet. "Let's go for a walk," he said gruffly. "I'm tired of sitting here."

I followed him off the porch. I had no intentions of going home before I learned what happened next, though I think that deep down in my heart, I already knew.

The rest of the week dragged by on leaden feet. There was no prayer meeting that week, and Dale skipped MYF. Somehow, the memories of the Bible conference were too special to spoil by the lightheartedness he knew would prevail at the Saturday evening gathering.

All week Dale carried with him a cloud—the knowledge of Sheila's struggle. He prayed much for her—asking God to help her find peace with doing His will, whatever that was. He prayed too for grace to accept whatever God had planned for him.

Sunday morning came and went—but no Sheila. She had stayed home from church, apparently. Even her parents avoided him, or so it seemed to him. But he was glad, because he didn't feel up to talking to Donald anyway.

The next week went even more slowly. Wednesday passed, then Thursday. Still no word from Sheila. Should he call her? Just to assure her that he was praying for her? He tried once, but no one answered, and he didn't have the heart to try again.

Friday passed. Still no word from Sheila. Saturday came, and still just silence. Dale pretty well gave up again when he came in for supper and still she hadn't called.

But in the middle of the meal, the telephone finally rang.

"Could you slip over tonight?" Sheila asked when Dale came to the telephone. "Please? I—I'd like to talk to you." Her voice sounded husky.

10

The End of the Road?

"Oh, the joy of leaving all to Jesus!
What a balm the broken heart to heal."
—Anna Ölander (adapted)

Now that the moment had come, Dale felt almost sick. He stood beside the telephone, trying to regain his composure before returning to the table.

His father looked up as he sat down. "Sheila wants me to come over tonight," Dale answered the unspoken question. "She didn't say why—she only said she wanted to talk to me."

No one talked for the rest of the meal. Dale knew that his parents were almost as concerned about the outcome of the evening as he was. They had grown to love the girl who had promised to be their daughter-in-law. Her pain was their pain, just as surely as Dale's pain was theirs. But there was little they could do to help. As

Richard had told Carrie the night before, sometimes young people had to iron out their own troubles, and the best thing that parents could do was stand back and pray and leave them in God's hands.

Somehow—even if they said little—Dale knew that tonight his parents would be praying for him and for Sheila.

As his car turned the corner from the road into the Lawrences' lane, Dale couldn't help but remember the first time he had gone around that corner and the far-reaching repercussions that had come from that evening. What would this evening hold?

He parked his car but stayed sitting for a moment, praying for strength to go in and face Sheila. But most of all, he prayed for Sheila, that she might find peace and that God would take the haunted look from her face.

Sheila met him at the door, where she had been waiting for him. He could see that she had been crying, but her face was expressionless—almost as if it had been carved from stone. Once again, he followed her down the familiar steps to the family room. Sheila almost seemed to read his mind. She looked wistfully around the room, then up at him. "You know," she said huskily, "this room has so many memories of us in it. I can never come down here without my heart beating a bit faster."

For a moment her face seemed to soften, but she didn't say anything more until they were seated—Dale in the leather-covered easy chair and Sheila on a chair across from him. This time she faced him, not the fire. But it was Dale who spoke first.

"So, have you had a chance to think things through?" he asked, coming right to the point. "How are you feeling about us by now?"

She ignored his question for a moment. Instead, she looked earnestly at him. "I'm sorry for making you wait this long," she said softly. "I'm sure it's been a miserable week for both of us."

"It was a long week," he agreed. "I thought of you a lot—and prayed for you."

Sheila's eyes flickered, and she almost glanced away. "I never want to spend another week like it," she said softly. "I've never felt so horrible in my whole life."

Then she dropped her gaze and came back to his question. "I thought I knew what I was going to tell you," she said wistfully. "Now I'm not sure if my heart will cooperate."

She sighed. "But I might as well tell you what I was thinking," she added. "It would break my heart to break our engagement. I so badly wanted this to work. But I just can't see myself in a cape dress and you in a plain suit. I just can't force myself to accept that."

She paused, but he didn't say anything, so she continued. "I thought I would put it this way," she said without emotion, as if reciting from memory. "If you would be willing to promise me that you won't start wearing a plain suit and that you'll never ask me to wear a cape dress, I'll marry you and try to be the best wife for you that I possibly can."

When she raised her eyes, he saw that she was begging him to understand, not just how she felt, but why. "If you don't want to do that, I'll understand," she whispered. "And I—I'll release you from your promise."

Dale was stunned. All week he had prayed for grace to handle such an answer, but now that she had spoken, he felt as if he had turned into stone. Surely this couldn't be happening. Not after all the happy times they had shared together, and all the deep waters they had gone through together. How could he walk away from her? His heart would be torn in two. Life wouldn't be worth living without her. She had been in his every waking thought for the past year. Every plan that he had made for the future included her. How could she do this to him? How could God allow it?

He moaned, almost inaudibly, and dropped his head in his hands.

Yet, how could he make such a promise? He didn't know if God was asking him to wear a plain suit for sure, but how could he promise her that he would ignore God if He did? How could she ask this of him? His heart almost lashed out at her for putting him in such a spot, but he could not—he loved her too much. Yet, how could he do this? It would mean denying his God.

Who comes first? It was only a still, small voice, but it got his attention. He also remembered what he had told her last time—he couldn't let anyone, not even her, get between him and God. There could be only one answer.

Dale looked up at her, dully. He saw in her eyes that she already knew what his answer would be, and that she was steeling herself for it. Dumbly he remembered the vow she had made to him in this very room: *The LORD do so to me, and more also, if ought but death part thee and me.* He could still see her saying it. What had happened to her, that she would back down on that? Then a sudden thought came to him—he tried to push it away, but it kept coming back—What repercussions will she face because of her decision?

Slowly he shook his head. "I—I don't know what God will ask of me," he said, his voice breaking. "But I can't make a promise like that. I'm sorry."

He thought for a moment that she was going to crumble before him, but she willfully pushed her weakness aside. "Then—then please release me of my promise." She tried to speak firmly, but her voice cracked a little. "I—I can't go through with it."

He nodded dumbly, and she looked at him one more time. "Please don't hate me," she whispered. "And—and please forgive me."

Even in his misery, he could see how unhappy she was. "Sheila," he said gently, "I couldn't hate you even if I wanted to. No one has ever meant as much to me as you do. I would have died for you, but I can't—I can't do this . . ."

They sat there quietly, and he wondered for a moment if she would really see it through or if she would back down on her decision, even yet. But she was resolute, so he slowly got to his feet. "I guess this is good-bye then," he said huskily. She nodded mutely but did not offer to accompany him to the door or to watch him go. The last he saw of her, she was staring into the fire. Blindly, with tears trickling down his cheeks, he found his way up the stairs and out to his car. He never knew afterward how he got back on the road or where he drove, but somehow he found his way home.

His parents looked up when he came into the kitchen. They did not need to ask any questions—they could tell what had happened by the look on his face.

It seemed to Dale that his father looked more haggard than he had ever seen him, and he realized that they were almost as disappointed as he was. His father opened his mouth to speak, but then closed it again. When he finally did speak, he sounded like an old man. "Why don't we pray together," he said. "God knows how to heal broken hearts."

Uncle Dale stopped and leaned over the fence to look at several cows with young calves. "To this day, I still don't know, for sure, what made Sheila do what she did that night," he said gruffly. "I doubt if she knows either. But when the going gets tough spiritually, only a real commitment to the Lord will see you through. I still think she wanted to do what was right. But that wasn't enough. I know that she loved me, but that wasn't enough either."

He watched a calf walking up to the fence. "I forgave her long ago," he added quietly. "She has reaped much from that decision. I only feel sorry for her. She'll answer for her choices in life someday soon, and I'll answer for mine."

I was full of questions, but he shook his head. "Not tonight. We'll talk again."

I understood. He needed some time alone.

11

Sunday Happenings

"The daughters of Zion are haughty,
and walk with . . . wanton eyes."
—Isaiah 3:16

Sunday morning came far too soon for Dale. He had slept little the night before and did not feel in the least like going to church. No one at church knew yet about the rift between him and Sheila, since she had not been at church the week before. But if she was there this morning, people would start to wonder. This would be especially so at the evening service, when the young couples normally sat together.

Could he face it?—the looks of pity, the curiosity disguised as concern, the knowledge that people were discussing him and Sheila behind his back. Well, like it or not, he had to get up for chores anyway. He would face that question after breakfast. He reached over to turn off the alarm, and got dressed. Then he sat on the edge of the bed and picked up his Bible. He flipped the pages idly, wondering dully what he could read that would apply to his present situation.

It all seemed so unreal. A month ago, he and Sheila had been busy making wedding plans and thinking about setting up housekeeping. Now it was all gone. His finest dreams were shattered—and worst of all, they had been shattered by the girl he loved. He sat and stared at the wall; then finally he got down on his knees beside his bed, burying his face in his pillow.

When he rose to his feet, a damp spot on the pillow testified mutely to the depth of his struggle. But his shoulders didn't sag quite as much, and his step was a little lighter. Resolutely, he went out the door and up the steps.

Even though Dale had resolved that he would go to church as usual and say as little as possible about what had happened, he found it pretty difficult to actually walk in the church doors. However, he stuck it out, and no one asked him why he hadn't brought Sheila that morning. Right after church, he slipped back the side aisle, intending to head for home before anyone caught him. But he got stuck behind a few men, and by the time he got to the lobby, a group of girls had already congregated there.

His heart sank when he spotted Sheila at the edge of the group, chatting with several others. He would have to walk right past her on his way out. How could he do that? And how should he act? Should he say hello to her? Or just ignore her?

Out of the corner of his eye, he saw Donald heading in his direction, and he knew he had to act immediately. On top of everything else, he could *not* handle a discussion with Donald that morning. Quickly he slipped into the lobby. For just an instant, his eyes met Sheila's; but she continued talking as if she hadn't seen him, while he slipped past and out the door. Just as he closed the door behind him, he heard a voice—he was almost certain it was Anne Carter's—saying, "Hey, Sheila, what gives? You two mad at each other or something?"

He didn't hear Sheila's reply, but he heard a burst of laughter as the door clicked shut. Heartsick, he walked across the church parking lot to his car. However, before he opened the car door, he heard someone else walking across the graveled drive.

Looking around, he saw Blake Martens. Blake was somewhat older than Dale, having turned twenty-six recently. Blake was a decent young man who had pretty well given up attending any youth activities some years before, due to the direction that they had taken. In fact, he had been to only one MYF meeting since Sheila had moved into the area—the time of the "Elvis" episode—and thus didn't know her very well. Blake usually stayed in the background and was often viewed as a loner—if he was noticed at all. Blake and Dale had never been close friends, but they had been together occasionally before Dale started courting Sheila.

Dale nodded a greeting and would have passed on, but he noticed that Blake stopped and turned in his direction.

"I heard this morning that Sheila broke your engagement," Blake said, a little awkwardly. "I just wanted to tell you that I'll be praying for you."

He cleared his throat again before continuing. "I don't know why Sheila did what she did, and it's none of my business. But don't give up—a few of the rest of us still appreciate you and the stand you're taking."

He turned on his heel without waiting for a response from Dale and opened the door of his car. Dale—a little dazed by this unexpected comfort—watched him leave and then opened his own car door. *I'll have to get to know Blake better. Maybe I should invite him over sometime. He doesn't have much social life, and I sure won't feel like it either, without Sheila.*

He was partway home before it struck him. Sheila was wearing a new dress. And even though he couldn't remember exactly how it looked, he was sure that it was a different pattern from those she had worn most of the past year. She had gone back to her old dress pattern. *She made that dress before ever talking to me. That means that she was planning to take her own way no matter what I did.* His heart turned a few degrees colder. Any lingering hopes he might have had that she would change her mind evaporated.

But deep inside, a small flicker of flame sprang to light. It would take some time, but already he was starting to see that perhaps the Lord had used this means to deliver him from a worse tragedy. Already, the healing balm of God's Spirit was at work.

> *Uncle Dale stopped and looked at me. "It wasn't easy, son," he said. "But mind you, God never asks anything of you that He doesn't give you strength to do. I knew that I had done the right thing and that God approved. That helped a lot."*

Several weeks went by, and Sunday came around again. Rather than spending another Sunday afternoon sitting around the house and battling with morose thoughts, Dale had invited Allister and Blake for lunch.

The three had the house to themselves for the afternoon. Dale's parents had been invited away. Jane had gone to a friend's house and was going from there to the singing. After raiding the refrigerator for the food that Dale's mother had prepared for them, the three settled down in the living room for an afternoon of visiting.

By now, most people in church knew that Dale and Sheila had broken up, and the novelty had already begun to wear off. The current story—passed around mostly by Anne Carter and a few others of that ilk—was that Dale had insisted that Sheila start wearing a cape dress and that she had finally put a well-deserved end to his bossing her around. Dale heard the story from a rather indignant Allister but did not bother to try to vindicate himself. As usual in such cases, some people believed the story, some doubted it, and some didn't really care one way or the other. What Sheila thought of the story or what part she had in starting it, Dale never found out. But it evidently didn't bother her enough to cause her to take any active steps to squelch it.

That, in fact, was the subject that Dale and his friends were tossing around this afternoon. Since Allister had been along to Oregon with Dale and Sheila, he had seen some of Sheila's reactions during that trip. Even though Dale had never given him the complete story of his breakup with Sheila, Allister was astute enough to have pretty well pieced together what had happened.

Allister lounged back in his easy chair and propped his feet on a nearby hassock. He clasped his hands behind his head and cocked one eye at Dale. "So, has Anne still been needling you?" he asked. "She sure seems delighted that Sheila dropped you."

Dale shrugged his shoulders. "She keeps rubbing it in every time she gets close enough to get my attention," he said. "I can't figure out why she gets such pleasure out of making fun of me. But what bothers me even more is that Sheila seems to be spending a lot of time with her. I don't like that. Sheila is too nice to be corrupted by Anne Carter."

"Oh, I don't know," Allister said. "It's nice of you to defend Sheila, I suppose. But I think she's as much at fault as Anne is if she hangs around her. She seems determined to prove to the others that she is part of the in crowd. It sure did not take her long to start dressing like the rest after she dropped you. I think she's had a new dress almost every Sunday since, and each one is more like Anne's dresses than the last one was."

Characteristically, Blake had listened quietly to their exchange up to this point. Now, however, he spoke up. "Anne is at the hub of the peer pressure in our youth group," he said. "If you want to be popular, you have to be one of her friends. I think Sheila is eating her heart out at what happened. She loved you, Dale, and a person doesn't get over something like that overnight. I think she is trying to drown her feelings."

Dale nodded. "I'm afraid you're right," he said miserably. "I sure wish I could help her see it. She isn't that kind of girl at all, and I'm sure she's dreadfully unhappy. But I'm afraid where this will take her."

Allister frowned. "But how could she do what she did if she really loved Dale?" he objected, facing Blake. "Surely her love couldn't have been very strong."

Blake shook his head. "That's not necessarily true," he said. "But something else in her heart was even stronger than her love. It could have been fear, or a love for something else."

Dale got to his feet and walked over to the picture window on the other side of the living room. He clasped his hands behind his back and watched a few puffs of dust on the field across the road. "You're right," he said slowly. "She was afraid. She was afraid that I would become too conservative and that she would feel obligated to fit in with me. She was afraid of the power that her love gave me over her, and where it might take her."

He turned and looked at the others. "Actually," he continued, "I think she felt that she should wear a cape dress. But she didn't recognize that it was God working in her heart that made her feel that way. Instead, she thought it was my influence. She tried to make me promise that I would never wear a plain suit, so that she wouldn't feel obligated to wear a cape dress."

The room was silent for a moment while Dale's friends digested this information. Interestingly, Blake was the first to respond. "So she broke your engagement because you wouldn't promise that?" he asked quietly.

Dale nodded.

"That was the only right thing for you to do," Blake said. "No girl has the right to limit her husband's allegiance to God. Your marriage would have had no end of problems if you had entered it on that kind of premise."

Dale crossed the room and sat on the couch again. "I know," he said ruefully. "But it didn't make it any easier. I—I sure miss her."

His friends were quiet for a moment, respecting his grief. "It would almost have been easier to see her die than to see her take the course she's taking," Dale continued quietly. "I'm afraid she has no idea where she could end up. I don't think she has any resistance right now, because of her state of mind. And Anne Carter is smart enough to see that and take advantage of it."

He would have continued, but at that moment the back door slammed, and they heard the buzz of excited girls' voices. Jane and several of her friends burst into the dining area beside the living room. "Dale, you should have seen what happened at the singing!" Jane exclaimed as soon as she saw him in the living room. "Anne and some of the others were fooling around in the hospital lounge, and the activities director asked us all to leave. She said that we were disturbing the patients and their visitors too much and that we weren't to come back."

The other girls added some more details while the three boys looked at each other soberly. Finally, because he knew that Dale wanted to know, Allister asked Jane, "Was Sheila along with you?"

Jane glanced at Dale out of the corner of her eye. "Yes, she was," she said reluctantly, her excitement fading a little. "Anne was trying to persuade her to go for a ride with George in his new car. He wanted to take her home." Then she added quickly, "But Sheila wouldn't go, and Anne got huffy with her because right now Anne and George are buddies. Sheila got upset and walked out on her because she can't stand George."

Everything was quiet for a moment; then one of the other girls spoke up. "Sheila went off with Andrew Martens instead," she said, adding quickly, "but we figured that was just to spite Anne. We're sure she isn't interested in him."

The girls headed off to Jane's bedroom, still chattering about the afternoon's excitement. Dale's face had blanched when he heard about Sheila, but he said nothing, and the other two weren't sure what to say.

Finally Blake broke the silence. "Well, it's too bad

that our church is leaving that kind of testimony," he said soberly. "But maybe this will help some of our young people realize how their antics look to other people."

Allister grimaced. "Wonder how the bishop will view this," he said. "He usually finds some way to water down what happens. He might find it a bit harder this time."

That evening after church, Dale brought up the subject again as he and his parents sat around the kitchen table, drinking tea. "So our young folks got kicked out of the hospital," he said. "I wonder what people will think of that."

His father nodded soberly. "I heard about it," he said. "I must say that they have been pretty long-suffering, according to what Jane said. I guess they liked the singing all right. But the way the young folks acted—especially afterward—bothered them."

Dale hesitated. "Did Jane say anything about Sheila being involved?" he asked slowly.

A pained look crossed his father's face. "A little," he admitted. "But it sounded to me like Anne Carter was pestering her again. I wish our ministry could see what that girl is doing to our youth group. I have talked to them a few times about it, and they always act concerned, but nothing ever happens. They say they don't want to turn her away, so that we can help her. That sounds good, but look at all the young folks that she's influencing in the wrong direction."

Dale nodded. "I know," he said. "I think Anne was

the first of our girls to wear a gym suit in high school, several years ago. And I know that she and some of her friends sometimes wear slacks, depending on what they are doing. I don't think Sheila has ever done that, but she'll get sucked into it if she keeps running with Anne's crowd."

His shoulders sagged. "I've been trying to accept it that it wasn't God's plan for me to marry Sheila," he said. "But wouldn't there be some way for someone to help her see what's going to happen to her if she keeps on this trail?"

He looked at his mother. "She used to respect you," he said. "Couldn't you talk to her?"

His parents looked at each other. "I don't know," his mother said softly. "I've tried to meet her after church different times. But she seems to avoid me. I could try again, I suppose. I don't have much hope though. She seems to have made up her mind what route she wants to take."

12

Donald Visits Dale

"Had I the choosing of my pathway,
In blindness I should go astray,
And wander far away in darkness,
Nor reach that land of endless day."
—Charles Naylor

The next Sunday afternoon, Dale was downstairs in his bedroom reading when he heard a car drive in. Moments later, he heard a knock on the door and his mother going to answer it. He was engrossed in his book, however, and didn't pay any attention to the murmur of voices overhead. But when he heard rapid footsteps coming down the stairs toward his bedroom, he looked up, puzzled, and set his book down on his desk.

Who could be coming to see him today? Before he could get up from his chair, there was a sharp tap on his door, and a voice asked, "Can I come in?"

"Sure," said Dale, and to his amazement, Donald walked in. Dale half rose to his feet, but Donald waved him back. "Don't get up," he said. "I can sit on the bed."

Uneasily, Dale watched him settle down on the bed and cross his legs. Whatever did he want? Had he come to try to get Dale to try Sheila again?

Donald didn't leave him wondering long. "Well, young man," he said, with some of his old joviality, "I've tried to track you down at church the last number of Sundays, but you seem to be as slippery as an eel. You do an awfully good vanishing job whenever I come back the center aisle."

Dale shifted in his chair, and Donald chuckled and then looked at him searchingly. Noting Dale's uneasiness, he became more serious. "Actually," he continued, "I don't really blame you for that. But I did want to talk with you, so I took the liberty of inviting myself and coming over. This is better than talking at church anyway, since people won't be eavesdropping and gossiping about us."

Dale relaxed a little as Donald dropped his pretense at lightness.

"I suppose the past few weeks haven't been easy for you," Donald said sympathetically. "I know that Sheila hasn't been happy either. I had a long talk with her last night, and I thought I would talk with you too, to see if there was any way that we could patch this up."

He looked at Dale with a calculating eye. "I guess Sheila put you on the spot a little, from what she told me," he continued. "I think she was a bit foolish, and I told her so. She lost herself the best chance at a good husband that she might ever get, because of her actions. But she's always believed in being honest. I guess she felt obligated to tell you how she felt."

He continued to watch Dale's response and apparently noted the question on his face. "I wonder if we could put together a bit of a compromise," he said confidentially, lowering his voice a little. "I know Sheila loves you, and I know that you honestly loved her as well."

He paused, and Dale nodded without speaking.

"Well, like I said, I told Sheila that she took the wrong approach entirely," Donald continued. "She admitted to me that you never asked her to make any of the changes she made. She really had no reason to think that you would ever make her wear a cape dress—which is what she seems to fear."

His voice became more earnest. "I'd like to see you and Sheila get back together," he said seriously. "I've got no use for the gang she's getting involved in now, and I told her so. I'd much rather she stayed like she was, even if I don't share all your convictions."

He looked at Dale appraisingly. "I don't have a lot of use for the plain suit myself," he admitted. "Even though I admire your father for sticking to his beliefs. But I'd rather have a son-in-law with a plain suit any day than one of those shallow-minded characters who run around with Anne Carter."

He stood up and looked down at Dale, putting his hand on his shoulder. "Listen," he said huskily. "I know you are a serious young man and that you want to do what is right. But you gave up too quickly. I think Sheila would let you wear a plain suit if you wanted to, and still marry you, as long as you promised that you would never make her wear a cape dress against her will. At least it would be worth broaching the subject with her."

Startled at this sudden turn of events, Dale looked at him speechlessly while his mind whirled. Was there a chance that his relationship with Sheila could be restored after all? Was that what Donald was trying to tell him?

Donald walked restlessly over to a picture on the wall and looked at it for a moment before turning abruptly back to Dale. "I think I know what you're thinking," he said. "Sheila hasn't been doing too well since she broke up with you. But I hope you won't hold that against her. She's just been trying to drown her feelings. I really don't think she will ever be happy until you get back together."

He sat back on the bed and looked pleadingly at Dale. "Sheila doesn't fit with Anne Carter's crowd," he said. "I think she realizes that and would actually welcome you back. It would give her a good excuse to break up with them. All she needs is some moral support, which I know you could give her if you wanted to.

"Actually," he continued confidentially, "I have a feeling that sooner or later she might even get used to the idea and decide to wear a cape dress of her own accord. I personally don't care for the appearance of it, and I know Sheila's mother doesn't either. But we've kept my promise to you. We've never tried to turn Sheila against your convictions, and we won't."

He looked moodily at the floor. "I kept hoping you would rub off a bit on our boys," he added. "They aren't doing so well. But they thought highly of you, and you would be a good influence on them."

Abruptly he got to his feet. "Well, what do you think?" he asked. "Should I tell Sheila that you'll be over to talk to her? I think she'll be around this evening."

Dale's whole soul was in turmoil. He had given up Sheila and had found a measure of peace in submitting himself to what appeared to be God's plan. Now Donald was offering him a second chance. He longed from the depths of his soul to reach out and grasp that chance. But was it right? Was this God's direction, or would it lead him away from God? What should he say? Donald was waiting for an answer. He had to say something. Finally he shook his head, as if trying to clear away the cobwebs that kept him from thinking clearly.

"This is so sudden," he said huskily, speaking for the first time since Donald had entered the room. "I have to have some time to think and pray about it. I'd love to have Sheila back, but I don't know what to say. I have to have more time."

Donald saw the struggle mirrored on Dale's face and apparently decided that he had accomplished everything that could be done for the moment. He walked to the door as if to leave, but paused with his hand on the doorknob and turned back. "I haven't forgotten my promise to help you with a down payment for a farm," he said. "Keep it in mind."

Then he was gone.

Dale remained seated, his book forgotten. It seemed to him as if all the emotional defenses he had erected to protect himself had come crashing down like a sandcastle. All of his longings came rushing back. He thought of Sheila and all the good times that they had had together in the past year—the times of sharing together and reading the Bible together and planning for their life together.

But he also remembered again the searing pain that had pierced his heart when she asked him to turn against his convictions, and the agony of her subsequent rejection when he refused. Could he ever forget those moments? Could their relationship ever be the same again? Could he ever trust her again? Would it really be possible to reassemble their shattered relationship from the ashes that remained of their past?

And what about the things that had happened since? What about the rumors about him that Sheila hadn't bothered to squelch? And her new dresses? And her new friends? Was it his duty to try one more time to rescue her from the course she seemed determined to take? Was it really his fault? Should he have suggested a compromise and saved her from that? Would she even be willing to try to regain what they had lost?

The questions churned around and around inside his head until he almost despaired of finding sensible answers to them. Finally, in desperation, he sank to his knees beside his chair and tried to pour out his heart to God.

When he rose from his knees, he was calmer, but he still wondered what to do. Would Sheila respond as Donald had predicted? Even if she did, would that show that the Lord was leading them back together again? Should he at least try to talk to her?

He still hadn't made up his mind when chore time came. But while he was feeding the cattle, he remembered that there was no church that evening. Since Jane was visiting a friend, he and his parents would have the house to themselves. He would talk to them about it rather than visiting Sheila. He could still go to Donald's later if they thought it was a wise idea.

Later that evening, Dale told his parents about Donald's visit. They had known about it, of course, but had decided to let Dale bring up the subject on his own accord.

"So what do you think?" he asked in conclusion. "Should I try again? Will it be my fault if she turns out wrong and I didn't give it a second try? Donald wanted me to come over tonight and try to talk to Sheila. I suppose he talked to her too, to try to persuade her to go along with it."

Dale's father shook his head doubtfully. "I thought pretty highly of Sheila," he admitted. "But I don't like the course she has been taking. Maybe you could talk her into accepting Donald's proposition, but what would that accomplish in the long run? If she really isn't committed to living the Christian life for any other reason than marrying you, I don't see how it could ever work."

Dale's mother nodded in agreement. "I don't want to see you hurt again, Dale," she said softly. "If she finds her way and turns her back on her friends and her rebellion, I would maybe think differently. But she has shown no indication of wanting to do that."

Dale's father nodded. "I suppose Donald could be right in his evaluation that she is trying to drown her feelings in running after Anne and her friends," he said. "But that isn't the response of a committed Christian. I feel sorry for her, and I wish we could help her. But I wouldn't be ready to see you go back to her without seeing some genuine changes. A marriage normally lasts for a long time. It can be a very unhappy relationship if two people don't see eye to eye on spiritual things."

He looked thoughtfully at the table, as if trying to put his thoughts together. "Donald might be right," he said again. "But I think Sheila should give a pretty strong indication that she has changed her ways and regrets her actions, before you give any further consideration to asking her again."

He looked at Dale keenly. "Besides," he continued, "she's hurt you pretty badly. I think it would be pretty hard for you to regain your confidence in her, wouldn't it?"

Dale winced and looked at the table. "I know," he admitted slowly. "I've really been struggling with that. But I want to be forgiving too."

His father shook his head. "That's true," he said. "We need to be forgiving, but I think she is the one who should be coming to you rather than you going to her. Or better yet, she should be proving that she has voluntarily turned away from the course she is presently following. You'll have to decide for yourself, of course, but I can't advise you to go back to her with what she has shown herself to be in the past weeks. If she is what Donald thinks she is, she will give some positive indications without you making her promises like that. If she changes just to get you back, it won't last, and you will simply be hurt again. Or you might lose out yourself in trying to keep her."

Dale nodded soberly. "That's what I expected you to say," he said. "I just haven't been able to persuade myself that it would be the right thing to do, to follow Donald's advice. I'd still like to have her back, but I'm afraid we can't rebuild what we had in the past anyway. At least not without her showing more desire to live uprightly than she has so far."

Several weeks later, Dale bumped into Donald in town in the supermarket parking lot. Donald stopped to talk. "Let's go to the doughnut shop for a coffee," he said somewhat gruffly. "I think we should talk some more."

Dale followed him uneasily into the doughnut shop. What did Donald want now? Was he going to try again to talk him into a compromise? Was he upset because Dale hadn't gone to talk to Sheila?

Donald bought two cups of coffee and some doughnuts, and they found a quiet corner, where they had some privacy. They sat in silence for a few moments; then Donald sat back in his chair. "You never did talk to Sheila, did you?" he asked.

Dale shook his head. "I couldn't make myself," he said frankly. "I'd like to help her, but it didn't seem the right thing to do."

Donald looked out the window moodily for a moment, while Dale held his breath. "You were probably right," Donald said finally. "I can't talk any sense into her, even though I've tried several times. I can't understand it. She seems determined to prove a point or something. I've never seen her like this."

Dale was surprised at the look on the older man's face. "I'm sorry," he said quietly. "I honestly considered taking your advice. But I felt that if she changed just to get me back, it wouldn't be a very solid foundation for our marriage." He hesitated before continuing. "Besides, I—I just wasn't ready to take the risk of being hurt again. It would take a lot to regain my confidence in her now."

Donald was quiet for a long time. He drummed his fingers on the tabletop and avoided Dale's eyes. Finally, he looked up. "I've usually been able to persuade people to do what I think they should," he said. "That's why I'm such a successful salesman. But it just has not worked this time. I can't blame you for being cautious. Actually, I think she owes you an apology. What she did to you was pretty nasty. And her attitude since then hasn't been very good."

His eyes dropped again, and his shoulders sagged. "You're probably right," he added quietly. "You're too far apart. It would not work without a major change either in her life or in yours. It does not look very likely at this point that she is going to change much. And I really wouldn't want to see you give up what you have in order to win her back."

He pushed back his coffee cup and squared his shoulders. "Well, I must be on my way," he said, offering Dale his hand. "I guess this is good-bye. I would have really liked you for a son-in-law, and I hope there are no bad feelings between us. I did what I honestly thought was best for you and Sheila both."

Dale stayed sitting while he finished his coffee. Through the window, he saw Donald striding across the parking lot, and he noticed that Sheila's mother was in the car waiting. *So it was no accident that I ran into Donald out there. They must have seen me go into the store and waited for me to come back out so that he could talk to me. He didn't seem very happy. Even though he doesn't really agree with my convictions, he doesn't like the course Sheila is taking. I wonder if he realizes that his own lifestyle and lack of conviction might have something to do with her problems.*

He wondered again for the hundredth time what was really making Sheila act as she was. What kind of a point was she trying to make?[1] His heart went out to her parents. He knew that they were almost as unhappy about the situation as he was.

---

1 Sheila's actions are not an unusual phenomenon. A look of determination is often worn by those who were formerly earnestly seeking God's will, but have decided to follow the flesh and the crowd, as Sheila did.

13

Sheila's Prophecy Fulfilled

"The clothing people wear is an index of what is in their hearts."

—Adapted[1]

Wearily Dale closed his book, pushed himself back from his desk, and got abruptly to his feet. He stretched, yawned, and then stared moodily down at his desk, where his Bible, some notepaper, and a copy of the book *Doctrines of the Bible* lay in disarray. He had just finished reading—for probably the dozenth time—the chapter entitled "Nonconformity to the World."

He reached over to one side of his desk and picked up several sheets of paper—the notes he had taken during the message about Biblical nonconformity in Oregon. He glanced at these again and then tossed them on

1 Daniel Kauffman, ed., *Doctrines of the Bible* (1928; reprint, Scottdale, Pa.: Mennonite Publishing House, 1996), p. 495.

the pile, partly obscuring the neat list of references he had just copied from *Doctrines of the Bible.*

Why did the Mennonite Church promote the plain suit up until the last decades? Where did it come from? And why was it adopted?

Deep in thought, he clasped his hands behind his back and stared sightlessly at a motto hanging over his desk. Doctrines of the Bible *doesn't really say anything about it. And the minister at Oregon just took it for granted that a truly spiritual person would wear a plain suit. I want to be spiritual, and I want to do what is right. But I don't want to make a fool out of myself for no reason at all.*

He thought for a moment of the scene that Anne Carter would make if he showed up at church or an MYF meeting in a plain suit, and a whimsical grin crossed his face. *She'd have a time all right. Would she ever make a fuss!* Then a look of pain replaced his grin. *I wonder what Sheila would think. I suppose that would forever ruin my chances of getting her back. But then, I don't think I have a chance anyway—not the way she's been acting the last couple of months. Anyway, I couldn't take her back without some major changes in her life.*

He spent a moment in reflecting on some of the things that he had heard the last while about Anne's group. Sheila still ran around with them, though he had heard that she wasn't always wholeheartedly in favor of everything that went on.

Then he shook his head. *I'm getting sidetracked. What I really want to know is whether God wants me to wear a plain suit. How do I decide? I don't want to be a radical, yet I do want to do what's right. Do I really have a conviction for it, or am I just thinking this way because of the young folks I met in Oregon?*

The ringing of the telephone upstairs jolted him from his reverie, and he heard his mother answer it. He sighed and turned to the door. *Maybe I should go upstairs and have tea with the others. I'm spending so much time down here that I'm about going funny. I don't seem to be getting anywhere anyhow. Maybe my father would have some answers—though he hasn't really said much. He wears a plain suit himself, but he sure has not pushed me to wear one. I wonder why not.*

When Dale got to the kitchen, Jane was just setting up for a game of Chinese checkers with her parents. "Good," she said. "It's about time you spend some time with us, instead of just sitting in your bedroom, reading those dusty old books. Your personality is going to get warped, spending so much time alone."

Dale's father chuckled, and Dale grinned. "Set up a place for me too, Jane. I'll show you that I'm not too far gone to beat you in Chinese checkers," he said.

"You'll have to be good," Jane challenged, a glint in her eye. "I intend to walk all over you three."

Dale looked at her thoughtfully. "You know," he said, "there's an old proverb that says something like, 'Let not him who puts on his armor boast as him who takes it off.' "

Jane made a face at him, but her only reply was to sit down at the table and move one of her marbles. "Let's go," she said. Dale and his parents also took chairs around the table, and soon the game was in full swing.

Jane was a determined player, indeed, and she swooped all over the board with her marbles, managing—as she had declared she would—to overcome all obstacles and win every game.

After her third win, Dale pushed back his chair in pretended disgust. "What a welcome you've given me," he said, eyeing Jane with new respect. "Maybe tomorrow night I'll just stay downstairs and read again."

Jane wrinkled her nose at him in triumph. "You'll never get good at it if you do that," she said. "You need more social life. It'll be good for your soul to spend more time with me."

Dale's parents both chuckled at her, but soon sobered up. "Jane's right, Dale," his mother said. "You should spend more time with us. Studying is good, but you have been getting moody the last few months. You need to put the past behind you and get interested in life around you again."

Dale nodded. "I know," he said. "I've thought the same. That's why I came up tonight. But it's not that I don't enjoy family life—it's just that I have these questions that I am trying to sort out, and I don't seem to be making much progress."

His father added some sugar to his tea and stirred it; then he asked, "What kind of questions? Is it anything we can help you with?"

Dale clasped his hands behind his head and tilted his chair back on two legs. "Oh, it's the same old thing—nonconformity. I have been thinking of wearing a plain suit ever since I visited Oregon. But I've never really heard a good rationale for it. Why did the church start wearing it in the first place? Why do you wear it? I want to do what's right, and it appeals to me in a sense. But I know that a lot of people will consider me radical if I do, and I don't want to do something stupid."

His father considered him thoughtfully. "I've never applied any pressure on you to follow my example," he said. "I don't know if that's right or not. But I have reasons for wearing it, I guess, or at least I have reasons for not dropping it. However, I wouldn't want you to start wearing it just because I do."

He stopped to consider for a moment before continuing. "Why do you think you should wear one? Or what appeals to you about it?"

Dale scratched his head. "Well, that preacher in Oregon said that the plain suit is a sign of nonconformity. And he made quite an issue about the value of distinctive dress as a testimony to the world."

Dale's father nodded. "The Bible teaches separation," he said. "The Bible even teaches separation in our appearance.[2] You've studied that, I think."

Dale nodded, and his father continued. "The principles of separation go far beyond our appearance and our dress, however," he said. "In fact, the plain suit and cape dress would actually be a farce in our setting, if adopted by most. Too many of our people don't have the principles of separation in their hearts. For such people to put on plain dress would be hypocrisy."

He paused for a moment and then walked over to the living room closet, where they kept their Sunday coats. He pulled out his plain coat and, turning to Dale, he said, "I heard it illustrated like this once." He held up the coat and looked at it. "There's no salvation in this coat," he said. "None at all."

Then he put it on and buttoned the top few buttons. "But now, there *is* salvation in this coat. Because I've put it on. In other words, the coat has value only because of what I am, spiritually. If I were a sinner, wearing this coat would have no value whatsoever. But since I am a Christian and wear it as a symbol of my separation from the world, it does have some value."

Dale sat forward eagerly. "So you are saying that my life needs to line up with what the coat symbolizes, in order for it to have any value to me."

His father nodded. "That's right," he said. "I am not against your wearing it. But I don't want you wearing it

---

2 See *Doctrines of the Bible*, pp. 490–504 for an outline of this teaching.

just because it is a novelty or because you want to prove to the others at church that you are better than they are. If you wear it, wear it because it is an expression of what already exists in your heart.

"Separation from the world is an important Bible teaching," he added. "The Christian reads different books, goes different places, and has different values from what the world has. It only makes sense that he will also look different from the world."

He returned his coat to the closet and sat down again at the table before continuing. "In the past, when most church members wore clothing like the plain coat and the cape dress, they also gave a witness of uniformity and unity. Members showed their allegiance to the principle of separation by wearing distinctive dress. That has changed today, and it is up to each member to decide what he will wear. I wish we could get back to the old standard, but it will take nothing short of a miracle for that to happen, I'm afraid."

Dale nodded. "Would you be against my wearing a plain suit?" he asked. "Would that do the wrong thing?"

His father rubbed his chin thoughtfully. "I'm not against it," he replied slowly. "Just make sure that you aren't doing it because it's a novelty. Make sure that it indicates a course in life that you are dedicating yourself to travel—a commitment to a lifestyle based on truth. You will have to be willing to stand almost alone. If you don't have a deep-rooted conviction that you want to travel the road of separation with Christ, you won't be able to stand against the opposition you will receive. It will be much worse for you than for me, since I have always worn it. Your peers will challenge you to see if it's really real in your life."[3]

Dale nodded. "I'm used to that," he said. "Though this might be worse than some other things have been." He hesitated and then asked, "Where does the practice come from though? I haven't been able to find anything about it."

His father chuckled. "I did some reading on that some years ago," he said. "Actually, the plain coat is an adaptation of the old colonial suitcoat, worn by the pioneers. In earlier years, in Europe, distinctive dress wasn't as much of an issue. Most Anabaptists were peasants, and the peasant dress was regulated by the government. Since peasant dress was basically within Scriptural principles, it wasn't as much of an issue."

Dale cocked his head somewhat quizzically. "So they didn't necessarily have distinctive dress?" he asked. "I thought the minister in Oregon made it sound like that has

---

3 In our setting Dale's father might have worded his advice somewhat differently. We expect brethren to wear the plain suit because of the principles of uniformity and unity, as well as because of separation. However, the same principle applies now as did then. If you are separate from the world only because the church requires it, you would lose your separation quickly if the pressure to comply were removed.

Note also that the principle of separation goes far beyond plain clothing. Our entire life must line up with the principle of separation. We must act different, talk different, and drive different, as well as dress different, before the world will be convinced of our allegiance to this principle.

been a basic principle of separation throughout all time."

"It was in the Old Testament," his father replied. "In the New Testament era and since, the issues in focus have normally been modesty and simplicity. The true church has always promoted these principles. In Anabaptist times, their tailors were not allowed to make fancy or frilly clothing for rich people. But an Anabaptist could stand in a crowd of peasants and not be noticed. Local governments then passed laws requiring everyone to wear a sword so that they could recognize an Anabaptist. They knew that the Anabaptists would not wear swords, and that was one way of telling if a person was one or not. Their dress generally wasn't distinctive enough to identify them."[4]

He leaned back in his chair and hooked his thumbs into his belt. "Of course," he added, "as the world grew worse and worse, dress patterns changed, but the Anabaptists and Mennonites refused to change with them. The headship covering, the cape dress, and the plain coat were all adapted from items once commonly worn by the world, which the Mennonite Church retained as styles changed.

"I am for distinctive dress," he added. "I think that minister in Oregon was right—it is necessary in our day. In fact, it is probably impossible to dress Biblically without also being distinctive. But the church didn't see the

---

4 The same seems to have been true of earlier groups such as the Waldensians. The argument of distinctive dress seems to have surfaced mostly after the regular dress of the world started to violate the principles of simplicity and modesty.

need for it as clearly when modest, simple dress wasn't a problem. Distinctive dress for the Christian certainly fits the principle of separation and is a definite asset to any Christian in maintaining his testimony."[5]

Dale nodded again. "I can see that," he said. "But where would I get a plain suit? Can you get them made by a tailor?"

His mother had the answer to this. "A tailor might be able to make you one," she said. "But it would be much cheaper simply to remodel your suit. I have done that for your father different times. I'm sure I could do yours too if you want me to."

Dale's face brightened. "Would you do that?" he asked. "I'd like to go ahead if you don't mind trying it."

Blake and Allister dropped by one evening while Dale's mother was working on his suit, and the three discussed the idea some more with Dale's father. In the end, Blake somewhat bashfully looked at Dale's mother. "Would you consider making over a suit for me too?" he asked.

Carrie looked a little startled, but she answered, "Sure, if you think I can make it good enough for you."

"If you can do it good enough for Dale, I'm sure it will be good enough for me," Blake said. So it was settled, and Blake brought his suit over the next evening.

---

5 In our time, Scriptural dress will invariably be distinctive and will give us a Scriptural identity. Uniformity of dress will also be an aid to Christian identity.

Thus it was that several weeks later, when Dale set out for church wearing a plain suit, he knew that he wouldn't be facing the group alone. Still, now that the moment had arrived, he was battling some second thoughts. But he pushed them aside. *It isn't going to be as easy as I thought it would be, but I'm not going to back down now. I'm glad Blake decided that he would get a plain suit at the same time. It will make it easier. I only wish Allister had decided to join us. He didn't seem to be ready to go ahead, even if he agreed that it was probably the right thing to do. I wonder why.*

He parked his car and took a deep breath. *Well, it won't get any easier just sitting here. I might as well go in.*

He noticed a few eyes turned his way in surprise as he walked into the church building, but no one said anything until Sunday school. David Martens, the bishop's son, taught the youth class, which both Dale and Blake were part of. Dale noticed that David eyed him and Blake throughout the lesson. Then toward the end of the class, he worked his way around to the subject of clothing.

"Don't you think," he said, "that we have gotten to the place in church life where we no longer need old-fashioned clothing to bolster our self-image as Christians?" He glanced around the class a little cynically. "It seems to me that our forefathers used their clothing to give them a psychological advantage over the world. But I thought we were getting beyond that. If we are truly confident of our standing in Christ, we shouldn't need such psychological aids, should we?"

On this note, the class ended. Dale and Blake glanced at each other, but neither commented as they wound their way back upstairs into the auditorium for the preaching service. Both of them had known that they would face opposition to their position. Both also knew David Martens's antagonism toward plain clothing and tradition, so his statements weren't really a surprise.

No one else commented on Dale's new suit, though he was aware that various eyes turned his way. He worked his way back the aisle again to the lobby in the back. Here, like normal, a group of girls had congregated. Sheila was in the group, talking animatedly with some other girls. Dale happened to be looking her way when she noticed him, and he saw her reaction. The words she was saying died on her lips and she turned pale, almost as if she had seen a ghost. The other girls turned to see what she was looking at, and spotted Dale immediately. Several snickered, and one of them made a remark of some sort to Sheila. Sheila didn't answer. Nor did she laugh with the others. Dale suddenly remembered what she had said one of the last times they were together—that sooner or later he would wear a plain suit because of the kind of person he was.

Dale steeled himself and forced himself to walk down the steps and past the group of girls. No one said anything to him, but the group grew quiet as he came closer. He breathed a sigh of relief as he closed the church door behind him. *Well, at least that's over. Now they can talk about it, I guess. It should be easier to wear it the second time. At least Anne wasn't in church this morning.*

He continued to ponder the situation as he drove homeward. *Sheila looked almost sick when she saw me. And I'm sure I saw tears in her eyes as I went past, even though she wouldn't face me. I wonder if her decision is still bothering her. She cannot help but remember that vow she made to me that evening when she promised to be my wife.*

The memory of that evening still stung, but not quite like it had earlier. Instead, a feeling of pity welled up in his heart for Sheila. She had looked unhappy the last while, and especially so this morning.

That evening, it didn't go quite as hard to wear his new coat to church, though he met Anne Carter in the lobby on his way into the auditorium. She looked at him and snickered. "Well, well," she chortled. "So what do we have here? A new preacher? What's the sermon about tonight?"

Dale didn't bother answering her, but walked right on past. After all, why should he care what Anne Carter thought? He had expected some kind of a smart response from her. But he had to admit that her words rankled a bit. That had been his worst fear—that some would feel that he was showing a holier-than-thou attitude by wearing a plain suit.

After church, he happened to meet the bishop, Samuel

Martens. Samuel shook his hand and then hesitated. "I see you have a new suit," he commented. "Did you have a particular reason for changing suits?"

Dale hedged a little. "Actually, it's my old suit," he said. "My mother made it over for me. I felt that the Lord wanted me to wear something a little more distinctive. Plus, this is the traditional suit of the Mennonite Church. . . ." He ground helplessly to a halt, not sure what else he should say. Somehow, the reasons that had seemed so clear the day before were hard to put into words under his bishop's eye.

"That's true," the bishop replied. "I just hope you aren't trying to make yourself seem better than the rest of our young people. We have some fine youth in our congregation."

He paused as he looked Dale over again. "I wear a plain suit myself," he added, "but I don't promote it very much. I have seen a lot of pride expressed with plain suits in the past."

Dale nodded respectfully. "I suppose that could happen," he said. "I don't want to do that."

The bishop pursed his lips and opened his mouth as if to speak again, and then apparently changed his mind. He shifted his weight uneasily from one foot to the other and finally spoke again. "Well, give it some thought," he said. "I wish you would have talked to me first before you did this, but I suppose it's too late for that now." He moved on to shake someone else's hand, and Dale continued on his way down the aisle.

That evening as the family sat around the kitchen table, enjoying tea together before bedtime, Dale recounted his meeting with the bishop. "He seems to feel that I'm wearing a plain suit because of pride," he said. "He thought I should have said something to him first, before I started."

His father looked sober. "I thought of that," he said. "About talking to him, I mean, not that you're proud. But I was afraid he would just try to talk you out of it, and I thought it might be better just to go ahead and do it."

Dale nodded. "I wasn't expecting him to be against it," he admitted. "I guess I hoped that he would think I'm being a good influence. But he seems to think the very opposite."

"I'm not surprised," his father said. "You are, in a sense, a threat to him. As he said, he doesn't promote the plain suit anymore. I wonder how long he will even wear one himself. He probably is afraid that your plain suit will make turmoil in the congregation. He doesn't want trouble."

"But how can he take it off?" Dale asked. "I'm sure at one time he would have taught the importance of distinctive attire."

"Yes, he did," his father affirmed. "But it doesn't fit the course the church is taking today. He tries his best to avoid upheaval. If a traditional practice creates unrest, he would rather give it up than to take the chance of losing members.

"My guess is that forty years down the road, you won't

be able to see any difference between the members in this church and the members of the churches in town.[6]

"I wonder sometimes what kind of an account such a man will need to give to God someday."

6 It didn't take that long. Today, some nominal churches in Alberta are more conservative and Scriptural than the Mennonite church on which this account is based.

14

A Revival That Foundered

"Some men's sins are open beforehand,
going before to judgment;
and some men they follow after."
—1 Timothy 5:24

"It sure is hard to believe that it's 1963 already," said Richard one Saturday evening, while the family was sitting around the table, eating a bedtime snack. He looked a little sheepish. "I wrote out a check at the UFA[1] today and dated it 1962 instead of 1963. Last year sure went around fast."

Dale said nothing. In a way, the year had gone fast for him too, but in another sense, an eternity separated him from a year ago, when he had been dating Sheila. She apparently had forgotten about Dale completely. She

1 United Farmers of Alberta—a farm co-op.

still ran with Anne's crowd, and there was little difference anymore between her and them. She also dated occasionally, mostly Andrew Martens, a classy young man who attended the church services but wasn't a member. Occasional stories of wild parties or other troubling events that included Sheila had leaked into the Eberly household. But time had done its healing work, and Dale had settled back into his bachelor status, satisfied to remain there for life if necessary.

By now, most people had become accustomed to seeing Dale and Blake wearing their plain suits. Even Anne had nearly given up saying anything about it, though she still tossed Dale a snide remark occasionally when she thought it appropriate.

Dale's attention came back to the conversation abruptly when his father remarked to him, "One of Samuel Martens's old friends from the East is preaching tomorrow morning, I hear. He has a reputation for being a conservative man, even though he is still affiliated with a conference setting."

Dale set down his cup. "Really? Why would our bishop ask him to preach for us? And what's he doing out here?"

"I imagine he's traveling through the area and decided to stop and visit Samuel's," his father replied.

"As far as why the bishop would ask him to preach here, I'm not sure, I guess," he continued. "They're old friends, so that might be part of it. But it's nothing new for apostatizing communities to want conservative preachers to preach for them. I suppose it makes them feel like they are still trying to maintain the faith. They feel a nagging doubt in their hearts about the course they are taking, and conservative preaching tends to make them feel better, even if they don't do anything about it." [2]

Dale looked at him wistfully. "Do you think it's too late to make changes here?"

His father shook his head. "I suppose only God knows, but I'm afraid it might be. It seems that we have drifted so far that only a miracle could make changes now."

Dale was still mulling over this latest information as he drove to church the next morning. Sunday school passed by like normal, except that the youth teacher, David Martens, seemed strangely subdued. David, a young married man, was the bishop's son and had a reputation for being a spiritually-minded person. He was respected by most of the members—even by those youth who seemed to have little respect for spiritual values of any sort. However, he had little inclination for the traditional conservative values of the church—hence his earlier reaction when Dale and Blake began wearing plain suits.

---

2 This was not a unique phenomenon. One conservative minister noted that after he left the apostate setting, he was booked ahead a year and a half with appointments in liberal churches who wanted him to preach for them. Richard's interpretation of this is probably about as accurate an opinion as any. Note that these visits by conservative speakers seldom, if ever, accomplished much. Once a congregation reaches a certain point in the apostatizing process, it is well nigh impossible to reverse it.

He was an immaculate dresser and invariably appeared in a fashionable suit and tie.

David was as talented as he was handsome, and normally held the attention of the class. This morning, however, he seemed preoccupied and dismissed the class early. Dale wondered what was up, but he was still thinking about the visiting preacher and soon forgot about it.

The visiting minister and the bishop took their places on the bench behind the pulpit. The bishop stepped up to the pulpit, but instead of introducing the visitor or having a devotional, he looked across the audience with a troubled look. "David Martens has something he wants to tell us this morning," he said finally.

A chill passed through the audience. Voluntary testimonies and confessions were no longer the common occurrence they had been in an earlier generation, and everyone there knew that a church confession normally denoted a major failure.

David Martens was sitting toward the front. He got to his feet and turned toward the congregation. It struck Dale momentarily that his fashionable appearance seemed strangely at odds with the sober expression on his face.

David was obviously serious, but it was easy to see that he was having a hard time facing the congregation—perhaps because he knew how many of them would feel about what he was going to say. "I have been convicted recently that my relationship with the Lord is not as close as it should be," he said. "I find that it is easier for me to be interested in secular magazines or light reading than to be interested in reading my Bible. I have found it hard to maintain my personal devotions, and that has affected my whole life. I want to regain the closeness with God that I once had—so that I can walk unashamedly at His side."

He sat down abruptly, and the bishop cleared his throat. Obviously, he was displeased—Dale wasn't sure whether it was because of his son's drifting or because of his confession. The bishop cleared his throat again. "David has, I think, very adequately taken care of any problem that might have existed in his life," he said. "I wouldn't have thought it necessary for him to make a public confession, since he is obviously trying to live for the Lord, but he preferred to do this."

He opened his Bible, as if dismissing the subject, but then closed it again. "An old friend of mine from the East, Samuel Brubacher, will be preaching for us this morning," he said. "I think we will skip our usual devotional to give him some extra time. Let's just kneel in prayer together before we give the time over to him."

David Martens had been Dale's Sunday school teacher for several years. He had always admired his teaching and personal conduct, in spite of the remarks that he made the first Sunday Dale had worn his plain suit. Though many in the congregation undoubtedly felt—like the bishop—that David's confession was unnecessary, Dale admired him for it.

It was soon evident that the visiting minister felt the same way. He referred to David's confession in his opening remarks to the congregation. "You know," he said, "it's true that perhaps our friend could have kept quiet about his feelings. But I believe that his desire to confess them is a good indication that his heart is soft before God. If the Mennonite Church is to survive, we need brethren and sisters like this, who are ready to look at their lives and face up to the truth and then do something about it."

He paused and looked around at the congregation before continuing. "I feel strongly about that," he said. "So strongly that I am going to preach about it this morning. Our brother's confession has laid a perfect groundwork for what I want to say."

It was a message that Dale never forgot. The minister got right to the root of the problems that were facing the congregation.

He talked about Christian integrity . . . about honesty . . . about purity . . . about gossip . . . about thought patterns. He briefly mentioned outer appearance and dress, as indicators of what was going on in the hearts of those sitting before him. Then he spoke about the Christian's new heart. "That's where it all comes from," he said emphatically. "It's what is in your heart that makes you what you are. You can reform, you can wear plain clothing, you can even make confessions, but if you don't take care of the sin in your heart, *nothing will work for you*." His eyes flashed as he looked across the audience.

"I'm not against changing bad habits or against wearing plain clothing—in fact, I abhor the way many

Mennonites today dress. Nor am I against confessions—like I said, our brother did the right thing this morning, and it will help him this coming week. But I am going to tell you *this.*" He pointed his finger directly at the audience sitting spellbound before him. "If you aren't doing these things because of a changed heart, *you are simply wasting your time!"*

He paused again, and his dark, piercing eyes traveled along the rows of young people seated toward the rear of the church. Dale saw his eyes pause when they came to him and Blake. He also saw—out of the corner of his eye—that Sheila squirmed when the preacher's gaze passed over her and that Anne Carter subconsciously gritted her teeth.

The speaker's voice softened. "Young people," he said, "I know that in many ways you are the product of your environment. But I can see from comparing you with the older people here that this congregation will not long be the conservative congregation that it has been in the past unless something changes. I would challenge you to spend time with your Bibles and compare your lives with God's Word. Seek His will earnestly."

Dale noticed the bishop shifting uneasily on his pew, as if he were wishing he could stop the minister before he said too much more. But the visiting minister wasn't the kind to worry about what others thought when he was preaching God's message.

However, his eyes shifted back to the parents. "Your

young people are pliable and easily molded," he said. "The worldliness that I see in many of them probably isn't as much their fault as it is yours. That is why I preach to parents when I get to a church like this, even if the parents don't look as worldly as the young people."

You could have heard a pin drop in the auditorium, and Dale sat spellbound. He had heard his father talk of some of the powerful evangelists he had heard speak when he was younger, but Dale had never heard a message like this one. It gripped his heart, and he could see that it was having a similar effect on others around him.

No one watched the clock that morning, and when the speaker noted that it was time to close, Dale was shocked. But the visiting minister wasn't finished yet.

"I was impressed by our brother's confession this morning," he said. "Maybe there are others here who would like to clear themselves of sin or who would like to ask for help. I am going to open it up for you to say something if you want to."

Dale could almost feel the silence and tension in the room. Then a young man to his right got up—and confessed that he had been involved in smoking and drinking. It was like starting an avalanche—people could hardly wait for each other. Some confessed sinful thoughts, several confessed that they had stolen items when they were younger, and a few confessed immoral conduct with fellow youth. A married man in his upper twenties confessed to dishonest business practices and asked for prayer that he could make the proper restitution.

Dale was almost dazed by the time the service finally came to a close, over an hour later. Was this the miracle he had been praying for? Would the church really change? And what was Sheila thinking? He could see Sheila and Anne clearly. Both were white and shaking—but Anne was obviously very angry, while Sheila was battling . . . what?

The bishop closed the service. He had little to say about the landslide of confessions, which had left his congregation in a bad light. But it was clear that he had been shaken by what happened.

Blake spent the afternoon with Dale. His father came into the living room while they were discussing the morning's events, and they turned to him for his opinion. "Do you think this will mark a turnaround for our congregation?" Dale asked eagerly. "Surely things will have to change after a service like that!"

Dale's father rubbed his chin. "It was a good service," he agreed. "It certainly should have an effect on church life if we build on what has happened."

Blake looked at him keenly. "So you think that our leaders will let this die?" he asked quietly.

Dale's father raised his shoulders and let them drop. "I would like to think they won't," he said, "but their past actions don't give me a lot of hope."

He shook his head. "Also," he added, "did you notice that practically none of the confessions were made by older people? Lots of young people made confessions, and so did some young married people, like David

Martens. But I don't think a person over thirty did. I'm sure the confessions were sincere ones. But I wonder how much the parents and leaders really support what happened this morning."

Blake nodded. "And if they don't support it and help follow through with it, it will soon die," he said. "I see what you mean. But God did His part this morning. If we don't follow through, it won't be His fault."

Dale and his father both nodded. "I wish Sheila and Anne would have responded," Dale said wistfully. "Both of them looked dreadfully unhappy."

"I think Sheila might have if Anne hadn't been sitting beside her," Blake said. "For some reason, Anne seems to have a lot of power over her. But I'm afraid that she is further from it now than ever. Anne was quite upset, and she will see to it that Sheila doesn't break down now."

Dale looked unhappy. "I know," he said. "That's what I'm afraid of."

He dropped his chin in his hand. "It's not that I'm hoping to get her back," he added. "I've given her up long ago, and I'm not sure I could take her back even if she did change. But she was a nice girl, and I wish she could get out of the trap she's in."

Uncle Dale paused and shook his head. "It was a pity," he said. "My father was absolutely right. The parents and church leaders squelched that revival within weeks. The bishop told people not to bother making restitution for dishonesty, for instance. He said they had done their duty by confessing it to the church. And most of the fathers felt the same."

He paused and looked at me bleakly. "Most of those young people were sincere when they made those confessions. They were open for help, but they didn't get it. It was a crime, and only eternity will reveal the awful cost of that one mistake."

Several months later, Dale stopped at the grocery store in town to do some shopping for his mother. By now the effects of the revival had about vanished, and things were pretty well back to normal at church. Richard's prophecy had proven to be amazingly accurate. There had been one bright turn of events, however. The liberal-minded assistant pastor who had moderated the MYF when Dale gave his topic had decided to move back to the United States. He had been replaced by a quiet man in his early thirties, who was much more sympathetic with the traditional values of the Mennonite Church.

The new assistant pastor, Graham Albright, had already befriended Dale and Blake and encouraged them to continue in their good influence. Dale was mulling over these events and what they might mean as he came out of the grocery store that morning and almost bumped into Sheila.

Dale nodded and would have continued on his way, but Sheila stopped him. "Would you—would you—have a few minutes to talk?" she asked, a little stiffly.

Dale was stunned—he hadn't talked to her for nearly

a year, but he nodded. "Sure," he said. "I've got lots of time. My car is right over here."

Sheila followed him to his car and slipped into the once-familiar passenger's seat. Dale got behind the wheel and started the car, since it was cold outside. Then he turned partway in his seat so that he could see Sheila's face.

She didn't say anything for a few moments, and he had a good chance to study the profile of her face while he waited. She had changed, he could tell. Her face showed signs of unhappiness. He could see that she had been crying recently—her eyes were swollen—and her expression was serious and almost sullen. Yet, he sensed a softness about her that had been lacking during the past year—the determined set in her jaw that she had worn ever since she broke up with him was gone. Instead, she wore a distinct aura of sadness, and he sensed that she was brooding over something.

Finally, she apparently made up her mind about something and turned to look at him—though her eyes didn't quite meet his. "Are you still praying for me?" she asked, almost abruptly.

The familiar question took Dale totally off-guard, but he answered honestly. "Yes, I pray for you every day," he said. "Why?"

She bit her lip. "Oh, I just wondered," she said. "I was pretty sure you would be, knowing the kind of person you are. It used to make me angry—thinking about you praying for me. But—but I guess I needed your prayers."

She paused and took a deep breath. "I just wanted to tell you that I've broken up with Anne and her gang," she said. "It just isn't right, the things that they're doing."

Dale didn't ask her what she meant. The things Anne's group was involved in was pretty common knowledge—at least among the young people—and he didn't want to discuss them with her.

Sheila's eyes dropped, and she shuddered a little. "You've got no idea how horrible I've felt about the life I've been living," she whispered. "I don't even know why I ever got involved, except that I guess I was trying to forget our times together. I knew I had failed utterly to live up to what I wanted, and I couldn't face it. But I hate the life I'm living too much to keep on."

Dale looked at her compassionately. "I think I understood why you were acting as you did," he said. "Though it really hurt me to see you take that course. But if you ask God for His help, it still isn't too late to repent and become what He wants you to be."

Sheila bit her lip. "I really wish I had made a commitment and a confession like those other young folks did that morning," she admitted. "But I didn't have the courage. I talked to my parents about it, but my father wasn't very impressed with the service that morning, and he doesn't want me to make a fool of myself."

She clasped her hands, and Dale noticed that they were trembling. "I even talked to the bishop about it," she continued, "but he agrees with my father. He doesn't think that I was so bad—that I should just make a few changes, and I'll be fine. He didn't even encourage me to break up with Anne. He thought I could be a good influence on her."

She shook her head, as if trying to clear the cobwebs from her mind. "Do you remember the first time that we talked in our family room?" she asked. "Well, I still feel that way. I just can't seem to find God or His direction. I feel torn apart inside. Maybe if I had the kind of help you have from your parents, life would look different. But I just can't make myself take a stand like you have, even though I don't want to be like Anne."

She stopped abruptly as if she had said more than she intended. "Anyway," she added, reaching for the door handle, "I just wanted to tell you that I've broken up with that gang. I'm no longer willing to have Anne rule my life."

Before Dale could answer, she opened the door and got out. Her muffled "good-bye" was almost lost in the sound of the car door closing.

That evening Dale told his parents about the encounter he had had with Sheila. Finally, his father put down his cup. "I think I know why Sheila finally got to this point," he said. "I was thinking of talking to you about it anyway. Some of Anne's group have been involved in immoral conduct, and I just heard this morning that Anne is in trouble. Sheila apparently wasn't willing to follow Anne to that point."

Dale was stunned. "So that's what happened," he said. "I guess Anne's way of life has caught up with her then.

I'm just glad that Sheila saw through that."

His father nodded. "So am I," he said. "I was really afraid for her and where the course she was taking would end up. But I'm afraid she isn't out of the woods yet. She can't change her life in her own strength."

He shook his head and looked moodily at the cup in his hand. "What will it take to bring Donald to his senses?" he asked. "Or our bishop, for that matter? Can't they see how she's hurting? that she badly wants their guidance? If she's lost, whose sin will it be?"

That night Dale lay awake for several hours before falling asleep. Was God trying to tell him something about Sheila? Had he given up too quickly on her, as Donald had hinted earlier? Should he follow up on this contact and try to help her find her way? Was that what she was hoping for? Would it be his fault if he did not and she was lost?

He tossed and turned—and prayed. Finally, he decided to leave it in God's hands. *She probably just stopped me on an impulse. If I get involved with her all over again, I might not have the strength to give her up the second time—it was tough enough the first time. Surely God will send someone else to help her if she is really earnest about changing. She did make it clear that she isn't ready to become like me. That was probably her way of telling me that the old deal still stood. She would accept me—but on her terms. And I can't do that and stay faithful to my commitment.*

Even though he felt at peace with this decision, he couldn't quite banish her from his mind. He fell asleep with a prayer in his heart that Sheila could somehow, somewhere, find the peace and rest she was seeking, and that she would be willing to take the necessary steps to find God.

15

Distant Thunder

"He giveth power to the faint;
and to them that have no might he increaseth strength."
—Isaiah 40:29

It was a beautiful day in late winter, and Dale had just finished feeding the half-grown calves they kept in the corrals. Several inches of fresh snow covered the barren prairie, and the air was invigoratingly cold. Dale climbed up the six-foot board fence surrounding the corrals and seated himself on the top, watching the cattle eat for a few minutes before heading for the house to warm up with a fresh cup of coffee.

Dale enjoyed farm life. He loved the fresh air of the prairies and the freedom and the elbowroom of the wide-open spaces, the enormous sky, and the distant horizon that made the prairies unique in North American land-forms. The prairies are often intimidating to city dwellers, who need the comforting reassurance of nearby buildings or hills, but Dale was a typical western farm boy and loved his home.

He yawned—he had been up half the night with some new calves and was tired. But he was used to it, and somehow he never tired of the sight of a new calf taking its first steps. There were times, when the temperatures hit thirty below, or even lower, that he wondered if there wouldn't be easier jobs somewhere, but a few hours' sleep usually took care of that.

He yawned again and swung his legs over the top board, dropping lightly to the ground on the other side. "Better go get that cup of coffee," he said to the collie walking at his side.

As he headed across the yard, he heard the back door of the house close, and saw his father walking out to the car. *Hmm. I wonder where he's going this time of the day. He's all dressed up too. He's been awful quiet the last week or so. I wonder if he's still troubled about things at church. Things sure haven't improved.*

He kicked the snow off his boots on the back porch and stepped into the entrance. He pulled his boots off and hung his parka and cap on a nearby hook. Then he padded in his stocking feet up the steps and into the warm kitchen. His mother and Jane were doing some baking, and he stopped to pick up a warm cookie.

"How's everyone?" he asked, grinning at Jane as she shooed him away from the cookies. "Is the coffeepot on?"

His mother smiled at him affectionately. "There's hot

water in the teakettle," she said. "Your father just had a cup, so it's all ready."

Dale poured himself a mug of hot water and added a teaspoon of coffee from a jar on the counter. He sat down at the kitchen table close to the coal burner that heated the house. "Ah, this feels good," he said. "Nothing like a brisk winter day to get your blood moving."

He took a sip of coffee and looked up again. "Say, where's Father off to this morning?" he asked. "He looked all dressed up."

"He and a few others have a meeting with the bishop and the rest of the ministry this morning," she said. "He'll probably talk to you about it when he gets back. We've been burdened more and more with what is happening here, and he and several others are making an appeal to the church to try to stop some of these things."

She brought Dale several more cookies and sat down across the table from him. Dale picked up a second cookie and took a bite. "Mmm," he said appreciatively. "Nothing like warm cookies, straight from the oven, on a cold morning." Then he returned to the subject at hand. "So what are they concerned about?"

His mother waved her hand. "Oh, the usual things that we have discussed before," she said. "Only since that last confession meeting, they actually seem to be worse than before. A number of girls are trimming their hair now, and several have even been seen in town with their hair in a ponytail."

Dale made a face. "Really?" he said. "That doesn't sound

good. I thought maybe things would get better after that meeting, but it sure doesn't seem like it. I wonder why?"

Dale didn't get an answer to his question until that evening, when he and his father had a chance to talk about it over their bedtime cup of tea. Dale tipped back his chair and looked at his father, who was sitting with his elbows propped on the table, staring moodily into his cup. "So how did things go at your meeting?" he asked. "Did you get anywhere with them?"

His father sighed and took a sip of tea. "Oh, I don't know," he said. "They want to look like they are trying hard to be spiritual and orthodox. Graham especially seems sympathetic, but he can't do much by himself."

"How many of you went?" Dale asked. "You didn't go alone, did you?"

His father shook his head. "No, Blake's father and my brother James went with me. They are all very concerned about the way things are going. I think there were five or six girls at church last Sunday who had bangs. They had their hair up, so you couldn't tell for sure, but I suspect that at least some of them are trimming their hair at the back too so that they can let it hang open if they want to."

He sighed again. "I always thought that that would be the last straw," he said gloomily, "and that I wouldn't stay with a church that allowed women to cut their hair. But it's come in so innocently, a little at a time, that all of a sudden it's here, and none of us really found out when it happened."

He shook his head. "Communion is only two weeks

away," he added. "I don't see how I can take Communion this way. The others said the same, but Samuel wants us to hold off. He thinks we're too impulsive. He promised that he would have a members' meeting about it before Communion, so we finally told him that we would wait for that."

Dale nodded sympathetically. "He'll try anything he can to keep you happy without actually doing anything much to change things," he said. "I can see that it's hard to really know when the time is to make a break."

His father nodded. "That's the problem," he said. "Sometimes I wish something drastic would happen so we would know that it is time to leave, without any more questions."

Dale nodded. "I really thought that that confession meeting would help things," he said. "But instead, things seem to be worse than before. I just cannot understand that. Why didn't it help longer than it did?"

His father shook his head. "I'm not surprised," he said. "In fact, that's rather common."

Dale raised his eyebrows and waited for him to continue.

"If a revival isn't followed through properly, all it does is make hearts harder," his father said. "The people who made confessions were serious, but many of them fell back into their old habits again because of a lack of encouragement, teaching, or commitment—and they ended up worse off than ever."

Dale nodded. "I can see how that could work," he said. "So actually that meeting ended up being a hindrance rather than a help."

His father nodded. "In a sense anyway," he said. "Though we shouldn't really blame the meeting, but rather how we handled what happened at the meeting."

They sat quietly for a few moments before Richard changed the subject. "My brother James told me this afternoon that some people from Pennsylvania have started a conservative community in British Columbia. Apparently one of his wife's cousins has moved there. They have been corresponding some, and they have invited the concerned people from here to visit if we want to."[1]

Dale scratched his chin contemplatively. "How far would it be over there?" he asked.

---

1 A year or two previous to this, conservative communities had been started in Ontario and Pennsylvania and a few other places. As we noted in a previous chapter, there were also several conservative churches in Oregon. It probably will seem strange to some readers that Dale's parents hadn't taken more action to get into contact with these communities, if they were really serious about their convictions. We must remember, however, that leaving the conference was a new phenomenon—one fraught with spiritual danger in the minds of most people. Also, Dale's visit to Oregon wasn't entirely without difficult repercussions, and he evidently never went back, at least during this period of time.

There were actually two conservative communities established in British Columbia in the early sixties. However, families like Richard's, isolated as they were from the larger Mennonite communities, often knew little about what was taking place elsewhere. We cannot blame them for taking some time to evaluate what was happening before accepting these movements. We could also note that people did not communicate as much as we are used to, nor did they move around as easily. Richard's "inaction" was probably a fairly normal response, given the circumstances. Today, a five-hundred-mile trip does not seem far. To them it was a big thing. Also, Richard's community lacked a strong leader to lead out in the revival process, something that most of the larger Mennonite communities had.

"About four hundred fifty miles," his father replied. "A good day's drive, I suppose, since some of it would be mountainous driving."

"That wouldn't be too bad," Dale said. "Oregon was at least twice that. If Oregon were just a day away, I would probably go back there for another visit. Maybe Blake and I should take a trip to British Columbia sometime to look around."

His father nodded. "Maybe we should all go sometime," he said. "I think we are getting close to a break here if the Lord doesn't intervene. It would be good to know where to find other fellowship if that happens. A day's drive is pretty far, but it's sure better than nothing."

He stopped suddenly and looked at Dale. "Actually," he said, "James said that the church in British Columbia is planning a Bible school of some sort later in the spring. It's a bad time of the year, but maybe we could figure out a way that a few of you could go. That would give you a chance to get to know some people there and make some friends."

Dale nodded. "I'd like that," he said. "I should talk to Blake and Allister about it and see if they'd like to go."

His father looked up suddenly. "By the way," he said, "how is Allister doing? He seems sympathetic to conservative values, yet he doesn't seem to be adopting any of them personally."

Dale tapped his fingers on the table thoughtfully. "I know," he said. "I've noticed that too, and I'm troubled by it. In some ways, he reminds me of Sheila—he wants to do what's right, but doesn't quite have the spiritual strength to follow through. He's fine when he's with Blake and me, but he has a problem standing for what's right when he faces pressures alone. His parents aren't very helpful either. I don't think his mother would like it if he decided to wear a plain suit."

His father nodded. "I was afraid of that," he said. "His father is a lot like that too. I think that if his mother favored being more conservative, Allister and his father would both go along with it, but they don't dare to stand against her opinions."

The members' meeting the bishop had promised was a few evenings before the regular counsel service. Most of the young people didn't come, like usual, but many of the married members were there—especially the men. Dale and Blake were both there, but Allister wasn't.

The bishop opened the meeting promptly at 8:00. They discussed various semi-important issues. Finally, just before closing, the bishop got to the point that Dale was waiting anxiously for. "Several brethren have raised a concern recently that we wanted to address before counsel meeting," he said. "I'm glad that they came to us this way so that we can address their concerns without having a rift in the congregation over that matter. Apparently, a few young girls have been trimming their hair a little bit to allow for what they call bangs."

He paused and looked around at the group. "Actually," he said, "I haven't noticed it myself, but I trust the brethren who raised the issue. They are spiritual brethren who wouldn't do this without genuine reason for concern."

He opened his Bible. "Let's turn together to First Corinthians, chapter eleven," he said. "I want to read these verses as a basis for our discussion."

Expressively, he read the first fifteen verses. "Now the church has always held to a literal interpretation of these verses," he said. "How many of you believe that we should take the Bible literally?"

A forest of hands went up.

"So according to that, we aren't ready to drop this teaching," the bishop said. "How many of you feel that we should maintain the teaching of this passage?"

Again, most of the members raised their hands, though some weren't quite as eager this time.

The bishop smiled beatifically. "That's good," he said. "I was sure it would be this way," he continued. "But I thought it would be good for us to make a public declaration of that. I am sure that the brethren who raised the concern will be happy to see that our congregation is standing together with them on this teaching."

He made a few more closing remarks and added, "We will plan for our counsel and Communion services as usual."[2]

2 Note the approach Samuel Martens used—a common one in those days. First, flatter the concerned brethren, then call for unity and make a show of being orthodox, then follow through with taking Communion together. That supposedly sealed the matter, since people were expressing peace with the congregation when they took Communion. They were considered out of place if they brought up issues later that were known before Communion—since this opened them to the accusation of taking Communion under a pretext of peace.

Dale and his father had driven together that evening. Richard didn't say anything as he crawled into the passenger's seat, but as they drove out the driveway, Dale asked him, "Well, what did you think of that?"

His father shook his head rather bleakly. "I'm not sure," he answered. "Has anything changed? We believe in taking First Corinthians 11 literally, according to the show of hands. But do we believe in doing anything about it when some of our members don't cooperate? Yet he basically pulled the carpet out from under our argument that the church has changed its beliefs."

He looked out the window at the passing landscape. "We won't know until next Sunday if those girls will take Communion or not. And if they do, we won't know if they are still planning on cutting their hair from now on, or not."

Dale looked at him thoughtfully. "Maybe they will ask them to make confessions," he suggested. "Then we would know."

His father nodded. "That would help," he agreed. "But I also know that our bishop isn't too fond of confessions. When we were there to talk with him, he as much as said that the last confession meeting did more harm than good. He was right, of course, in a sense. But we both know that it wasn't the confessions that were at fault. It was the lack of follow-up that did the damage, not the confessions."

In spite of their concerns, the three men who had gone to the bishop—and their families—all took Communion in the end. Dale and Blake discussed it a bit, but reluctantly decided that it would do more harm than good for them to refuse to go to Communion on their own.

"I'm a bit disappointed in our parents though," Dale told Blake the evening after the Communion service. "I think they caved in too easily. I wish they had asked for more concrete assurance that something would actually change."

Blake nodded. "I know what you mean," he said. "But I guess it's better for us to let them decide. They are our parents. And it will show the congregation that we do want to cooperate. I suppose overreacting could do damage too."

Nothing further was said about girls trimming their hair—not even when several others started doing so, soon after Communion. Dale could tell that his father was more preoccupied than usual, but they didn't discuss the issue much. Then, all of a sudden, it was time to think about going to Bible school in British Columbia. Dale and Blake decided to go, but Allister was too busy helping on his father's farm. So the two headed out together.

They arrived on Saturday evening and stopped at the bishop's house to see where they should go from there. The bishop, Henry Anderson, was a chunky man with a gruff voice. He was waiting at the door to welcome them in, as if he had been expecting them. Behind him in the kitchen, the boys glimpsed a number of curious children and teenagers who could hardly wait to see who was at the door.

"Hello," Dale said, a little more bashfully than usual. "We're here for your Bible school sessions, and we need a place to go."

"Come in, come in," the minister growled cheerfully. "We'll put you up right here. You're from Alberta, right? Your uncle James called and said you were coming."

Dale hesitated, noting the number of children seated around the supper table, as well as several men who also appeared to be visitors. "You're sure you have room?" he asked. "We don't want to inconvenience anyone."

"Oh, we have lots of room," the minister boomed. "Come right on in. Bring your luggage. Have you had supper?" He called over his shoulder, "Mother, get out a few more plates; these boys are hungry!"

Thus it was that a few minutes later Dale and Blake found themselves squeezed onto a bench behind the table. To one side of them were several teenagers, and to the other side, a set of grinning twin brothers, who looked to be about ten years old. Dale studied them a moment and then rubbed his eyes.

One of the men across the table laughed and said, "Don't worry, you're not seeing double. They sure look alike, don't they."

It was an evening that Dale long remembered. He was especially intrigued by the conversation of the three men. The two visitors were ministers from Ontario who had come to teach at the Bible school. All three of the ministers had come from settings much like the one that Dale and Blake were from, and they were fascinated as the three discussed the issues they had faced—and how the Lord had helped them find answers to them.

Sure enough, in spite of the size of the family, Dale and Blake were given a little room with a mattress for the two of them. "We have only one washroom," their host told them, "but if you get to it by 5:30 or so, you'll probably find it empty. If you get there too much later, you might have to wait until after breakfast."

Dale, remembering the number of teenage and older girls in the family, vowed to get up early.

The Bible school was as interesting as Dale had expected, and his convictions were strengthened again. As he had been in Oregon, Dale was especially impressed with the young people. Since this was Blake's first visit to a setting like this, he was especially intrigued by it. "I can't get over these young people," he told Dale one night as they were getting ready for bed. "They have a totally different attitude from the young folks we're used to."

Dale yawned and nodded. "I know," he said. "That's how it was in Oregon too. It's a real breath of fresh air."

"I especially notice it with the girls," Blake said. "Most of them are friendly enough, but they are a lot more reserved than the girls in our youth group."

"I had to get used to that," Dale agreed. "I stopped to chat with a girl yesterday, and I almost wondered if she was going to faint. I think she's shy, which made it worse."

"Oh?" Blake said. "Which one was that?"

"I think her name is Rose," Dale said. "She's that slender, black-haired girl. She's so shy that she almost freezes if she sees a boy coming her direction."

Blake scratched his head. "I think I vaguely remember her," he said. "I'll look out for her tomorrow. Maybe she'd make a girl for you," he suggested cautiously.

Dale shook his head. "No, I don't think so," he said seriously. "First of all, I'm not ready to try again. I doubt that I'll ever feel about another girl like I did about Sheila. Anyway, even if I did consider another girl, I don't think I could handle having her be so timid. I'd want someone I can visit with."

Blake picked up his Bible in preparation for his evening Bible reading. "You might be surprised how she'd change," he said. "The way you describe her is about exactly how I am—or was, at least, when I was younger." He grinned. "Before I met you, in other words."

Dale grunted and picked up his Bible.

The week went by rapidly. One evening was especially meaningful to the two boys. They were sitting around the table at Henry's with the other adults, drinking tea before going to bed. Slowly the conversation turned again to the way the Mennonite Church in general had drifted from truth in the previous decades.

Dale put down his cup and looked at Blake. "I guess we've been fortunate, by the sounds of it," he said. "At least we haven't faced as much as some people have."

The younger of the two ministers was directly across

the table from Dale. "It won't be long," he said. "From what you've told me about your congregation, I think you are being forced pretty close to the breaking point."

Dale nodded. "I know my father feels that way," he said. "But it's so hard to know when it's the right time. We don't have any leaders that are actively helping us, and we feel pretty alone sometimes."

The minister toyed with the handle of his cup. "I can see that," he said. "In our case, we at least had five of us leaders standing together. It wasn't easy, but at least we did have that."

Dale sipped his tea before answering. "We actually thought for a bit this spring that we had reached the breaking point," he said. "But in the end, they managed to manipulate things again so that we ended up all taking Communion. I don't know what will happen this fall, but I know my father is pretty discouraged with it all."

He went on and recounted the events that had just taken place. "It was pretty discouraging," he finished. He glanced at Blake again. "Actually, we were a bit upset with our parents. We thought they should have held out for more. But we decided we had better support their decision, even if we didn't understand it."

The minister smiled. "Sometimes young people find it hard to be patient," he said, chuckling. "Though I can understand why you felt that way. I think we have all faced those times of not knowing when it was time finally to draw the line. It was good you stood with your parents, but I do suspect that the time is coming pretty soon that they will have to draw the line even if it looks as if they were unreasonable."

The other visiting minister agreed. "They have a way of always making it seem like the wrong time or the wrong method," he said. "But finally, I think we need to bear our cross and do what is right anyway. But your parents do have a difficult situation on their hands if no local leader is willing to take a stand on the issues. It puts them on their own."

The two ministers looked at each other. "You know," the younger of the two said, "it wouldn't be that far out of our way to stop in there on our way home."

The other one nodded. "I was thinking the same thing," he said. He turned to look at the boys. "Do you think your parents would be glad to have us come and do some counseling with them?" he asked. "We can easily change our train tickets to come around that way if you think they would want us to."

It didn't take Dale long to answer. "I'm sure they would appreciate that," he said. "In fact, we have lots of room in my car. Why don't you just ride along back with us? It would save you a little bit of money, and we'd enjoy the company."

The two ministers looked at each other again. "I think we ought to do that," the older one said. "Remember how we felt?"

The younger one agreed. "That's right," he said, turning to Dale again. "Why don't you call your parents and talk to them about it," he added. "If they don't have a problem with that, we'll plan on it."

So it was that the next Monday morning, when Dale and Blake left for home, the two ministers were riding in the back seat.

16

The Storm Advances

"To every thing there is a season,
and a time to every purpose under the heaven."
—Ecclesiastes 3:1

It was an interesting trip home. Nearly half the trip, they traveled on winding roads through the scenic Rocky Mountains. Dale, accustomed as he was to the prairies, almost felt at first as if he were penned in. In fact, it almost seemed as if the horizon could fall on him and bury him. Yet the rugged mountain territory filled him with awe, and he soon joined the others in pointing out new points of beauty as they wound their way between the towering mountains.

During the trip, Dale and Blake saw a side of the two ministers that they hadn't seen before. The older minister's name was Arnold Martin. He was the quieter of the two men, but when he did speak, his words carried a lot of weight. He spoke slowly and gravely, but the two boys discovered before the day was over that he also carried a distinct sense of humor, buried just below the surface of his gravity. They had been a little afraid of him during the classes the week before. But by the time they arrived at home, they wondered why they had ever felt that way.

Amos Good, the younger minister, was serious in his own way, but an avid conversationalist. A former schoolteacher, he pointed out and explained many points of interest that the group would have missed otherwise. He also was an enthusiastic storyteller, and the miles rolled by as he related events from his childhood and younger married days.

Dale and Blake were fascinated. The characters of the two men were so different from each other, yet they complemented each other so well. Amos told the stories, and Arnold often added the moral, yet neither one seemed preachy or stuffy.

Arnold had known Samuel Martens in years gone by and had actually preached at Dale's church some years before, while he was still in the Ontario Conference. Dale remembered it well, and he knew that his father would too—he had talked about Arnold's sermon for months afterward. As they traveled out of the mountains, through the foothills, and into the plains, Amos went to sleep; and Arnold brought the conversation around to the local church situation.

"Your congregation used to be known as a fairly conservative group," he said. "But I noticed when I was there the last time that it had really drifted. I suppose it has continued to go in that direction."

Dale nodded. "We had a bit of a revival after you were there," he said. "And we had another one about half a year ago. But neither made a lasting difference. In fact, I think after both revivals, things soon got worse than they were before."

Arnold looked grave. "So in other words, no one carried it on," he said. "A revival will not do much on its own if a congregation doesn't follow through with it."

Dale nodded. "That's what it seemed like," he said. "The people who responded seemed sincere enough, but they didn't get any encouragement. Today most of them are back to doing the things they confessed, and they don't even seem to feel guilty about it."

Arnold shook his head. "So, do you think Samuel is happy with the situation as it is?" he asked. "He was a fairly conservative man in his younger years."

Dale shrugged. "My father could answer that better," he said. "I can't see how he could be happy about it, but he really fights making any genuine changes. I suppose in order to really change things, he would need to start with his own family. Maybe that's what keeps him from doing anything."

"It could easily be involved," Arnold agreed. "It is amazing how many conservative men have lost out when the time came to deal with their own children. I am disappointed in Samuel though. I didn't expect that of him. He was well-known throughout the conference as a good speaker and administrator."

By now Amos had come to again and was listening interestedly. "That could be part of the problem," he injected. "Popularity has ruined many a man. Since the conferences no longer appreciate conservatism as they once did, Samuel needed to adjust his ways to maintain his popularity."

"It might be," Arnold agreed soberly. "Though it might also have been internal pressure. You know what that is like."

"I certainly do," Amos said. "When I was still a pastor in the conference, I tried to keep back some people from Communion because they had sin in their lives. But the congregation appealed to the conference executive committee, and they allowed them to remain in fellowship."

He glanced out the window at the prairie for a moment before addressing Dale again. "You know, Samuel Martens was a hero of mine when I was younger," he said. "He had revivals in our home church when I was a boy. Years later, he came through the area when the five of us brethren were involved in our disagreement with the Ontario Conference, so we had a meeting with him."

"That's right," Arnold said. "I was rather disappointed in his advice. He offered us positions in the Saskatchewan–Alberta Conference if we would move west. He said he didn't like divisions, and I guess he thought we might fit better into the Western Conference than we did into the Ontario Conference."

Dale looked startled. "Do you really think he expected that you would be happy in the church out here?" he asked. "I sure can't imagine that."

Amos shook his head. "From what you have been saying, I'm sure we wouldn't have lasted long out here," he said. "I don't know where he would have put us, but most of the western congregations are actually more liberal than yours, aren't they?"

"The ones that I'm acquainted with are," Dale said. "There might be some that are more conservative, but I sure wouldn't know where."

The two ministers had arranged with Dale's father to have a small service at Dale's home that evening. So much of the rest of the trip they spent in silence while they studied and meditated in preparation for the meeting. However, Dale and Blake had much to think about by then, and the remaining several hours went by quickly. It was almost suppertime when they pulled into Richard's driveway.

As Dale had expected, his father was very glad to see the two ministers. Their coming seemed to give him new hope, and suppertime was a joyous occasion. Richard still vividly remembered Arnold Martin's earlier visit to the congregation, and they reminisced a little about it.

Amos mentioned to Richard, as he had to Dale, that Samuel Martens had been a boyhood hero of his. "He was an evangelist at my home church when I was young," he said. "I'll never forget those meetings. They left a tremendous impression on me. It is very disappointing to me that Samuel has taken such a course. I would really like to meet him again."

The two ministers looked at each other. "I was thinking the same thing," Arnold said soberly. "I don't suppose it would be of any value to have an interview with him."

"We could contact him, I suppose," Amos said. "Though you're probably right—it probably wouldn't do any good. It might even hinder the work of the brethren here."

They left it at that because it was almost time to start the service. Richard had passed the word around to various families that he thought might be interested, and soon several arrived. It wasn't a large group, but more came than he had expected—about five or six families and several older couples who still had an appreciation for the older ways.

Since Arnold was known in the area, Amos had urged him to have the main message of the evening. Amos opened the meeting with some singing and a short devotional. Then Arnold got up to preach.

That picture of Arnold standing gravely in front of the kitchen counter stayed with Dale for a long time. Arnold opened his Bible; then he looked searchingly at the little group before him. "I want to look at God's Word for some inspiration tonight," he said soberly. "God's

Word has the answers for all of life's dilemmas."

He turned a few more pages and began to read from Psalm 139:23, 24: " 'Search me, O God, and know my heart: try me, and know my thoughts: and see if there be any wicked way in me, and lead me in the way everlasting.'

"I'm starting here," he said, "because that is where we need to look first when we face life's perplexities. Is my heart right?

"God knows my heart, and He knows your heart. He knows our thoughts and our deeds," he continued. "Perhaps we do not realize that we have failed and that we have areas where we need to change, but God knows us through and through. If we are genuinely honest with Him and pray this prayer with the psalmist, God will be faithful to show us these areas."

He paused and looked from person to person again, and it seemed to Dale that Arnold could almost read the minds of the people facing him. "I have a friend in the ministry who prayed this prayer," Arnold continued. "He was honest about it. And the Lord went to work on him.

"Now this friend of mine was a good Christian. At least all those of us who knew him thought so. But when he opened himself to God like that, God went to work. God knew that He could make a better person out of him—a more useful person.

"My friend was amazed at all he learned about himself when he let God go to work. He grew more in his Christian life in the next six months than he had in the six years prior to that. Mind you—he was a widely used man in the Lord's work, but that didn't matter. What mattered was that he opened himself to God and allowed God to work in his life."

He paused for a moment. The group waited silently. "This friend of mine is one of the most humble people I know," he continued quietly. "Once we see ourselves as God sees us, we just can't be proud anymore. Pride is one of the first things that God picks out in our lives when we open ourselves to Him."

He referred to other Scriptures and pointed out various areas where God wants to cleanse His people. The sermon gripped Dale—it was a powerful appeal to his desire to be what God wanted him to be. And he began to realize—somewhat dimly, but nevertheless surely—that God wanted to continue to do a work in his heart.

It was a sober group that fellowshiped together after the service. Most of the audience had almost forgotten what it was like to hear such a sermon.

Some of the families left soon after the service was over. But the ones who stayed decided that they would meet again with the two visiting ministers the next day to see if they could give them some further advice on a plan of action.

Dale decided to go to bed right after a snack. He was tired from traveling and was eager for a night's rest in his own bed. Besides, he sensed that his father wanted some time with Arnold and Amos, and Dale hoped that if he went to bed, his father would be able to pour out his heart to them.

When Dale got up from the table and said good-night, Amos smiled at him. "Brother Richard," he said, "you have a good boy there. I have really appreciated getting to know Dale this past week. We had some good talks, and I know his heart is in the right place."

Dale was taken aback and blushed a bit, but his father replied, "I know. I often thank God for him. I think I would have been tempted to give up long ago but for Dale's desire to do what is right. He is a challenge to me, and I don't want to let him down."

Arnold nodded gravely. "It is a tremendous challenge and responsibility to be a good example and teacher for our children," he said soberly. "And often that spurs us on to greater efforts to be faithful ourselves."

Dale left them then, but the discussion went on. Dale woke up once during the night and heard the distant sound of conversation. He rolled over and looked at his alarm clock and then shook his head. *Two o'clock, and they're still talking. I'm glad they decided to come.*

Uncle Dale stopped for a moment. "You know," he said seriously, "you young people today have no idea what it would be like to face what we faced that summer. Our congregation was going to pieces spiritually. We could have done almost anything, and the leaders wouldn't have cared enough to try to stop us."

He shook his head. "Now some of our young people grumble when church leaders won't let them do things

> *that might lead them astray," he said. "They have no idea how good they have it, son. It's a terrible feeling to be on your own like that and to have your spiritual leaders think you're radical for doing what God wants you to do."*
>
> *He shook his finger under my nose. "If you ever put this in a book," he said, "you make sure that the people who read it understand the blessings they have. I could count you several dozen people right now who are lost today because their parents and church didn't care enough to give them the kind of support that our young people take for granted and sometimes grumble at!"*

The fathers who met the next morning invited Dale and Blake to join their meeting. "You're in the middle of this," Amos told Dale before the meeting started. "And your parents need your encouragement. Don't let them down."

It was a heart-rending meeting. They started with a time of prayer, and it was the first time that Dale saw grown men break down and pray with tears running down their cheeks. They prayed for the church, for their leaders, and for their friends and relatives. But most of all, they prayed for their children. Dale realized for the first time how deeply his father felt about their situation when he prayed with tears for his grandchildren, which might be born in the future. The way things were going around them, what hope could there be for them? "God, make a way for my family!" Richard pleaded.

After the prayer service, they discussed various alternatives. One person suggested that they start having services separate from the church. But most felt that they should try another appeal, only this time put it into writing.[1] So together they drew up a letter to present to the ministry.

Dale and Blake stepped outside after they were finished, and sat on the back porch steps while Blake waited for his father.

"So what do you think of that?" Blake asked.

Dale eyed a cloud on the horizon contemplatively. "Well, it's another step, I guess," he said. "Though it seems to me that we've let this drag on about long enough." He shrugged and leaned back against the porch railing. "We'll end up at the same place anyway," he added. "It'll just take a bit longer this way. Personally, I wish it were over."

Blake nodded. "I suppose we all do," he said. "But it's probably better to take our time. There'll be enough accusations as it is if we start a separate congregation."

Dale sighed and agreed. "You're right, I suppose," he said. Then he switched the subject. "I'm glad we were in that meeting today. I knew our parents were burdened about the church, but I didn't realize that they felt this strongly about it. Sometimes I have been tempted to feel that my father didn't care enough. But I can see now that

---

1 This was the approach taken by most groups who withdrew from the conference. Probably none actually expected that the appeal would accomplish much, but it seemed a proper way of doing it. The text of most of these letters is still in existence, including this one.

he cares a lot more than I realized. He just felt it was hopeless. I can't imagine what torture he must have gone through the last few years."

Blake soberly watched a magpie land on the corral fence. "It must be quite a feeling to know that you are responsible for your family, but have nothing to offer them," he said. "I think our parents did pretty well under the circumstances."

Dale stood up as the door behind them opened. "That's true," he said. "But I sure hope I'll have something better to offer to my children, if I ever have any."

Dale drove Arnold and Amos to the train station that afternoon to continue their interrupted trip home. His father and the other two fathers delivered a copy of their letter to Samuel Martens. He promised to discuss it with the other ministers and to get back to them about it. However, he was not very happy that his old friends from Ontario were involved in the area. Dale's father told the family about it that evening.

"I suppose I can't really blame him for feeling that way," Richard said. "He thought they were friends of his, even though he knew what course they had taken back in Ontario. He felt that they should have asked for his side of the story or at least asked his permission before getting involved."

He sat back in his chair with a sigh. "I guess it's like Arnold said before he left—no matter how we do this, it'll be wrong." He drummed his fingers on the table and added, "At least it's this far now. Samuel promised that he would discuss our concerns with the others and maybe even call a members' meeting. We'll probably hear back from him in a day or two."

As it turned out, Richard's expectations were overly optimistic—by far. It took several weeks for the bishop to bring up the letter at a ministers' meeting. And then all they did was send a written acknowledgement to the concerned brethren. The letter stated that the ministry had taken note of their concerns and that they were considering what action to take. (It was almost August before the bishop finally told them that the congregation would discuss their letter in a members' meeting several weeks later.[2])

Dale, understandably, chafed under the suspense of waiting to see what would happen. He brought up the subject one day late in July when he and his father were returning from delivering another load of hay.

"Why don't we just up and leave if they're going to ignore us anyway?" he asked. "I think they're just stalling for time."

His father nodded. "I know," he said. "I've thought

2 This was a common tactic—to treat the concerns like ordinary business and to make sure that the concerned ones realize who is in control, then leave them in suspense for a while, since they would probably not leave until their concerns had been discussed and answered. The final step, as we will see, was then to try to make the concerned ones feel guilty of the sin of sowing discord in the brotherhood. Thus, when the concerned ones finally did leave, they were normally given a black name in spite of their attempts to handle the situation honorably.

the same. But we've waited this long; I think we can wait a little longer yet. They will have to look at the issue before fall Communion, if not earlier."

Dale slowed and pulled into their driveway before answering. "I have tried hard to be patient," he said with a sigh. "But sometimes it gets tough. I hope we don't need to take Communion again without something changing. It almost doesn't seem right to take Communion with some of the people—it's almost an unequal yoke."

His father picked up his lunch box from between the seats. "I know," he replied. "I've struggled with the same thing. Yet, the Bible does tell us to examine *ourselves* before taking Communion, rather than telling us to examine everyone else. It's true that in the long run it isn't right to remain in an ungodly setting. But I do think it is right to give some time if there is a chance that things might yet turn around.[3] I don't think it would be right to leave before they give us an answer to our letter."

So Dale tried to be patient and spent much time in prayer for the upcoming crisis and for himself. However, all things come to him who waits, and this was no exception.

Finally, on the first Sunday morning in August, the

---

3 We would temper Richard's statement a little today. First Corinthians 11:31, 32 states, "For if we would judge ourselves, we should not be judged. But when we are judged, we are chastened of the Lord, that we should not be condemned with the world." In these verses, it is clear that if we do not judge ourselves, others will need to do that to keep Communion clean. However, Richard's statements here portray how many felt during this time, and explain why many stayed in impure Communions as long as they did.

bishop added a postscript to his message. "Several families in the congregation seem to have an ongoing problem with the leaders of the congregation," he said, somewhat gruffly. "They have written us a letter about their concerns. We have looked at this as a ministry and decided that we would have a members' meeting on Friday evening to look at the situation. Since it reflects on our administration, we are asking Frank Peters to lead that discussion.[4] We would like all the heads of the home to be at this meeting so that we can put these things to rest, once and for all."

Dale felt a chill go up his back. The bishop seemed to be taking their letter as a personal affront to his administration. Would he excommunicate those with concerns rather than dealing with the sinners in the congregation?

For the first time, Dale realized that this might be a distinct possibility.

---

4 Frank Peters was a respected laymember of about middle age in Dale's congregation. He was a successful businessman in the local community and an outspoken supporter of the local administration. In this case, the bishop apparently intended for him to be an arbitrator between the ministry and the concerned brethren in the congregation.

17

The Storm Breaks

"Ye fearful saints, fresh courage take;
The clouds ye so much dread
Are big with mercy, and shall break
In blessings on your head."
—William Cowper

It was a long week for Dale—actually, it was a long week for all the concerned families. Now that the moment of confrontation was at hand, it looked like a big hurdle.

The members gathered at 8:00 on Friday evening, and for once, most came. Samuel Martens opened the meeting, looking grim. After some introductory remarks, he opened the letter that the concerned families had given him and curtly read it to the whole group.[1]

---

1 The following letter is abbreviated somewhat, but capitalization, spelling, and punctuation are taken directly from the original document. Used by permission.

To the Bishop Brethren of the Alberta - Saskatchewan Conference

Dear Brethren
Greetings:

We the undersigned desire to petition you relative to pressing concerns and interests in the welfare of our Brotherhood.

We understand that our Church was born of God-inspired conviction and God-given courage in the hearts of Brethren, who united together under truly Biblical Doctrine and Practice. And that the Church was furthered in it's cause and spread by those who gave their lives for the sacred principles and daily practice enjoined by the word, even unto death.

We further believe that historically, the faith which the Mennonite Church subscribed to, based on the eighteen Articles of Faith as stated in the Dortrecht Confession of Faith, A.D. 1632, and affirmed at Garden City, Missouri, in 1921, is in true and in full accord with the Sacred teachings of all the Scriptures; and that the Scriptures are the sole and final authority of the individual and Church life. We cherish the readiness of our Church, during the days and times of revived Spiritual life and the 'great awakenings', to apply time-proven principles of Christian life and conduct to every area and part of their life, however unpopular or radical it was deemed by others.

The call to Christian Discipleship and cross-bearing is still a valid and inescapable duty today, as formerly. We believe that Holiness of Spirit and life is a direct result of a genuine new-birth experience, and that Holiness and Righteousness will always be present where Christ lives in the heart through His Spirit. The new-birth will always result in a continuing desire to conform to the ways of God, and will be manifest in our thoughts, interests and actions having a definite similarity to God's while diverging clearly and unmistakably away from this evil world and all it's practices.

Although not stated in so many words perhaps, we fear that there is a tendency to make room to somehow join together in common unity all types of thinking and we sense an effort being made to hold together all the various interpretations and practices existing among us. We with you share the concern expressed by the Church and it's plea for Church loyalty. Yet in spite of all pleas, the field of disrespect and disobedience to conference standards grows wider and wider.

We wish to insert at this point an expression of keen disappointment concerning the neglect of action following the concerns expressed by we, the undersigned.

We believe the following to be unscriptural:

1. The continued use of men known to be unsound in doctrine, both in our local pulpits, and in conference-wide meetings.
2. Organizational affiliation with other conferences and in the World Council of Churches, and all other unscriptural ecumenical movements.
3. The interdenominational affiliation and emphasis in our mission programs such as open communion, fellowship meetings, use of teachers and counselors of other faiths.
4. The continued expression and development of our mission program with some personnel definitely not in harmony with our doctrine and standard. This being verified by reports, and various circumstantial evidence.

5. Implied scholastic requirements of missionary personnel placed on missionaries which necessitates the patronizing of unsound educational institutions.
6. Continued close cooperation with the mission board, the organization programs and seminars. The Mennonite Central Committee, the publishing interests, and unscriptural school alliances.
7. The many programs on the radio that are of a evil nature and not conducive to holiness, and many religious programs are dangerous because they proclaim only a partial gospel.
8. The entrance of television without discipline in some bishop districts.
9. Laxity in discipline on modesty of dress in both men and women, such as: mixed bathing practices; men appearing without shirts; fashionable suits, ties, short sleeved sport shirts; haircut fads; use of transparent materials; sheer hosiery; women wearing slacks; low-necked, short sleeved, capeless, worldly adorned dresses; the flagrant violations and complete lack of consistency and uniformity in the covering and hair dressing practices, gym clothing, and all other departures from our accepted standards.
10. Organized sports such as ball teams, bowling teams, patronizing bowling alleys,

attendance at any and all public games, and entertainment such as ice capades circuses and rodeos.

11. Desecration of the sacred ordinance of marriage by worldly weddings.

We believe the above mentioned with others to be symptoms of the terrible disease of sin that has penetrated to the very heart of our church life.

We have committed ourselves to the aims and ideas set forth herewith.

1. A church directed by Jesus Christ in glory and in spirit here on earth.
2. A church after the apostolic and Anabaptist pattern.
3. A church through which God can work His purposes unhindered.
4. A church made up of voluntary freely committed believing members.
5. A sin conscious church deeply striving for holiness of life.
6. A church balanced in inner spiritual life and external practices.
7. A church requiring practical evidence for applicants for membership have already willingly embraced our standards before being received with the clear understanding that if they at any later time persist in disobedience they lose their membership.

8. **A church of vision, hope, faith and courage is in God's great promises.**
9. **A church partaking of and bringing others to the marvelous grace of a supernatural power of the divine nature in human hearts.**

Samuel was an expressive speaker and reader. He outdid himself this time, emphasizing certain words, drawing out certain others, and inserting little remarks such as, "And *then* the author goes on to say . . ." at a few spots.

From his seat toward the back, Dale could see the varied reactions across the congregation. With a sinking heart, he realized that many of the members viewed the letter as a slam against their congregation and its members—much as the bishop had viewed it as a slam against the ministry.

Had they overstated the facts? As the bishop continued, Dale heard the letter for the first time with the same ears the ministry and members were hearing it. It did sound bad. Yet, what it said was true. In fact, from his perspective as a young person, Dale knew that the truth was worse than what the letter stated, even though he hadn't had the courage to say so at the meeting when they drafted it.

When the bishop finished reading the letter, he also read the names of those members who had signed it. Then he looked across the group. "I'm not going to say more at this point," he said. "I think you can understand how we feel about it. But I don't want to be unfair, so I have asked Frank to lead out in discussing this. I think he will be fair to both sides. When he is finished, we will ask for a vote of confidence in the ministry."

Frank rose to his feet as the bishop sat down. He laid his copy of the letter in question on the lectern in front of him and paused until he had the audience's undivided attention. "I want you to know before we start that I support the church and its leaders," he said. "However, when Samuel asked me to moderate this meeting, he also asked me to give a fair hearing to those who wrote this letter. So I'll try to do that."

He picked up his copy of the letter. "I'm going to take this a piece at a time," he said. "You give me your comments on each part after I read it again."

He reread the introductory part of the letter first. "I noticed some errors in capitalization and punctuation and some ambiguity in sentence structure," he said. "This letter is written as a formal letter, but it doesn't quite make it. That illustrates my first point. The people who drafted this letter are—for the most part—uneducated farmers or inexperienced youth.[2] It seems a little presumptuous on their part to try to teach our leaders what is Scriptural and what is unscriptural."

Some snickers and a few amens arose from the audience. Dale felt sicker than ever. He could see already that the concerns in the letter didn't mean a thing to

---

2 The latter evidently referred to Dale and Blake, who had signed the letter along with their parents.

many of those present. He remembered the topic he had given several years before, and the response of the young people afterward. The response of their parents to the letter of concern wasn't much better, though it was a little more polite perhaps.

But Frank was continuing. "Note what this paragraph says," he said. "It begins with, 'Although not stated in so many words perhaps, we fear that there is a tendency to make room to somehow join together in common unity all types of thinking. . . .' Note that they have no proof of their statement—they only 'fear' that this is true. But worse yet, the writers evidently feel that their concerns are the only 'types of thinking' that should be tolerated."

He looked around the room, and someone close to the front spoke up. "I noticed that too," he said. "That was one of the big problems that men like Daniel Kauffman and George Brunk had—they had no toleration for any opinion but their own. Conservatives are almost always like that. But if we want to bring Christ to the world, we need to broaden our perspectives. Lots of good Christians aren't Mennonites and don't dress like them. We've got to get over this compulsion to equate Christianity with appearance."

Frank nodded. "My sentiments too," he said. "Are there any more comments on this introduction?"

The same man spoke up again. "That last paragraph—the one complaining that no action was taken about their concerns. Is that really true?"

Frank looked at the bishop. "Maybe you wanted to

comment on that?" he asked.

The bishop stood up. "I wasn't going to say anything about it," he said. "However, I suppose the answer depends a little on your perspective. From our perspective as a ministry, I feel we tried hard to accept the concerns that came and to work with them to the extent that we considered proper. However, we didn't feel led to force the congregation to comply with their concerns, so I suppose that from their perspective the writers felt that they could truthfully say what they did."

Another murmur of assent rose from the benches. But Frank at this point remembered that his prerogative included being fair to both sides of the question. He looked questioningly at Richard, who, of those who had signed the letter, happened to be the one sitting closest to him. "Maybe one of the writers would like to speak in defense of the letter?"

Richard shook his head. He and the others had agreed beforehand that they would not argue in favor of their points, but would let the letter be their statement of concern.

Frank frowned at this rejection of his generosity. "I don't want you going from this meeting thinking that we haven't treated you fairly," he said. "If you have anything to add to the discussion, please say it."

Richard glanced at the others, who were close by, and then spoke up. "It isn't our purpose to argue our position," he said courteously. "We tried to put our concerns down in the letter, and we will let it speak for us. I'm sorry if there are places where it isn't clear. But all we ask is that it be accepted and discussed in the spirit in which we tried to give it."

This put the damper on the discussion for a little, and Frank looked a little abashed. He turned to his paper again. "All right," he said. "If that's what you prefer, we'll go ahead with that understanding."

He picked up his paper and proceeded to read the first point. "So how do we feel about this one?" he asked. "They feel that we are using false teachers in our pulpits. But they don't say whom they are talking about. Are they referring to our ministers? Or visiting ministers? Do the rest of you feel that we have had false doctrine preached here in the past several years?"

Dale noted that with this last question he neatly shifted the focus from men who believed false doctrine to whether anyone had actually preached any false doctrine. His mind went back over some of the speakers that he remembered—such as the local pastor from the nearby town, who didn't believe in nonresistance or nonconformity. He probably hadn't preached anything false, but that wasn't really the concern behind the question.

Frank looked across the audience and repeated his question. "Can anyone remember any false doctrine being preached here or at a conference-wide meeting?"

A younger man sitting close to the front snorted. "Of course not," he said. "We may not totally agree with everything that every visiting speaker believes, but it is highly unlikely that anyone would presume on our hospitality to such a degree. And anyway, Jesus said that whoever isn't against us is for us. I think the writers are straining at a gnat and swallowing a camel. I understand that they allowed some non-conference men to preach for them at Richard's home. We could complain about that too."

Again a murmur of assent came from around the room.

Frank nodded. "So that pretty well covers that point, I suppose," he said. "How about the next one? Naturally we are affiliated with other conferences—we have never believed that independence was a good idea—so there is little value in discussing the first part of this statement.[3] But what about the World Council of Churches? Are we really affiliated with them?" He looked again at the bishop.

This time Samuel's answer was a little slower in coming. "Well," he said judiciously, this time not getting to his feet, "I suppose it depends a little on our interpretation of the word *affiliated*. Our conferences do at times send delegates to their meetings. This is mostly so that we can stay in touch with what is happening and maybe

3 Dale wasn't quite sure what this part of the statement meant. It could have been referring to some of the liberal conferences, such as the one in the East that the Lawrences had been part of. More likely, it may have referred to membership in the Mennonite General Conference, which tied together the various North American Mennonite conferences with little regard as to the individual worthiness of a conference. Note how this concern was brushed aside—at this point there was little sympathy for taking an individual stand for holiness in the church.

have some input into the decisions they make. We don't necessarily support everything that the World Council of Churches stands for."[4]

Frank hesitated a little before continuing. "I suppose there was a time when our churches would have stood against even attending the WCC meetings," he said. "But it does seem that in our day there is a need to stay abreast of current events in the world around us. How many of you are willing to accept the bishop's explanation?"

A forest of hands went up, and Frank nodded—apparently satisfied. He picked up his paper. "Let's go on then," he said. "The next point speaks to interdenominational activities on the mission field. Also, they are concerned because our missions use teachers and counselors from groups other than our own."

Several hands went up, and one man spoke up heatedly without waiting for recognition by the moderator. "That's about the same as we were talking about in the first point," he said. "We can't ostracize others—who are probably just as Christian as we are. I'm sure our mission directors use discretion, but they are on the field and are in a better position to judge their needs than we are. They can hardly wait for a church council to make a decision when they need help."

4 Remember that Samuel, as a noted conservative in his time, probably had some personal difficulties in supporting the status quo of the conference in some of these areas, though he was unwilling to admit it. The leading edge of the North American conferences would not have waffled on this question as Samuel did here.

Again there were several amens, and heads nodded across the auditorium. Dale could see that the irritation of the group was growing with each point that was raised. He was surprised—he had expected opposition, but he hadn't realized how deep the animosity to Scriptural principles had become in the congregation.

Frank glanced at his paper. "Well, that takes care of this point and the next one as well," he said. "Even 5 and 6 would be included in that. If our mission boards feel that an education is an asset to the work, they should have the privilege to implement that. I am also sure that our publishing houses and the Mennonite Central Committee have given careful consideration to these issues. There is little use in us trying to judge them."

He acknowledged another man who was waving his hand. "What do they mean by 'unscriptural school alliances'?" the man asked indignantly. "I think most of our missionaries and publishing personnel attend one of our own colleges or universities, such as Goshen or Hesston. It seems pretty judgmental to call our own schools unscriptural."

Again there was a chorus of agreement. Frank acknowledged this with a nod. "Everyone seems to agree with that," he said. "Let's go on to number 7—the point about the radio. Our friends seem to feel pretty strongly that the radio is evil—though if I am not mistaken, I think each of the homes represented in these signatures has a radio of its own."

Dale cringed a little and thought of the radio on their

kitchen counter. He knew Blake's family had one too. But he also knew that none of them ever listened to the programs the point referred to. Still, maybe Frank had a point—maybe they should have gotten rid of them. He noticed a funny look on his father's face and wondered if the same thoughts had crossed his mind.

A younger man spoke up, rather disgustedly. "Is it even worth our time to go over these points?" he asked. "All of us know that there are some bad things on the radio, but the same is true of the daily paper. You see bad things in town too. You can't even walk through the grocery store without facing them. Should we have a church standard against going shopping too?"

The chorus of snickers and amens that followed this remark clearly showed where the members placed this concern. So Frank went on to number 8. "I don't know of any television sets in our congregation," he said. "I suppose some of the more urban churches may have some, but there is little value in discussing something that we can't do anything about."

He glanced at his paper again. "Now, number 9 is probably worthy of some discussion," he said. "It raises the dress issue again, which I think is a rather central issue in this letter."

He glanced across the congregation. "It's true that we have changed a fair bit in this area," he admitted. "I won't deny that. But my question is—does it matter?"

Again a number of hands waved. With a chuckle, Frank chose the arm that seemed most animated.

"William, you'd better speak before you hit someone on the head," he said, smiling.

William rose to his feet to better emphasize his point. "I am *tired* of all this noise about appearance," he said. "Sure, we've changed our appearance some. We'll change more in the coming years, I'm sure. But so what—it's been said several times tonight that lots of good Christians aren't Mennonites. Insisting on sticking to the old ways in our appearance can actually hinder us from serving the Lord."

Here Dale noticed that a few of the older men looked a little uneasy and even the bishop shifted a little in his seat. But no one spoke up to contradict the statement, so Frank continued. "It seems that people are tired of talking about our clothing. How many of you feel that way?"

Again, a majority of hands went up. Frank picked up his paper again. "That seems clear—we will not bother coming back to that subject this evening," he said. "Point 10 talks about organized sports. Do you have any comments?"

The group was quiet for a moment, and then one of the younger ministers spoke up. "I suppose there is some danger in anything like this that we get involved in," he said. "But really, isolating ourselves from the world isn't the answer. Our young people enjoy life, and they need to mix with other youth. Such involvement can actually be good for them and the church. We have several youth who come to church here because of friends they made in school or on ball teams. We don't want to squelch that."

This was a new thought for Dale, but then he remembered various other young people who had left the church throughout the years because of friends they had made in town during such activities. He wondered why no one mentioned that.

Frank had no such qualms, evidently. "Sounds right to me," he said, and across the auditorium the heads nodded vigorously.

Frank looked at his paper again. "The last point probably is referring to dress again," he said. "Though I suppose there might be other parts of a wedding that might be considered worldly. How many of you are satisfied with our weddings?" Again most of the hands went up.

Dale noted that a lot of the people looked almost bored. He wasn't sure which was worse—the boredom or the irritation.

But Frank had picked up his paper one more time. "I don't think we need to spend much time on the latter part of this letter," he said. "They listed their vision of the church, and I don't think it's much different from mine or from that of our leaders." He glanced at Samuel for confirmation of this, and the bishop nodded his head.

"Probably the only point that we should look at is number 7," Frank continued. "It's evident that the writers are thinking in terms of a congregation with a concrete membership and a rigid statement of standards. Actually, both of those ideas are on the way out in modern Mennonite circles. By limiting our Communion to only a select group who have their names on our church roll and who have agreed to live by a stringent protocol listed in a rule book, we are limiting the grace of God in a way that God did not intend." Again he glanced at the bishop for confirmation.

This time Samuel spoke up. "I think you are both right and wrong," he said. "Certainly the day has long passed that the church speaks to every point in a member's life. As has been mentioned, dress is not considered nearly as important today as it used to be. I don't think we should be too rigid in any of these things, and Communion would be included in that. However, I do think for the sake of order, it is good to have a congregational membership roll. It helps in sorting out issues such as we are looking at tonight, for instance. But that should not be used in a judgmental fashion."

Frank nodded. "I can see your point," he said. "I don't think anyone here has a problem with that."

He picked up his paper again. "I have one more issue I want to raise," he said. "Right after the list of eleven things that the writers feel are unscriptural, they state, 'We believe the above mentioned with others to be symptoms of the terrible disease of sin that has penetrated to the very heart of our church life.' I have a big problem with that statement, as I told the ministry before the meeting. To me, that seems judgmental and unloving. I would go so far as to say it is unchristian."

Frank was deadly serious now, and the room was quiet. "It is true that we leave room for some variation of thinking," he said. "Probably these families have a right to their concerns. But I don't think it is right to make statements like this about a Christian congregation. Even though it does not mention our leaders, it implies that they have been unchristian in their administration. I feel—and have suggested to the ministry—that this statement would be grounds enough to discipline the writers of this letter. They feel that we are lax in discipline. Maybe we should start here."

Dale was startled at the growl of assent that rose from the benches.

Frank glanced at the bishop. "I'll give the meeting back to you now," he said to Samuel. "But I think it is quite evident how the congregation feels."

He sat down, and the bishop rose to his feet. It was evident that he had some reservations about the turn the meeting had taken. "I do appreciate the evident consensus of confidence that has been shown in the ministry tonight," he said. "It is gratifying to see our group so unified in this."

He paused for a minute and drummed his fingers on the lectern. "Frank raised his last suggestion to us earlier," he said. "We discussed it somewhat. But we feel it is a little drastic. I do believe that these men raised their concerns in all good faith that we would understand why they were doing so. I hardly know what to say, in the face of the feeling expressed here tonight."

He paused again, glanced at the other ministers, and then seemingly made up his mind. "Here is what we are recommending," he said. "We feel too that their criticism of the congregation and its leaders has gone too far. However, Christ has appealed to us to be forgiving, so this is what we are offering. We are asking that each of the cosigners of this letter take Communion with us next Sunday to prove to us that they do not hold any personal ill will against the congregation or its members. If they refuse to do this, we will have no choice except to deal with them as transgressors."

He looked across the crowd. "Do we have your support for this?" he asked. Again a forest of hands went up.

Dale's heart plummeted. So that was the end of it, and they would probably be forced into taking Communion yet again with all their concerns unanswered.

18

Finished?

"What appears to be the end
may really be a new beginning."
—Unknown

The men who had cosigned the letter met the next evening at Richard's home to discuss their response. Before they met, Richard called to Ontario to get some advice from the two brethren who had helped them draw up the letter. He passed this on to the others. "Brother Arnold and Brother Amos both agreed that they would support us in whichever course we decide to take," he said. "They don't have a problem with our taking Communion one more time to prove that we have no personal animosity toward the members here. We have made our concerns clear, and there is little else we can do. But they feel that we should be looking for a further solution, rather than just continuing like this, since the situation is obviously not going to get better."

His brother James agreed. "The meeting last night made it pretty clear where we're standing, I think," he said. "There was almost no interest in returning to a Scriptural position. If it weren't for the fact that I would like to leave on a clear basis, if possible, I wouldn't go back at all."

The others felt the same. Dale had a few qualms about it, but he and Blake again decided that they would support the decision their parents made.[1] Thus it was that a little over a week later, Dale and Blake were sitting at the back of the church, waiting once more for Communion to be served. None of the concerned families had been asked to make any confessions or expressions that they weren't comfortable with. It seemed that the ministry knew that they had pushed them about as far as they were willing to go.

Yet Dale felt uneasy for some reason. Did God really want them to take Communion? Were they going back on their commitment? Was this an unequal yoke? He struggled with that all week. He prayed often that God would reveal to them if they were going against His will. But he respected his father too much to go against his decision.

Dale pondered the face of Graham Albright, the assistant minister, sitting on the pulpit bench. Graham had

1 Probably some readers will question this decision. It certainly is possible for people to wait too long to act. Yet we need to admire their desire to go the second mile to prove their Christian attitude to their congregation. There certainly is a time to refuse to commune with sinners, and probably some people during this era waited plenty long to act.

always been friendly, even sympathetic, to the conservative brethren. What was he thinking at this moment?

The bishop got to his feet after the normal preliminaries. The thought crossed Dale's mind that he too seemed a little uneasy.

Samuel opened his Bible and took out a sheet of paper. "I have a few things that I want to say before I serve Communion," he said. "First of all, I am glad to see that those members who were involved in drawing up the letter that we discussed the other week are all here with us this morning. I trust that this is a sign that they do not have any animosity toward the rest of us. We do not want to brush aside anyone's concerns, and I certainly want them to feel free to share with us."

Dale wondered briefly why he bothered to emphasize this, since it didn't seem as if their concerns had meant anything at all.

The bishop shifted from one foot to the other. "Also, we have some visitors with us this morning from northern Alberta," he continued. "Most of you know Walter and Susie Snider. They are passing through the area again, and we have decided to offer them Communion on a visitor's basis. However, Walter wondered if we were sure that the congregation here would accept their participation, since he and his wife both wear wedding rings. He doesn't want to make a problem. So I promised him that we would verify it with the group before continuing."

He paused and glanced around the group. Dale sat frozen in his seat. He knew immediately that this might be the final straw—they had never before been faced with this. He was almost certain that his father would never voluntarily take Communion with someone wearing a wedding ring. Dale had often heard his father tell the story how his mother—Dale's grandmother—had needed to give up her wedding ring to become part of the church. Dale's grandparents had been raised in the Lutheran Church, and his grandmother had struggled with the issue for quite a while before deciding that it was right for her to give up her wedding ring. Surely his father would not disregard his mother's sacrifice by taking Communion now with Walter and his wife.

But the bishop was continuing. "Let's take a show of hands," he said. "Those of you who are ready to welcome Walter and Susie to take part in Communion, please raise your hands."

A forest of hands went up, and Samuel looked relieved. "Well, I think that is a strong vote in favor," he said. "We will proceed at this time."

Everyone sat silently as he stepped from the platform.

Then Richard stood up. For a moment he stood there, and Dale thought at first that he was going to say something. Then he stepped out into the aisle and deliberately walked toward the rear of the building.

The congregation went dead silent, and the bishop stopped in his tracks. Then Dale's mother stood up and followed her husband. Dale and Blake looked at each other. Blake nodded, and they both stood up to join Richard and Carrie. Out of the corner of his eye, Dale noticed Blake's parents and his uncle James's and their children also straggling back the aisle.

The other families went quietly outside, but Dale's parents remained standing in the lobby. For a moment, Dale wondered if his father was contemplating going back in. Then it struck him. Jane was still in the auditorium. A chill went up his back. Would Jane stay in with her friends and defy her parents' action? What would his father do if she did?

His father just stood there, and Dale noticed that he was praying.

It was one of the longest moments of Dale's lifetime. Then there was a stir in the auditorium, and Dale saw Jane hurriedly coming back the aisle, her head down. Relief washed over him, and he heard his father whisper, "Thank You, Lord."

Uncle Dale paused. "I suppose only another nineteen-year-old girl could understand the test my sister faced that day and how many deaths she died while she was walking back that aisle, with everyone looking at her," he said. "She turned her back forever on almost all of her old friends that day—for the sake of her father's convictions. It wasn't as hard for me, because I was sick of the situation. But she didn't understand all of that. She probably faced the hardest test of any of us."

He wiped a few beads of sweat from his forehead—mute indicators of how deeply his memories had stirred him again.

In the oddly silent parking lot, the other men talked briefly with Richard. He looked at Carrie. "Shall we meet again at our place?" he asked. And so it was decided. They finished the morning with a time of prayer for further guidance. Everyone stayed for lunch.

In the afternoon, the men sat in the living room to discuss what they should do next. "I suppose we should call Arnold and Amos again, to see if they have any further advice for us," Richard said. "It's going to be a long road from here."

Everyone agreed. "We should also call the group in British Columbia," James suggested. "They are the closest conservative group, and we will want to work with them if possible."

Dale remembered his time in British Columbia and agreed.

Blake's father, Malcolm, was a lot like Blake—not quick to speak, but worth listening to when he did. "I wonder if any other families at church will want to be part of this," he said soberly. "I think all of us know of some others who do not like the course the church is taking. Maybe we should plan a meeting for Wednesday night and get word around about it, in case some others would like to be involved."

The others recognized the wisdom of this. "It sure would be nice to have a few more families," Richard said wistfully. "But most of all, I wish we had a leader. It is going to be difficult to make our group seem like a viable alternative if there are only a few families and no ministry. We would be better off all moving to other communities than doing that."

Dale had listened quietly, but now he spoke up. "You know," he said thoughtfully, "Brother Graham has been pretty sympathetic with Blake and me. He's encouraged us several times to remain faithful to our convictions. You don't suppose he would be willing to join us?"

The older men looked at each other. "It might be worth pursuing," James said. "He's not the aggressive kind, and he's never taken a public stand on our side; but I know he's talked like that to me too."

Richard nodded. "I think we should talk to him," he said. "If we have a leader, some of the other families will be more likely to consider joining us. He hasn't been here long enough for us to know for certain if he is sympathetic enough to take such a step, but I think it would be worth talking to him."

So it came about that the three fathers decided that they would ask for a meeting with Graham Albright. "Let's leave our other plans until after we talk with him," Richard suggested. "If he goes along with us, we'll want his contribution in our further plans."

So they left it.

The sorting out began quickly. Dale ran into Allister in town the next day and stopped to talk with him. Allister was decidedly uneasy, and Dale couldn't help but notice it. "What's wrong?" Dale finally asked. "You act like you're scared of something."

Allister looked around hurriedly. "Well, it's this way," he said. "My mother is dead set against what you folks are doing. She's badly upset, and if she saw me talking to you, I'd really catch it! And she's around town somewhere, shopping."

Dale was startled. "Why would it matter for you to talk to me?" he asked curiously. "She never said anything before, did she?"

Allister hedged a bit. "Well," he said slowly, "she never liked it when I was with you after you started wearing a plain coat. I would have liked one too, but she really put her foot down. Now she wants me to go to the university in the city and get those notions out of my head."

"Really?" Dale was nonplussed. "You aren't going to do that, are you?"

Allister shrugged. "It looks like I'll probably have to go," he said. "My father won't stand up against her. Actually, I think he would be interested in your new group, but he wouldn't dare say so. I can't expect any help from him."

It took Dale a while to forget the misery on Allister's face. It hurt too, to think that a friendship of a lifetime was over, just like that.

It wasn't the only friendship to go up in smoke that day, however. When Dale got home, his mother was crying in the kitchen and his father was sitting soberly at the table across from her. He looked up wearily when Dale came in. "Your mother just had a telephone call from Lucy," he said.

Dale looked puzzled. Lucy was one of his mother's

closest friends at church.

"They want nothing more to do with us unless we come back to the church," his father explained. "In their minds, the sin of destroying the unity of the church is worse than any other sin could be. And they blame us for it."

Dale's mother wiped her eyes. "I shouldn't have let it get to me," she said shakily. "But it hurt so badly. Lucy was one of my best friends. We've been friends for thirty years."

Dale sat down at the table and looked at his mother sympathetically. "I lost a friend today too," he said slowly. "So I guess I know a little how you feel."

His father looked up quickly. "I met Allister in town," Dale continued, answering the question on his father's face. "His mother has forbidden him to have anything to do with us as a group or with me. In fact, they're sending him to the university in a few weeks, to make sure he doesn't get any funny notions about joining us."

His father shook his head. "Oh, no! I don't like that," he said. "With his personality, that could be spiritual suicide."

Dale nodded. "I think he knows that," he said. "But he's been so used to letting his mother rule his life, that I doubt if he'll stop now. He said he would have worn a plain suit, but for her."

They sat quietly for a few moments. "You know," Dale's father said, "I don't think we have any idea what all this is going to cost us. Both you and your mother have lost longtime friends, and it is only the day after our break. I wonder what else is going to happen."

Dale changed the subject. "I wonder what happened to the Communion service after we left," he said. "I suppose they kept on going?"

His father nodded. "They tried to anyway," he said. "I talked to Graham today. He said it put quite a damper on it, but they finished it and tried to pretend nothing had happened."

Dale looked up quickly. "So you talked to Graham, did you?" he asked. "How is he feeling about it?"

"I can't say for sure," his father answered slowly. "He was friendly enough. He also said he didn't know that the bishop was going to spring that on us, or he would have protested. But I gathered he went through with Communion himself. I explained what we were thinking, and he has agreed to meet with us tomorrow evening. So we'll see then."

"I suppose a lot of people are blaming us for making such a spectacle of it," Dale said. "But we didn't know what they were going to do."

"That's what Graham said," his father answered. "Apparently some sympathized with us, but felt we should simply have registered a protest afterward. But I just couldn't do that—not after what my mother suffered in deciding to stand for truth."

Dale looked at him thoughtfully. "You know," he said, "I prayed all week that the Lord would reveal to us if we should be taking Communion. I guess the Lord answered that prayer."

His father smiled, a little bleakly. "He certainly did," he said. "And I think God knew that we needed that last push to make us do what was right.

"You know," he added, "we have been taught all our lives that to leave the conference is about the worst thing a person can do. I have even heard of people on their deathbeds who made their children vow that they would never leave the conference. Leaving the conference is something you *never* do. But we have."

His shoulders drooped a little. "And it was one of the hardest things I ever did," he said. Then he straightened up and smiled. "But I feel better than I have for years," he added, almost triumphantly. "I have prayed for years for an answer. Now it has come."

"But we aren't through the deep waters yet," Dale's mother said softly. "The worst hardships might still be ahead of us."

"I know," Richard acknowledged. "That's probably right. But there's hope now. That makes all the difference. God won't let us down if we stick with Him. We will probably be the offscouring of the community for a while, but I'm willing to go through that if that's what it takes to find a way for my family."

Dale looked at his father thoughtfully. He had seen a new look on his father's face since yesterday—almost as if a mountain had rolled off his back. He was like a younger man. Dale had thought about that all day, and now his father had put his finger on it—he had a hope for the future now. Sure, there was a lot of work ahead.

Maybe a lot of tears even. But together they would see it through because God was with them.

The next night the three men met with Graham Albright. Dale was still up when his father returned. He looked up from his cup of coffee as his father came in the door. "So, how did it go?" he asked.

His father sat down, poured some hot water into a mug, and added a teaspoon of coffee before answering. "Pretty good, actually," he said. "He and his wife both expressed an interest in the stand we are taking. We're planning to have a meeting on Friday evening to decide where to go from here. That will give us time to contact others who might be interested."

So it was that on Friday evening, Graham Albright and his family were at the meeting. Four new families came also, along with the three original ones.

Dale enjoyed the meeting. He had a feeling that they were making history. But beyond that, it was almost the first time that he could remember feeling comfortable with the spiritual atmosphere in a meeting in his local setting. He could sense an intense desire to stand for truth that permeated the meeting. Even those who were there for the first time had, in a sense, cut their ties to the old church simply by showing up. All of them knew that the local administration would view this meeting as outright mutiny.

Richard opened the meeting and then called on Graham to lead in Scripture reading and prayer. Graham read

1 Kings 17:1–9—the account of Elijah at the brook Cherith. After the reading, he looked across the audience. "You know," he said, "I see some parallels for us in this passage. For most of us, our brook has just dried up. By being here this evening, we have lost the goodwill and support of our congregation. It might seem to us that now we have nothing.

"I suppose that many of you have seen that brook slowly drying up in the last years. Yet it was your sustenance, and you kept clinging to it. But now it's gone dry. What now?"

He paused again, thoughtfully evaluating the group's expressions. "Well," he said finally, "God had an answer. It did not look like a very good one at first. How much could a widow with no visible means of support do for Elijah? In fact, she was totally destitute herself—she was using up the last of her resources when Elijah first met her, and she was without any hope of getting more.

"Maybe that's a little how you feel tonight," he said. "This little group is a poor-looking substitute, as far as numbers go, for the brook we left behind. But God miraculously supplied the needs of the widow and Elijah. He will do the same for us if we trust Him as they did."

Graham was not a dynamic speaker. His vocation not requiring any manual labor, he was rather flaccid in comparison to the muscular farmers in his audience—and peered nearsightedly through thick glasses. But tonight the group didn't notice his shortcomings. They drank in the message as the parched desert drinks in rain after a summer of broiling heat.

> *"I'll never forget that meeting," Uncle Dale said. "The birth of a congregation takes a lot of time and effort. But we were all so glad to be unshackled from the burden of impure church life and the strain of communing with members living in open sin, that it all seemed like a breath of fresh air."*

They accomplished a lot during that meeting. They decided to ask Henry Anderson, the bishop in British Columbia, to help oversee their group. For the time being, they would use the conference statement of faith and practice, but they would consider revising it within six months, once they had found bishop oversight.

Of more consuming importance was the need for a meeting place and for appointing people to lead out in the work of the new congregation.

Laverne Jackson, one of the newcomers, solved the first problem. "I've got a big, heated, three-car garage at our place," he said. "All we do is park our car in it. We could set up some benches or chairs in there. It's big enough for all of us. We could have Sunday school in the house or even outside, for now."

Everyone was agreeable to this. Graham was appointed to be in charge of the services and to contact the bishop in British Columbia, and Richard was placed in charge of the Sunday school. James was appointed trustee, and Dale was appointed to be song leader. Further, they decided to have regular Sunday morning services, weekly prayer meetings, and Sunday evening services twice a month.

A time of fellowship followed the meeting. Dale and Blake stood off to one side and watched. "Well, everyone seems pretty enthused," Dale said. "It's sure nice to have a group this size."

Blake nodded. "It feels right," he said. "It will take some time to get everything organized properly, but with a bit of time, things should settle into a routine of sorts."

As they stood there, Jane wandered around the edge of the group and approached them. Dale smiled at her. "Feeling lonesome?" he asked her. "I guess none of your close friends are here."

She sighed. "No, there isn't anyone my age," she said wistfully. "I had hoped Neil's would come tonight, but they didn't."

She wandered off again. Blake's eyes followed her. "She's been a good sport about it, hasn't she," he said. "I can see it would be tough for a girl like her not to have any close friends. She's so outgoing and vivacious."

Dale glanced at him a bit curiously, but he didn't voice his thoughts. Instead, he watched Jane slip into the hallway that led to her bedroom. "We'll have to make sure she doesn't get too lonely," he said thoughtfully. "Maybe we'll have to take her along when we go places. She's been a good sister, and I'm glad she isn't complaining about this. There was a time she would have."

19

Settling In

"An encounter with God—a real one—means change."

The people in the "little church"—as the community called the new group—stuck together closely.[1] Partly this was for survival. They met a lot of opposition. The members of the "old church"—as the members of the little church now called it—were an important and well-thought-of element in the community. Many people who otherwise took little interest in the Mennonite Church sided with the old church and spoke disdainfully about the members of the little church—snubbing them to their faces and calling them rabble-rousers and radicals behind their backs, occasionally even adding contemptuous or

1 One member of the old church coined the phrase "chicken coop splinter group" to refer to the little church. The name held on for some years, even after they moved into a larger building.

unprintable modifiers.

But the group became close-knit for another reason. They were close because they had a genuine love for each other, which had been lacking for years in the old church. They discovered that during the week they missed each other, and so members often dropped in on each other with little or no excuse.

Thus it was that Dale wasn't particularly surprised when Blake drove in one day while he was out working around the corrals. But he was a little puzzled when Blake stopped to visit with his father instead of coming out to see him. And he was even more puzzled when Blake turned on his heel and headed for the house. *Oh, well, he'll find out that I'm not in there; then he'll come out and find me.*

But about five minutes later, Blake jumped back into his pickup truck and headed off in a cloud of dust. Dale scratched his head and then shook it. *Whatever's gotten into him today? You'd think he just came to talk to Jane. . . .* All of a sudden, his face cleared as the thought hit him. Maybe Blake *had* come to talk to Jane. Maybe . . . He tossed his straw hat on a fence post and headed for the house. *Time for a break anyway. You're not going to keep any secrets from me, sister of mine!*

As it turned out, his father had decided on a break at the same time. When Dale got to the kitchen, his parents and Jane were in the middle of a deep discussion. Jane turned to him as he came into the room, her eyes flashing. "And what do you know about this?" she demanded.

Dale noticed that she was blushing and that she looked more shocked than upset. "Me?" he said, acting bewildered. "What are you talking about?"

She looked at him searchingly. "You mean you *really* don't know?" she asked.

"Well," Dale hedged a little, "I have some *ideas*. I saw Blake come into the house and then go hustling down the road about five minutes later. But I don't *know* what he wanted. He never told me anything about it. Why are you upset?"

Jane sank into the closest chair, as if in need of its support. "I'm not upset—just surprised," she said. "I thought maybe you were in on this. Blake just asked me if I would consider a visit with him to get better acquainted."

Dale sat on the kitchen counter and looked down at her. "I wondered if that was what he was after," he said. "You can rest assured that he's serious about it. He doesn't do anything like that without thinking and praying about it for quite a while. He has no use for flippancy in courtship. What did you tell him?"

"I didn't tell him anything, really," she said. "It was a totally new idea for me, and I think he knew that it would be. He didn't ask for an answer—just told me to take my time and let him know once I had decided."

Her blush deepened. "He—he said he would be praying for me, but that I should feel free to do however God led me," she said softly. "I guess I always thought of him as your friend. It never dawned on me that he might be interested in me."

Dale contemplated her for a moment from his perch. "Well," he said finally, "take your time, and be sure. Rather say no now than break his heart later."

The others knew why his voice went husky as he said this. But a moment later he added, "But give him a good chance. He's really a nice person, once you get to know him, and he is a genuine Christian too."

He grinned suddenly. "But you'd have to share him with me because I need a friend too," he said.

Jane smiled back. "We'll cross that bridge when we get to it," she said. Then her face went serious. "In the meantime, I'd appreciate if you'd pray for me. I honestly don't know what to do about it."

Several months later, the whole family sat around the table for tea one Sunday evening before retiring. Dale had been musing over the day's events. "You know," he said, "church life is sure different from what it used to be."

His father put his cup down. "In what way?" he asked. "Better or worse?"

Dale grinned. "Better, of course," he said. Then he thought a little before continuing. "One of the big differences is meeting in a garage, I suppose," he added.

"And in having a congregation of thirty people instead of two hundred," said his mother. "That took me a while to get used to."

"Another big difference is that we all have the same

convictions," Dale said. "I don't have to feel on edge anymore because of what I believe. I really like that part."

His father nodded. "That's right," he said. "That's what I have prayed for, for years." He paused thoughtfully, before adding, "I like the openness of our people, especially since Brother Graham has started leaving time for testimonies and confessions after the sermon."

Dale nodded and then grinned mischievously at his sister. "Of course, we daren't forget Jane's courtship," he said. "She's grown up about two years in the past six weeks since she has an ongoing friendship with Blake."

Jane wrinkled up her nose at him, good-naturedly. "You're just jealous," she retorted.

Dale winced a little. "Actually, you're right," he admitted. "Not that I'm jealous of you and Blake—I'm glad for you. But I do miss not having more young people around, especially now that Blake is tied up with you part of the time."

His father nodded. "I think we will have to reach out farther for some additional fellowship," he said. "The British Columbia church has more youth. We'll have to make sure you get over there sometimes."

Dale's thoughts continued in this direction after he went downstairs to go to bed. He had to admit to himself that Jane and Blake's friendship was hard on him. He could see for himself the bloom of young love developing in Jane. So often she reminded him of Sheila—the way her eyes lit up when Blake came in the door and the buoyancy in her step, even during the week when Blake wasn't around. Dale had thought he had forgotten, until he saw how Jane and Blake enjoyed being together. They spent much of their time with the whole family, and even then they didn't get together nearly as often as Dale and Sheila had. But they still couldn't hide the growing attachment they had for each other and their joy in being together.

He stood up and paced back and forth across his bedroom a few times, his hands clasped behind his back and his head down. What really had gone wrong with his courtship with Sheila? He had tried so hard to follow his parents' advice and to maintain a spiritual relationship. They had had a pure courtship. They had spent a lot of time studying the Bible together and talking about spiritual topics. Sheila had obviously had a deep spiritual interest and a desire to grow spiritually. What had gone wrong? Why had they hit such a brick wall?

He thought back over the weaknesses in Sheila's home, and he realized again how difficult it must have been for her to cope with the spiritual indifference of her parents. True, they hadn't interfered with her growing convictions, but he could see how the cold indifference of her family might have been harder to overcome than outright opposition. But surely they could have weathered that together. His encouragement and their mutual love should have been able to overcome that.

Did Sheila have a spiritual weakness? His whole being revolted against the thought. He remembered the times she had shed tears because of her inner struggles and her desire to do what was right.

Finally, he shook his head. Maybe there were no answers. Maybe it simply boiled down to the fact that she was unwilling to follow God past a certain point. He remembered her struggle with finding God—and her assertion that He didn't seem real. Was it because she had subconsciously rejected what God wanted to show her?

He remembered her battle with the idea of wearing a cape dress. *I suppose she honestly desired to follow God and to have Him be real in her life. Yet if she put a limit on what she was willing to do if He did reveal Himself to her, I suppose God would hold back. He did take her a long way, and she was happy while she was traveling in that direction.*

He suddenly remembered an illustration that one of his Bible school teachers had given—that the Christian life was like climbing a ladder. A person might be a long way from the top, but as long as he kept climbing at the speed God took him, he was in God's will. But if he refused at any point to take the next step, he was in danger of destroying his relationship with God, no matter how far up the ladder he was.

Dale remembered vividly the picture of a ladder the teacher had drawn on the blackboard one day. Then he had drawn a stick man close to the top of the ladder. "You may have been a Christian for a long time," the teacher had said. "You may be almost at the top of God's ladder.[2] But if you stop moving up at God's bidding, you are in worse shape than the immature Christian at the bottom of the ladder, who is slowly but surely climbing higher at God's bidding." He drew another stick man at the bottom of the ladder.

Maybe that was the answer. If only he could have helped Sheila past that next hurdle. But she had shut him off, almost as if she was afraid that he would succeed in helping her, and she didn't want him to. He dropped his head into his hands for a moment. If only she had made a different choice! He tried for a minute to imagine what life could have been like, had she done so, but he sensed almost immediately the danger of such a train of thought.

He sighed. There was no use going over that again. She was gone, and gone forever, by all appearances. Anyway, it was no use blaming her. From his reading and study in the past year, he realized that he had made some mistakes too. *I suppose we were together so much that it destroyed our perspective of each other. Our emotional attachment for each other grew so rapidly that it interfered with our spiritual evaluation of each other, and we didn't realize how far apart we were. Even our times of Bible study together were based on that emotional attachment. I thought her desire for truth was motivated by a right spirit, and she did too. But maybe it was more from a desire to please me than she realized. If I ever keep*

---

2 Of course, we never reach the top. No human being becomes perfect on earth. But the illustration gives an important point.

company with a girl again, I think we will spend less time together so that we can have a more balanced perspective of each other. I'm glad Blake and Jane are taking their time.

Slowly he got ready for bed. Somehow, the last several weeks, his life had seemed lonely. Did God really intend for him to spend life alone? At one point, he had been sure of that and had even deliberately rejected any other idea. But all of a sudden, he wasn't so sure. Somehow, a bachelor's life looked like a long, lonely trail.

He dropped to his knees beside his bed. His prayer was an intimate one—his heart cried out to the best Friend he had. He knew from long experience that this was the best place to take his burden, and tonight again he knew that God heard him. But tonight his prayer included a hesitant plea that he had not included in his prayers for some time. *Lord, if it be Your will, please send me a friend. A girl who will understand my desire to serve You, and will encourage me in it—a girl who will be willing to share life with me and serve You with me.*

Dale finally grew restless enough that he decided to go on a trip. He talked to Blake about it one Wednesday evening after prayer meeting. "Why don't we go to British Columbia again for a weekend?" he suggested. "I'd like to have some outside fellowship for a change."

Blake had noted the struggles his friend was going through, though typically, he had not said anything to Dale about it. He had also made a reasonably accurate assessment of Dale's problem. "I think that would be a good idea," he said. "It would be good for both of us."

Dale hesitated a little. "Should we take Jane along?" he asked, watching Blake for his reaction.

Blake answered immediately, without batting an eye. "No," he said. "Let's go alone. We haven't done anything like that for a while. It'll be good for both of us."

So the plans were made. It turned out that the British Columbia church was planning a Bible conference in several weeks, and they decided to be there over that weekend.

They left early Friday morning. As the miles ticked away, Dale found himself relaxing and enjoying the scenery. They reached the foothills and then turned north. From there on, the driving became more rugged as they entered the Rockies. Again, at first, Dale almost felt claustrophobic, but gradually the sheer grandeur of the mountains won him over again. "This is sure different from the prairies," he said, breaking a comfortable silence that had lasted for almost half an hour. "Just look at that." He waved his hand at the mountain beside him and then grabbed the steering wheel with both hands again as they rounded a hairpin curve. "Oops," he added, "I've got to get used to this kind of driving again."

Blake chuckled. "It's worth the trip just to see this again," he said. "And to watch your hair stand on end when you almost miss a curve."

Dale cocked his eye at him and would have returned a similar remark, except at that minute they hit another hairpin curve that required his full attention. One back wheel dropped off the pavement for a moment. Blake grabbed for the door handle and then suggested innocently, "If you'd like me to, I could drive for a while, and you could enjoy the scenery."

Dale snorted. "Just for that I ought to make you drive the rest of the way," he retorted. But he kept his eyes on the road this time. "I don't see why they don't put guardrails on these curves," he grumbled. "We'd go a thousand feet straight down if we got three feet off the track." He pulled closer to the edge as they met a large truck coming around the next curve.

Blake looked out his window and down. "Hmm. It looks more like half a mile to me," he commented. "Maybe you'd better just let me watch the scenery. I'll report on anything interesting. You watch the road."

In spite of the roads, they both enjoyed the trip, and the day went by rapidly. "I wonder who all we'll meet this weekend," Dale commented when they finally drove into the valley that led to their destination. "I always like meeting new people."

Blake sighed. "That's not as easy for me as for you," he said. "I'll just trail along after you. I'm looking forward to the teaching."

Dale nodded. "I always enjoy that too," he agreed. "But I miss the larger youth group we used to have, even if most of the time I didn't go to their affairs."

They arrived at Henry Anderson's in time for supper.

Again the house was full, and again Henry would not hear of them going elsewhere. "Come in," he growled cheerfully. "We've been waiting for you. Supper's right ready." He saw Dale eyeing up the size of the crowd in the living room and kitchen, and smiled. "They're not all staying here for the night," he assured him. "We've got lots of room for you."

And so Dale and Blake once again found themselves seated at the familiar table for supper.

On Saturday, some of the young people and young married couples from the church decided to hike to the top of one of the mountains, behind Henry's farm, for a picnic. They invited the visitors to go along. This gave everyone a chance to get to know each other better.

Dale and Blake both enjoyed the hike, but Dale especially was glad to broaden his friendships. Before the morning was over, everyone was chatting as if they all had known each other for years, though Dale noticed again that the youth were more reserved than he had been used to.

They ate their lunch on a ridge that ran along the top of the mountain. It had been a strenuous climb, and everyone was glad to take some time to relax, visit, and admire the view. It was a beautiful spot, overlooking the entire valley. They could see the farms on the valley floor, lying lush in the late fall sunshine. To the east, they could see a small town and the winding road that ran the full length of the valley. On the far side, miles away, but looking much closer, were the mountains that made up the other wall of the valley. Such a sight can be seen only in the mountains, and in spite of being a prairie boy at heart, Dale could not help but admire the beauty spread out in such a panoramic scene before him.

Blake seated himself on a rock close by. "Beautiful spot," he remarked. "Jane would love this."

Dale smiled. "Missing her, are you?" he asked. "I guess we should have brought her along. She was a bit nettled at me for running off with you."

Blake smiled. "We can come again sometime," he said, looking out across the valley. "You're a friend of mine too, and she understands that."

"She was a good sport about it," Dale agreed. "She's a good sister, all around."

They sat quietly for a few minutes; then Dale turned to the others. "Why don't we sing for a while?" he suggested. The others were agreeable, so they sang some hymns together. Everyone enjoyed it, and even the echoes sounded cheerful.

But finally one of the married men looked at his watch. "I guess we'd better head back," he said reluctantly. "By the time we get back and get cleaned up, it'll be suppertime."

On the way back down the mountain, at a steep spot, one of the girls slipped and almost fell. Without thinking anything of it, Dale reached over to steady her. Instead of graciously accepting his help, she shrank back from him and was only saved from falling when several girls managed to catch her from behind.

Dale had thought it was proper to help a girl in such a situation, and her reaction startled him. In fact, it puzzled him enough that he brought it up after church, when he and Blake were sitting in the living room, visiting with Henry. Dale told Henry what had happened. "I didn't mean anything by it," he ended up. "I would have done the same for anyone. I thought it was proper to look out for others like that, especially girls or women."

Brother Henry chuckled. "I can see your predicament," he said. "We have done a lot of teaching here about the need for reserve between young men and women. Especially, we have taught a hands-off standard for courtship, because of the laxness that we faced in the old setting. I'm glad the girls have taken that to heart. I would, however, consider it proper for a boy to offer to help a girl who is slipping or falling."

Brother Henry stopped to scratch his head. "We left our apostate settings determined to have a pure and holy church life," he added. "We have preached and preached about those things, and I would rather see an over-cautiousness than the carelessness we saw in our former setting. But I trust we can find the right balance."

He smiled. "Anyway, I know you didn't have any bad motives. Don't let it trouble you."

Dale felt better after that, but he and Blake continued the discussion while getting ready for bed. "I guess I thought we had solved our problems by leaving the old church," he said to Blake, "but maybe it isn't going to be that simple."

"I doubt it," Blake answered gravely. "This thing of finding a balance can take a long time. Especially if there is difference of opinion on what we mean by being balanced."

They looked at each other soberly. "We're only getting to that point," Dale said finally. "I wonder what all we'll face in church life yet until everything settles down."[3]

---

3 Dale's premonition was correct, as later history proved. In fact, though none of these brethren realized it or could have guessed it, it took most of twenty years before the worst of the sorting out across North America was finished. This is probably typical of a revival movement. Some lessons seemingly can only be learned by experience.

20

Growing Pains

*"There are some things which only God can do. . . .
There are other things which only man can do."*
—*A. W. Tozer*[1]

Soon after Dale and Blake returned home from British Columbia, the six-month inauguration period was up. The congregation had originally decided to do two things at this point: organize officially, with a fixed membership roll, and revise the statement of standards. Several Sundays later, Graham made an announcement about this.

"Our bishop, Brother Henry, is planning to spend a week with us," he said. "He will be with us for the next two Sundays. He will outline the procedures further next Sunday, but I think he plans to meet with each family individually during the week sometime. On Monday night

1 *Paths to Power*, p. 15.

we will meet to consider revising the constitution, as we decided we would when we first started meeting together. If necessary, we will meet again on Wednesday evening to finish. Then on Friday night we will have our first counsel meeting and finalize the membership roll. On Sunday we will have our first Communion service."

He paused a bit. "If you have any questions, you can ask them after the service," he added slowly. "But it might be better to wait and ask Brother Henry. I'm not sure exactly what all he has in mind, and this is just as new for me as it is for you."

Henry had visited the little church several times before, so everyone knew him. He was a dynamic speaker, and the contrast between his preaching and Graham's took the congregation a little to get used to him when he came. While doing it compassionately, he also had a way of saying exactly what he thought. Dale, of course, knew him better than some of the others did, since he had stayed at Henry's place overnight both times that he visited in British Columbia. But even Dale was startled at Henry's comments during his sermon at the evening service the next Sunday.

"I feel that some definite changes are needed here if the congregation is to continue under the blessing of God," he said. "This is especially true in some of the dress practices and in the continued use of the radio."

He paused and looked across the congregation. "I have seen growth here in some of these areas," he said, "but I would like to encourage more. We don't want to just drift along twenty-five years behind the conferences. We will plan to discuss some of these issues in our meeting tomorrow evening."

The congregation was unusually quiet after dismissal that evening. Dale and Blake discussed Henry's comments for a little. "I wonder if anyone knew Henry felt like that," Dale said to Blake. "I knew that we looked a little different from Henry's home congregation, so I guess I should have realized a bit more what his expectations are."

Blake nodded. "This will give Jane a bit of a jolt. I guess we were all so much more conservative than the old church that none of us realized that we should be changing even more."[2]

---

2 Note that this process varied somewhat from group to group. Some people expected the church to become much plainer when they left their apostate settings, and some only wanted to step back a little from their previous practices. When these expectations both existed in the same congregation, they often clashed.

There was some variation as to how these situations were handled in the new settings. Some leaders took quite a bit of time making changes, hoping to keep their congregations together. A few of these congregations never did get the changes made at all. Other leaders felt it was their duty to insist on almost immediate compliance, as pictured here. Most of these congregations lost some potential members in the process. It seems that all of this was an unavoidable part of the sorting-out process, and it is difficult to judge at this distance what the best approach would have been. Note that this sorting-out process gradually led to various levels of conservatism over the first several decades after the divisions. Most of these basic levels have grown into church fellowships that are more or less sympathetic to each other but have few formal ties, by the time of this writing. The tensions and disagreements of this sorting process have never been totally healed, and still exist, in many cases—at least to a degree.

Dale bit his lip. "Not everyone is going to be happy about Henry's message," he said. He glanced across the room to where Laverne Jackson's wife was talking animatedly with another church sister.

Blake's gaze followed his. "She's one who will have to make a lot of changes if we take this route," he noted. "And she looks pretty upset at the idea. I hope this doesn't make too much trouble."

Dale looked a little troubled. "We've been getting along so well," he said. "I hope it can continue that way."

Dale had a troubled night. Would this destroy their little congregation before it really got started? Why did this have to hit now? Was this really what God expected of them? He didn't think he would have a personal problem complying with any of the things that might come up, but he knew some of the other members might.

The next day Graham and Henry came to Richard's for lunch and interviewed the family afterward. During this interview, Henry seemed to take for granted that there would be a number of changes. Toward the end, he looked at Jane and asked her kindly but also frankly, "Would you be willing to start wearing cape dresses?"

Jane looked a little flustered. "I—I'd have to do a lot of sewing," she said. "It would take a bit of time. I'd have to replace my whole wardrobe, almost." Her voice trailed off, and she looked at her father helplessly.

Richard noted her unspoken plea and spoke up. "How much time would you expect to give if we go ahead with this?" he asked. "It would take some time to make a change that drastic. Could she wear out her present dresses or use them for work?"

Henry frowned a little, and Dale noted that Graham shifted uneasily in his chair. Evidently they had had some earlier discussion on the subject. Dale wondered all of a sudden how favorably Graham felt toward these ideas.

"Well, I'm not sure," Henry said. "I guess it would depend a bit on what the congregation decided. But if we give too much grace, it might never get done. I didn't think you would question this, Richard."

Richard weighed his words carefully. "I'm not questioning it," he said. "I've been hoping for some improvement myself in some of these things. It's just that I hope we don't push it too rapidly. Would there be a place for giving some time for voluntary changes?"

Henry thought a moment before replying. "I have mentioned most of these things before in sermons somewhere along the line, in hopes that this would bring about some voluntary changes," he said. "Shouldn't that have been enough? Do you really feel that a lot more time is necessary? Things are not happening very quickly. My fear is that we will keep giving more time, and the changes may never happen."

He swung his gaze to Dale. "What do you think, Dale?" he asked.

Dale was taken aback a little at this direct question. "I guess I was a bit startled," he admitted. "I didn't realize that you weren't satisfied with what we were doing.

Church life has been going so well that I did wonder why we needed to make many changes now. But maybe I'm not seeing everything."

Henry looked a little surprised—he had evidently expected Dale to support him. "Maybe I haven't explained things as clearly as I thought," he said. "I see several things in all of this. First, unity of practice is a help to any congregation. If the world looks in at your group presently, they won't know for sure what your standard of practice is. That's confusing."

He paused a little before continuing. "But more important," he said, "if we don't take a deliberate stand on issues and draw a line, what is there to keep us from going down the same trail we were following before we left the conference? My fear is that we have just stepped back twenty-five years and will follow the old groups down the trail. In other words, in twenty or thirty years we will be right back where we came from."

He scratched his chin thoughtfully. "Well, let's see how things sound this evening," he said. "I do want to work with the congregation, but I was thinking it looked like people were needing a bit of a push."

Graham looked distinctly relieved at the direction the conversation was taking. "Maybe we could revise the constitution with the understanding that the changes would become mandatory after a certain period of time," he suggested, somewhat meekly. "That might make it a bit easier for a few people."

Henry still seemed a little reluctant. "I suppose," he

said. "But that period may not be too long, or it might never end."

Evening came, and with it the meeting about the constitution revision. Dale felt rather uneasy as he drove to church. Somehow, in the back of his mind he remembered the last meeting at the old church, when the group had gone down over their letter of concern. As he looked across the waiting congregation, he sensed that some of the others were tense as well. But he also noticed a determined look on the faces of several members, which puzzled him.

Henry opened the meeting and asked Graham to lead in prayer. Dale noticed that Graham seemed hesitant and uptight. *I wonder why. He seems afraid of something. I wonder what he and Henry have been discussing. Henry does seem to feel we need to make some changes here. But he might not be the only one. A few of the others seem to agree with him. But some are definitely against making many changes. I wonder if Graham is afraid we will have a major disagreement.*

As soon as Henry opened the meeting for discussion, a young married brother named Robert Fox rose to his feet. "I have a few things that I think we should be changing," he said energetically. "First, a number of our sisters are not wearing cape dresses. Second, we have several brethren who still have not started wearing plain coats. Third, many of our homes still have radios and use them. Fourth, most of our sisters are wearing flesh-colored or sheer stockings instead of black.

"I think we should make these things a test of membership. My uncle in Pennsylvania says that this is what their congregation did when they left the conference setting. In fact, he was surprised that we hadn't done so before this."

Henry nodded. "That is the stand we take in our congregation," he said. "Not every conservative congregation has gotten to that point, but most have."

Another brother spoke up. "If that's what the others are doing, then we should too," he said. "If we don't, they might not want to fellowship with us."

Richard raised his hand at this. "I don't think we need to be concerned about that for now," he said quietly. "I agree that we should be thinking in that direction. But I called Amos Good this morning, and he told me that the Ontario churches haven't made any of those four points a test of membership. He said they are encouraging growth in these areas by teaching, but haven't yet taken it any further. Nor did he think they would, for now. And their congregation has been in existence for three years longer than ours."

Henry frowned a little at this. "I know the Ontario churches have been a little slow in drawing the line in these areas," he said slowly. "I don't understand their hesitation to take a firm stand. But Richard is right—the group here is not likely to be cut off for now."

Laverne Jackson raised his hand. "I'm not quite sure what the fuss is all about," he said laconically. "I'm pretty well satisfied with how we are now. Why do we have to make changes? We seem to be getting along fine."

Robert Fox and the other brother who had spoken earlier exchanged glances, and then Robert spoke up again. "Some of our members still look the same as they did in the old church," he said, somewhat pointedly. "If we aren't going to be more conservative, why did we even bother changing churches? My wife and I have made a number of changes since we left the old church."

Dale knew this was true. Nor was he surprised that Robert was speaking up on these issues. He had always tended to be somewhat outspoken. In spite of this though, Dale appreciated Robert's determination to stand for truth. But he noticed the grim look on Laverne's face and wished Robert would soften his approach just a little.

Laverne didn't speak up again, but Blake's father did. "I suppose most of us agree that we would like to see some growth in these areas," he said. "I would be willing to add them to the constitution if we could give some time before they come into effect. Some of our sisters would need to do a lot of sewing and spend a lot of money if we make such a change effective immediately. But if we were to give a year, they could wear out some of their older dresses and do a more gradual changeover."

Richard nodded. "I would go along with that," he said. "It would make the transition easier. Also, it would give time for spiritual growth. Not everyone sees it this way, and we don't want to make it appear as if we were pushing anyone out."

Robert Fox's frown deepened. "I'm not so sure," he

protested. "No one should need a year to stop doing something that's wrong. I'm not sure that we are taking these areas seriously enough."

Dale could see that Henry tended to agree with Robert. "I can sympathize with your feeling," he answered Robert slowly. "I would have thought so too. But it does seem that our seasoned brethren would prefer an approach that is a little more cautious. I agree that they also have given good advice."

He bit his lip thoughtfully. "Let's do it this way," he said finally. "First, we'll take a vote on whether or not we want to see these four changes made. If that carries, we will vote on how soon to make them mandatory."

The first vote carried, with everyone but Laverne Jackson in favor. Graham and Henry did not vote.

"All right, that carried," Henry said. "Now let's vote again. How many want to give a grace period before making these changes mandatory?"

This vote also carried. Laverne voted in favor, and Robert Fox voted against it. Again, Graham didn't vote. Henry glanced at him and then turned his attention back to the group. "That has carried," he said. "Now we need to decide how long this grace period will be. Let's not make it too long, so it doesn't end up neverending."

Robert Fox said, "Six months," and Laverne Jackson said, "Two years," at the same time. Henry smiled, and a ripple of amusement ran across the audience.

After a moment of silence, Richard suggested, "How about one year?"

No one else spoke up. "All right, let's vote on those three suggestions," Henry said. "If we don't have a fifty percent majority for one of them, we'll drop the lowest and vote again."

The vote carried for a year. Laverne voted for two years, and Robert for six months, but everyone else, including Graham, voted for a year.

Henry smiled. "We're fairly unified on that," he said, relief evident in his voice. "So we will plan that way. I would encourage you not to wait for the deadline to start changing. The reason for the grace period is to make it possible, especially for our sisters, to make an orderly transition to the new stand. I don't think it should be necessary to wait a year to get rid of a radio. That doesn't really present a hardship in my opinion."

The meeting relaxed after this, though Dale noted that Laverne and his wife didn't seem happy at the decision. The rest of the members, including Robert Fox, seemed relieved at the position they had taken. Henry was obviously pleased after the service and seemed to agree that it was the right decision.

The week went by rapidly. Jane didn't say much more about the changes she would have to make, while Dale was around. But she was very quiet all week, and Dale sensed that she was going through a struggle. He might have been tempted to brush it off as being a little touchy on her part, but he remembered too well Sheila's struggles with the same issues and what it had cost him. He realized that such changes looked like a much bigger hurdle to a girl than they did to him, and he spent some extra time praying for her and the other sisters, that the change might not be too hard for them.

Friday evening brought counsel meeting. Dale could see that Graham seemed under pressure when he opened the service. But it wasn't until Henry stood up to take charge of the open expression, that he understood why.

Henry looked across the audience. "First, I am going to read the list of those whom we have accepted as charter members," he said. "This includes all those who have been regularly attending, except Laverne Jackson and his wife. They said they want a little more time before deciding. So we will give them another six months."

He hesitated. "Also," he added, "I neglected to say that anyone applying for membership from now on will be expected to go through a six-month proving period and to measure up to the new standards before being taken in. This will apply to Laverne and his wife as well."

Dale's heart sank a little. So there would be some casualties. He had hoped that the congregation's willingness to give a period of grace would solve the difficulties, but apparently Laverne's wife hadn't gone along with the idea. All of a sudden, it dawned on him—they were meeting in Laverne's garage. What if Laverne's stopped coming altogether and went back to the old church? Would they lose their place of worship?

His mind came back to the present as Henry started giving instructions for the counsel service. He wanted every member to give his personal testimony, as well as a declaration that he was at peace with God, with the church, and with his fellow man. "These areas are important," Henry added. "They are a basic synopsis of our Christian experience. In the old churches, members often took Communion when they hadn't taken care of issues in their life. We want to be sure that everyone is worthy to partake of Communion, as far as he knows."

Dale became more and more sober as member after member gave his testimony of peace. This was what he had longed for, for so long—a pure church. But somehow he hadn't realized what a responsibility this would place on him to ensure that he was a worthy member. Was he at peace with God? As far as he knew. With the church? As far as he could tell. With his fellow man? He couldn't remember anything that stood between him and anyone else.

The congregation was quieter than normal after the service. Dale could see that he wasn't the only one who had taken it seriously. He turned to Blake. "That was different from any counsel service I have ever been at," he commented. "Everyone sure took it seriously."

Blake nodded. "It's what we wanted," he said simply. "It's what we have longed for." But then he added seriously, "You know, though, I never realized how it would affect me. Each one of us has to do his part if we are going to keep the church pure."

Dale nodded. "I sure hope Laverne's don't back out entirely," he said. "I had hoped that we could all take part in this service. They have been with us all along, and it hurts to see them drop out at the last minute like that."

Sunday's service was meaningful too, but almost an anticlimax after the counsel meeting. At the close of the meeting, Henry made another announcement that startled Dale.

"Just one more thing before we have a closing song," Henry said. "When I come back in six weeks, I want to take your counsel about ordaining a deacon. Brother Graham is all alone in the leadership here, and we believe that it is good to have a plural ministry. So you spend some time thinking and praying about that in the meantime."

It soon became obvious that Laverne and his wife were not happy with the direction the new church was taking. They didn't make any efforts to make the changes that the church had agreed on. Even though the services were held at their home, they weren't always there, and the congregation discovered that they were going back to the old church at times.

It all came to a head when Henry came back six weeks later. He and Graham went to visit them. No one ever found out what all happened during that visit, since the ministry didn't discuss it. But that Wednesday evening, neither Laverne nor his wife was present. However, after the benediction, Laverne entered the room, walked to the front, and asked for the group's attention. "I'm sure all of you know by now that we aren't real happy with the direction this group is taking," he said. "It isn't quite what we had in mind when we came along with you. I thought maybe things would ease off a bit after the novelty wore off, but it doesn't look like it will. So we have decided to go back to the old church. I'd like to have my garage back, so I'd appreciate if you would look for somewhere else to get together. I won't kick you out, but I'd like to store some stuff in here; so if you could be out in three weeks or so, it would be great."

This started a buzz of conversation. Now what would they do? Was there a building around that they could rent? For a moment the deacon counsel scheduled for the next evening was forgotten.

The next evening the group met early for a time of prayer together. Dale could tell that Laverne's announcement had jolted the little group. Even though they had known for a while that Laverne's weren't happy, the parting of ways went hard—almost as if they had lost part of the family. Then too, there was the sudden need of finding a new place to worship, as well as the decision about an ordination that faced them.

Dale felt a little depressed that evening. Somehow, he had not been ready for such realities, even though he had realized that church life would never be perfect. But he had liked Laverne, and Laverne's action opened the old wounds of losing Sheila's and Allister's friendships. Was this what Scriptural church life consisted of?

He listened to the prayers of the brethren, and he sensed that they felt the loss. Henry also seemed very burdened when he prayed. Yet Dale sensed—and the others apparently did too—that God had not left them. The prayer time drew them together and strengthened them, giving the congregation renewed courage to enter the work of the evening.

Brother Henry closed the prayer time. During his prayer it finally dawned on Dale that the peace that came with the commitment to do God's will mattered more than the pain it brought. He continued to ponder that thought during the service and finally decided that this was a basic tenet of Scriptural church life—being ready to do what was right even if it was painful. Though they had been spared that pain in the old church, he knew well enough that such church life had never satisfied him. Anyway, he had suffered pain in the old church too—the pain of rejection by his fellow youth and the displeasure of his leaders. He finally decided that he would rather have the pain that came with being part of a Scriptural setting. The peace and satisfaction he enjoyed presently were worth it, even if church life wasn't the utopia he had somehow expected it to be.

Henry preached a short message on the need for a plural ministry. Then he and Graham went out into the entrance between the garage and Laverne's house. One at a time, each brother then went out to share with them his counsel concerning an ordination.

Dale had never been part of such a procedure. When

they had had a counsel in the old church, the younger men were never involved. But Henry expected every brother who was twenty-one or older to share in the decision-making process, so he and Blake were part of it. The responsibility of being part of a Scriptural congregation impressed Dale yet again. Somehow, he had not realized that members—including him—needed to be an active part of the process of making their new congregation be what God wanted it to be. It seemed to him that he was running into this realization at every turn, and it shook him.

He noticed that the other members felt much the same. The men were sober and left the room as if they were carrying a weight on their shoulders. They came back in stepping lighter, but still sober.

Then all of a sudden, it was his turn. He had come to the meeting feeling strongly that they should go ahead. But as he walked out to the counsel room, it dawned on him that it was quite possible that the decision of the evening might rest on his shoulders. The constitution required a seventy-five percent majority to go ahead. In a group their size, the outcome of the vote could easily depend on one or two people. Had he really read God's will properly? What if he was wrong? Was there anything in his life that might hinder this work or keep God from blessing it?

He almost shuddered as he stepped into the little entryway, but Henry's smile reassured him. "So what has the Lord laid on your heart?" Henry asked him. "I realize that something like this probably seems big to a young man like you, but we want you to tell us exactly how you feel."

Dale took heart. "I feel we should go ahead," he said, "even though this is a new process for me. I would much rather have let the older brethren make the decision, but I want to do my part too."

Henry smiled again. "Never underestimate God's power to lead you," he said. "Every member is important in this process."

Dale had been the last member to go out, and the ministry soon re-entered the room. Henry went straight to the front. "The Lord has given very clear direction tonight," he said simply. "The voice of the brethren is unanimous to go ahead. So I will plan to return in six weeks to ordain a deacon. We will have nominations on Friday evening and the ordination on Sunday evening. I will try to be here to have a Thursday evening service as well. I asked one of the bishops from Ontario to help with this, and it looks as if that date will work for him."

21

A New Family and a New Leader

"All things work together for good,
When God's ways are understood."

—Adapted

"I saw Laverne Jackson in town today," said Jane. The family was sitting around the kitchen table before bedtime. "He even said 'Hi,' but he seemed to be in a hurry."

"A lot of things have happened since Laverne's left us," Richard remarked. "That was almost two months ago."

It was true. The little congregation had moved out of Laverne's garage a month ago and was renting a building in town. And the Jacksons had—as Laverne had announced—gone back to the old church.

"I wonder how they're getting along in the old church," Dale said. "I heard that people don't quite accept them, even though the old church tried hard to win them back while they were with us."

"I'm not surprised," Richard said dryly. "We offended a lot of people who were trying to pretend that nothing was wrong, when we started our congregation. People don't forget that kind of thing very easily."

Uncle Dale paused here for a moment. "You know," he said thoughtfully, "some of those people still haven't forgotten it. Several years ago—about thirty-five years after that division—someone told me that he had relatives in the old church who still justified themselves for staying there because of the 'mistakes' we made when we left!"

He shook his head. "He used that as a lever to try to turn me against the group here," he added. "Imagine. Thirty-five years later."

At this point Dale's mother brought the teapot and some cups to the table. "Did I tell you that we will have company over the weekend of the ordination?" she asked. "Graham called today and wondered if we could put someone up. Apparently several families are coming from British Columbia to show their interest in the ordination."

Dale looked up quickly. "Who's coming?" he asked. "Anyone I know?"

His mother smiled and pushed the teapot toward him. "I don't know if you know them or not," she said. "The family that's coming here is from some small congregation in a sawmill community. They have a girl a little older than Jane. That's why they decided to put them here."

"Oh, goody," said Jane. "I need a good friend."

Dale grinned across the table at her. "Getting tired of Blake, are you?" he teased her. "Maybe I can have him back then."

Jane made a face at him. "Blake is more than just a friend, and you know that," she told him. "But I'd like to have a *girl* friend my age." She turned to her mother. "What's her name? Have I met her?"

"Her name is Rose," her mother answered. "I don't suppose you have met."

Dale set down his cup. "Did you say Rose?" he asked. "I've met her. She's as shy as—as Blake."

He turned to his sister. "You should get along great with her." He grinned. "You can do the talking, and she can do the listening."

Jane wrinkled up her nose at him. "Blake is *not* shy," she returned. "He's merely learned when to hold his tongue and when to speak. Anyway, you get along fine with him, so I don't see why I shouldn't get along with Rose."

Dale chuckled at the fire in her eyes. "You'll get along fine, I'm sure," he said more seriously. "She's a nice girl, as far as I know. If you can help her get over some of her timid ways, you'll be doing her a favor, but I think you'll get along."

Gary Yoder's—Rose's family—arrived on Wednesday evening before the ordination services started. After prayer meeting, the two families gathered around the Eberlys' dining room table for an informal time of visiting before going to bed. Dale noticed to his surprise that Jane and Rose were visiting enthusiastically at the other end of the table, with Rose doing quite well in holding up her end of the conversation. Jane noticed his glance and winked at him. He grinned at her and turned his attention to the conversation between Gary and Richard.

Gary was a light-haired man, with black glasses that constantly slipped down his nose, causing him to push them back with his index finger every several minutes. Surprisingly, Gary apparently was as vivacious as Rose was taciturn—though from the way things looked at the other end of the table, Dale had to admit that maybe he had been a little mistaken about Rose. . . .

"Actually, it appears that our community is going to disintegrate," Gary was saying. "The sawmill is going to shut down, and that will leave everyone without work."

Richard raised his eyebrows. "So can't you do any farming or truck gardening?" he asked. "Does the whole community depend on the sawmill?"

Gary shook his head. "We have about exhausted every

conceivable idea," he said. "The only way in and out of the village is by rail, so that makes it hard to get produce to market. It isn't really a farming area."

"That's too bad," Richard said sympathetically. "So you'll probably have to relocate."

Gary nodded and took a second cookie. "That's right," he said. "That was one reason for this trip. We would like to look around and see if the Lord might supply our need for a home here."

"Say, that would be great," Dale said. "It would be a switch to have a new family come, rather than have people leave."

Gary smiled. "Have you had a lot leave?" he asked.

"Not really," Richard said. "Laverne Jackson's went back to the old church recently, and that was a blow for all of us. But I agree, we would be happy for a family like yours to join us. Would you like us to take some time and show you around tomorrow? I know of some quarter sections with buildings that are for sale. There are a few acreages available too—country properties without farmland."

"That would be good," Gary said. "I'd be happy about any leads as far as work goes too. We have lost most of our savings just existing where we are, and we'll have to start almost from scratch. So I suppose farming is out of the question for now. But I've done construction work and carpentry."

"You shouldn't have a problem finding work," Richard said. "We can stop at a few places while we're looking around, and see what we can scare up."

They left it at that, and a few minutes later they broke up to get ready for bed. Down in his bedroom, Dale thought over the events of the evening. *Hmm. So Gary's are thinking of moving here. That's interesting. It would be nice to have another family here.*

He yawned and then remembered something else. *Say, that means that Jane gets a friend! And Rose—what kind of girl is she really? She seemed a lot more friendly tonight than I thought she was. She sure isn't boisterous, but neither was she as quiet as I thought.* He chuckled to himself. Trust Jane to get her out of her shell. Jane had often been the center of attention when she was young, and even now things were seldom quiet when she was around.

Dale was up with the sun the next morning. He had the chores to take care of and then a load of hay to deliver. They had a pre-nomination service scheduled for that evening, and he wanted to get back in good time to get ready. Richard and Gary were planning to spend the day looking around for a property and a job for Gary.

Dale got home in good time for supper, and Richard and Gary returned soon after he did. Dale could see from Gary's smile that their day had been successful. "I can work for a local carpenter crew," he told his wife cheerfully. "And the boss owns a house on the outskirts of town where we can live as long as I work for him. He made me a good offer, but he would like me to start within a month. I told him I would let him know before we left for home."

His wife smiled. "That sounds nice," she said.

"Maybe we should go and look at the house tomorrow," Gary said. "He said I could get the key from his wife if you wanted to see it. But I thought it looked pretty good."

"That would be fine," his wife said. "Though I'm sure if you're satisfied with it, I will be too. At least you would have a good job, and we could be part of a good church."

Richard chuckled. "You haven't really seen the church yet," he reminded them. "Maybe you should wait to decide until the weekend is over."

Gary pushed his glasses into place. "We will," he said. "But I'm sure that won't be a problem. I appreciate what I see in your home, and Brother Henry recommended the area highly."

The visiting bishop had the opening devotional that evening, and Brother Henry preached on the qualifications of church leaders. It was a serious message, emphasizing the leader's responsibility to God and his God-given authority in the church. Dale had never heard a message from this perspective before. He noticed the way Graham kept shifting in his seat, and his heart went out to him. *He's probably never heard anything like this before either. It certainly puts his job in a different light. I'm glad I'm not in his shoes. He's always just led out as sort of a moderator and allowed the congregation to make the decisions. But from what Henry's saying, he's not really filling his leadership role by doing that. I wonder if Henry is trying to give Graham some pointers indirectly.*

The message generated some discussion after the service. Dale had been sitting right behind some of the older men. He noticed Blake's father rub his chin thoughtfully and turn to Richard. "So, that's a bit of a different perspective," he said slowly, and Dale perked up his ears.

Richard nodded. "It's not what we were used to," he agreed. "I'm not sure what to think about it."

Robert Fox was right in front of them and overheard them. He looked surprised that the two older men would express any doubts. "Why, it's right there in the Bible," he said. "It's our part to submit, not to question."

The two older men looked at each other. Richard finally answered. "Well, yes and no," he said slowly. "We always submit to truth, but we do have a responsibility to be sure that it is truth before we just blindly submit. Remember, the men of Berea listened to Paul's preaching, and then they went home and studied the Scriptures to see if he was teaching the truth. The New Testament calls them honorable because they did this."

"But what about the leader's authority then?" Robert asked. "How can a leader have authority if we don't submit? That's what was wrong with the old church—no one listened to the ministry."

Richard smiled. "Submission is vital," he said. "But the men of Berea came back to Paul because they found he was teaching truth. Actually, the fact that they had tested his doctrine and found it sound made Paul's authority more effective. When a group agrees with its leaders and voluntarily submits, the leaders' authority is respected much more than if leaders just force people to agree and submit."

"That's right, brother." The hearty voice beside him made Dale jump, and the other three men looked startled too. Henry had apparently overheard most of the conversation. "I wasn't trying to force the congregation out of the picture," he added. "I was simply showing what a leader has to be ready to do if necessary. That was one problem with the old conferences—too much of the church conviction was simply leadership conviction. If the people had shared that conviction rather than simply submitting to the leaders' convictions, the church would never have drifted as it has. But when the strong leaders like Daniel Kauffman died, too much of the church's conviction died with them."

Blake's father nodded. "That's why we have situations like we had in the old church," he agreed. "Now the people lead the leaders, rather than the leaders leading the people. But it was all lost a generation ago by a lack of genuine conviction and commitment to follow truth. No amount of authority in the hands of the leaders would ever really change the hearts of the congregation."

Henry nodded. "I can see what you are saying," he

said. "I will have some things to say about that on Sunday morning, in my message about the congregation's response to their leaders."

Dale was very thoughtful the rest of the evening. Did any of the brethren really qualify for such a responsible position? He had thought he might nominate Blake's father the next evening, but now he realized that it might be easier for a more outgoing brother. Would it be proper for him to nominate his father?

The question went to bed with him. He had excused himself from the normal evening get-together in the kitchen so that he could spend some time in prayer before going to bed. He was beginning to realize that the future of their congregation could hinge on the man who was chosen to fill this position. He had never thought of it before, but it was probably important that the new deacon would be able to offset some of Graham's weaknesses as a leader.

His sleep was troubled that night.

The others in the little congregation must have had similar thoughts. Some of the men decided that they would fast at lunchtime and gather at the church for a time of prayer. It was strictly voluntary, but all the brethren, including the visitors, were at the meeting.

Graham led out, to Dale's surprise. Was Henry trying to give him some practice in being a leader? Whether this was the case or not, Graham did well in putting the group's concerns into perspective.

"I think we all feel the seriousness of what we are facing," he said simply. "The future of our little group may well depend on the choices we make tonight. I am sure we all wish someone else would make those choices for us, but God has made us responsible. So let's kneel together and ask God for wisdom."

Dale was impressed again by God's closeness as he listened to the prayers. *I'm sure God is hearing us. And I'm sure He will give us the wisdom we need tonight. He is just as concerned about this meeting as we are.* He started to relax. He would leave it in God's hands. Unless God showed him clearly that he should give a name that night, he would simply express his willingness to submit to God's choice.

In spite of his sense of peace, it was a long evening for Dale. First, the visiting bishop preached. Then he and Henry went into the anteroom and received the nominations of the members. Again, all the brethren twenty-one and older were expected to give their counsel. After everyone had gone out, it was another few minutes before the bishops came back in. Dale felt his heart beating faster from the suspense as Henry faced the congregation.

"We have two names," he said soberly. "Brother Richard Eberly and Brother Robert Fox have both been nominated."

Dale was sitting right behind his father. His heart went out to him as his father's head sank into his hands. Even

Henry seemed to be struggling for words. "Pray for our brethren and their wives," he said. "This will be a heart-searching time for them and for their families."

Dale did that. He prayed much for his parents and for Robert and his wife. He hadn't thought of Robert being included, but he could see that he had some qualities that would help to stabilize the congregation.

Dale's sense of peace stayed with him, and he submitted himself to God's choice. He wasn't sure how he would feel about having his father be a church leader. But he respected his parents and would support them any way he could, whether they were chosen or not.

And Robert? He would do the same for him, he decided. After all, God would choose, and God's choice would surely be for their best.

So it was that on Sunday evening, Richard Eberly and Robert Fox were sitting on the front row of chairs, facing two books—one of which contained a slip of paper that would change someone's life. The building was full. Several families had come from British Columbia, and some families from the old church had decided to come as well, swelling the ranks of the little congregation.

Then the moment arrived. The preliminaries were past, and it was up to Richard and Robert. Both men sat with bowed heads, trying to discern God's direction in choosing a book. Then Richard stood up and took the book closest to him. As soon as he sat down, Robert took the remaining book.

Dale held his breath as Brother Henry reached for his father's book and slowly turned the pages. He found nothing and returned the book; then he reached for Robert's book. Again, he turned the pages, and then he held up a slip of paper for all of them to see.

There was a catch in Henry's voice as he said, "The lot has been found in Brother Robert's book. The Lord has chosen."

The building was silent except for the muffled sobs of Brother Robert's wife. Then Henry continued, "Brother Robert, the Lord has chosen you to fill the office of a deacon. Please stand to receive your charge."

Dale could see the depth of emotion on Robert's face as he stood in front of Henry. *He's only six years older than I am. This would be a real challenge. He's probably wondering why God chose him instead of one of the more experienced brethren.*

After the meeting, Dale joined the row of people who wanted to meet those who had shared the lot. He could see the relief on his father's face, and he could feel it in the firmness of his handshake.

"Thanks for praying for us," Richard told him sincerely. "I could tell that you were. It means a lot to your mother and me to have a son who supports us like you do."

Dale's mother nodded but did not trust her voice to speak. But the grip of her hand spoke volumes to Dale.

He moved on to Robert and his wife and shook their

hands. "I'll be praying for you," he told them.

Robert shook his hand wordlessly. But then he caught himself before Dale moved on. "I'll be depending on your support," he said. "I really appreciate your contribution to our congregation. I don't feel that I am as qualified as your father would have been, but I will try my best, with God's help."

Dale could tell that he meant it.

22

Good Times, Bad Times

"To every thing there is a season,
and a time to every purpose under the heaven."
—Ecclesiastes 3:1

Gary Yoder's moved in about a month after the ordination. Jane and Rose became close friends, just as Jane had hoped. They spent a lot of time together—it seemed to Dale that whenever Blake wasn't around on a Sunday, Rose was.

But Dale was still puzzled about Rose, and he opened the subject one day some months later when he came into the house and found Jane alone in the kitchen. "What does Rose have against me?" he asked Jane. "When you two are alone together, you chatter away like two magpies. But the minute I sit down in the same room and try to visit, she shuts up tighter than the Calgary jail."

Jane laughed. "Are you jealous?" she asked. Then she

sobered down. "Actually, I think she just doesn't feel comfortable around boys she doesn't know. She tends to be shy by nature—she's talked some about the struggles she had when she was younger."

Dale shook his head. "Okay, I can see that," he said with a baffled look on his face. "But how can a person get to know her if she treats him as if he were a—a *leper*?"

Jane laughed at his emphasis. "She doesn't think you're a leper, I'm sure," she said. "I guess I hadn't thought of it before, but I know what you mean. But I'm sure she doesn't even think of it. She just automatically fades into the background when you come around."

She looked at Dale quizzically. "What's up?" she asked. "Why are you so worried about it? Or don't you want to talk about it?"

Dale walked over to the kitchen window and looked out across the back yard. "I don't know if anything is up," he said finally. "But I keep thinking she's a nice girl, when I see her around you, and I'd like to get to know her better. But when I come around, she seems to turn into someone else. I've never run into a girl before who simply wouldn't talk to me except to answer my questions."

Jane thoughtfully stirred the soup she was heating for lunch. "Just give her some time," she said finally. "Really, I think she admires you, but she doesn't want to be a 'boy-chaser.' I don't think she wants to be unfriendly, but she has good convictions about Christian reserve. Actually, I've learned a lot from her in that area."

She turned and looked at him directly. "Are you

interested in her?" she asked. "I couldn't think of a nicer girl for you."

Dale hesitated, and dodged her question for a moment. "You felt the same way about Sheila," he said. "How would you compare the two of them?"

Jane stopped stirring the soup and took it off the stove. "I really liked Sheila," she said slowly. "It still hurts me that she acted like she did. I thought she would make a good sister-in-law. If only she had gotten the kind of help from her parents that you and I did, I think she would have made it. She would have made a wonderful wife for you, but the way she is now . . ."

Dale nodded, and she continued, "I think the best thing you could do would be to find someone else. And I think Rose would be just what you need. She is a conscientious, spiritual girl. She's a thinker. She's not loud, but she is pleasant and friendly. In a lot of ways, she has many of the same good qualities Sheila had, only she has faced up to the struggles in her life and has conquered them. Sheila has never done that—and never will if she keeps on traveling the road she's on."

Dale looked out the window again. "I've been thinking and praying about it," he admitted. "But I'm going to wait a little longer. I want to be sure before I do anything more. But I wish I could get to know her a bit better first."

"I know," Jane said. "But you can be sure of one thing—if it does come to that point, she'll never do to you what Sheila did."

She set two soup plates on the table. Richard and Carrie had gone to the city to do some shopping, so the two were alone for dinner.

Jane waited until they had prayed and Dale had filled his plate. "You know," she said thoughtfully, "I've thought a lot about Sheila the last few months. I can understand some of the fear she had about changing her appearance. Wearing a cape dress and black stockings for the first time wasn't easy for me either."

She shuddered a little as she remembered that Sunday again. "And then that family from the old church was there to visit that morning," she added. "I was sure that they would go back and tell everyone that I was becoming a goody-goody."

Dale looked at her curiously. "Why does that kind of thing bother girls so much?" he asked. "I mean, I guess I was a bit nervous the first time or so that I wore my plain suit, but it wasn't as big an issue for me as Sheila made it."

Jane sighed. "I guess it's how we're made," she said. "Girls like to look nice, and we like to think other people think we look nice. Somehow, cape dresses and black stockings always seemed ugly to me. I didn't mind my mother wearing them, but it was really hard to decide to wear them myself.

"I suppose that's how Sheila felt too. And because of her background—and the way her parents felt—it was even harder. At least I knew my parents supported what I was doing. Blake helped me a lot too, of course."

Dale looked troubled. "I tried to help Sheila too," he said. "But maybe I didn't do enough. I told her I would never force her to change against her own will, but I think God was speaking to her about it. Anyway, it seemed that she just wanted to get away."

Jane nodded. "I met her in town the other day," she said. "She was friendly, but she was soon finished. I think she saw that I was wearing a cape dress. At least she looked at my dress and then left. She looked dreadfully unhappy. I felt so sorry for her."

Dale refilled his plate. "Well, Sheila is in the past," he said, a little tersely. "For her own sake, I wish she could find her way. But I don't think I could ever feel about her again like I used to."

He paused and buttered a slice of bread. "On the other hand," he added wistfully, "for the last half a year or so, I've had a real longing for someone to share life with. But I'm not sure I could ever feel like that about anyone else either. "

Jane looked at him sympathetically. "I really think Rose could fill that place," she said softly. "I'll pray about it with you."

So Dale kept on praying. But several months after this, he had a conversation with his father that gave him even more to pray about. They were delivering a load of hay together, and Dale was driving, as usual.

His father looked across at Dale. "So how do you feel about things at church by now?" he asked.

Dale steered around a gopher before answering. "I appreciate what we're doing," he said. "Robert's ordination has actually helped, though I had some qualms earlier." He paused and glanced in the mirror before dodging a pothole in the road. "Though I wonder about Graham sometimes."

His father's eyebrows lifted a little. "Oh? In what way?" he asked.

Dale pushed his hat back thoughtfully. "I'm not sure," he said slowly. "It's mostly a feeling I have. But he seems to be more and more in the background. He lets Robert lead out a lot of the time. And last Sunday, I sat beside him in Sunday school. He was still working on his sermon while the rest of us discussed the lesson."

His father nodded. "I was wondering if you were seeing some of that," he said soberly. "I've been pretty concerned the last while. Even the quality of his sermons has been slipping. They are more emotional and entertaining than helpful. I wonder how much time he really puts into them."

Dale nodded. "They were better at first," he admitted reluctantly. "I thought last Sunday's sermon especially was rather inane. I wonder how happy he really is here."

The group soon learned. Several weeks later was time for Communion again, and Henry was back to visit the congregation. The congregation never learned what all took place behind the scenes, but at the counsel meeting, both Graham and Robert made acknowledgments to the congregation.

Graham was first. "I realize that I have been shirking my responsibility. I was a bit offended when the group decided to choose another leader, and I have been pushing some of my duties off on Brother Robert. Also, I haven't been taking a lot of interest in preparing solid sermons. I guess you could say I've been lazy."

His head dropped. "I'm sorry for this," he added. "I want to do better. I do appreciate Brother Robert's help, and I want to work with him better."

Robert bounced to his feet in his characteristic way. "I too have some things to make right," he said. "I felt that Brother Graham was letting things slide. But instead of trying to encourage him to take care of them, I just went ahead and took care of them. Because of this, he felt I was pushing him aside in the ministry. I am sorry for this, and I too want to do better. I appreciate what Brother Graham has done for us since we started this group, and I want to support him in his leadership. I know I tend to be overbearing and intolerant, and I want you to pray for me that I will be loving and patient as God wants me to be."

These admissions shocked the congregation somewhat, though Dale noted that some didn't look as surprised as he felt. *I guess some of them realized what was happening. I'm glad that our leaders are willing to admit their weaknesses like this. It makes me feel closer to them.*

Henry looked over the group. "Both of your leaders have acknowledged failure," he said. "Those of you who are willing to forgive them and to assure them of your ongoing support, please stand up."

Dale stood, along with everyone else. Henry nodded for them to take their seats again. "Thank you," he said. "That was everyone."

He looked at the two rather downcast leaders on the front bench. "I trust you will allow God to work in you so that it doesn't need to happen again."

He looked at the congregation again. "All of us are human," he said. "That includes us as leaders. For instance, I know that I have a tendency to be gruff and unbending. I work with that all the time. Your leaders have confessed their tendencies. We all have similar weaknesses to work with. That does not trouble me as long as all of us—including those of us in the ministry—are open with each other and willing to accept help from each other."

This was a new thought for Dale. He had always found it hard to admit that he had a weakness. But now Henry made it sound like being open with the rest of the congregation about his struggles was a part of brotherhood.[1]

The Gary Yoder family was taken into membership that weekend as well, and Dale's mother invited them for lunch and the afternoon. The two families had become

---

1 This is an important point that too many church members today do not understand. God understands that we are human, and every member knows it too. If we pretend that we do not have human tendencies, we put a barrier between us and the brotherhood.

close friends, and it seemed a fitting way to commemorate the event. Jane invited Blake to come as well.

That afternoon, while the parents visited and the younger children played outside, Jane, Rose, Blake, and Dale sat around the dining room table, visiting and playing Chinese checkers.

During the game, Dale saw a side of Rose that he had never noticed before. In the first place, she was an astute player, winning two out of the first three games. And secondly, in the intensity of the game, she forgot herself a little and allowed her real person to show through the shell that she usually drew around herself when Dale and Blake were present.

In fact, she smiled triumphantly as she jumped a row of marbles that he had inadvertently lined up for her.

Dale moaned.

She grinned shyly at him. "Sorry, but I just couldn't resist it." Then she dropped her eyes in confusion as she realized what she had said. But her involuntary comment and Dale's answering laugh seemed to break the ice between them.

A little later, Blake and Jane went to the kitchen to make popcorn. Dale noticed Rose's hesitation—should she intrude in the kitchen, or should she stay in the dining room with Dale?

Casually he began placing marbles on the board again. "Which color do you want?" he asked. With another shy smile, she picked up some white marbles and started to place them on the board. He could tell that she was nervous; but as the game progressed, she forgot herself and increasingly relaxed. In the end—in spite of her bashfulness—she managed to win.

Dale turned his mouth down at the corners. "Where did you learn to play like that?" he asked. "I thought I was a good player until I saw you play."

Rose seemed a little embarrassed and pleased at the same time. "Chinese checkers was one of the few games we took along to British Columbia," she said. "We played it and played it in the wintertime. It was often too cold to do anything outside, so we sat around the fire in the evening and played games."

Dale pushed the game aside. "Well, it's no use my trying to beat you," he said. Then he changed the subject. "How long did you live in British Columbia?"

The conversation went on from there. Rose remained circumspect, but not distant, and Dale felt that he was actually getting to know her.

Jane and Blake returned too soon with the popcorn, but the conversation went on—though it became more general.

That night Dale had a hard time going to sleep. As he recalled the events of the afternoon, the image of a fine Christian girl with a shy smile kept surfacing in his mind. Was God answering his prayer? Was Rose the girl for him?

He went to sleep with a prayer in his heart.

Dale talked to his parents about his thoughts and

feelings the next day. "So what do you think?" he concluded. "Am I foolish to think of trying again?"

His father shook his head. "No, you aren't," he said deliberately. "I've thought of the same thing, and so has your mother. We both think highly of the Yoders and their family, and Rose seems like a good Christian girl. None of the things that troubled us about Sheila are a problem this time."

Dale nodded. "That's what I thought too," he said. "Still, I'm not in a hurry. I don't want to spoil things by rushing into this. Anyway, another month or so of praying about it can't hurt. I want to be sure God is pleased about the idea."

"That sounds good," his father said. "We'll pray about it too. But we have nothing against it once you feel ready."

A month later, Dale was still trying to decide whether to ask Rose for her friendship. Then his feelings were brought to a head by an event that put the whole congregation into a temporary tailspin. It seemed to be a normal Sunday morning, and no one in the little church had any inkling of the trouble that was just around the corner. Graham had the opening meditation, and Robert preached—something that happened several times a month. But at the end of the service, right after leading in closing prayer, Graham pulled a piece of paper from his Bible. "I have a statement that I would like to read to the congregation yet before we part," he said soberly. "I hope this isn't too big a shock, but I feel it is the proper thing for me to do."

He picked up the paper and read, " 'I have been having second thoughts about my involvement as a leader in this congregation. I do not feel that I can totally support the course that we seem to be taking under Brother Henry's administration. Due to this, I would like to be released from the responsibility of being your pastor. I am sorry where I have failed in my responsibilities, and trust that God will direct the group here according to His will. I am planning to take my family back to the congregation where we came from, for now, until the Lord sends us further direction.' "

A thunderbolt out of the blue sky could not have shocked the congregation more. Brother Graham—in spite of his weaknesses—had been their leader, and they had tried to support him. How could he do this to them? Where had they failed?

Dale could hardly remember being more despondent than he felt that day. Rose had come along with Jane for dinner and the afternoon, and all of a sudden he felt a deep longing for someone to share his feelings with. *Sheila was always ready to share her feelings with me, and I always found it easy to share mine with her. I wonder if I could really have a relationship like that with Rose. I wonder what she would say.*

After lunch Dale went down to his room, but he couldn't rest. He could hear Jane and Rose chattering upstairs as they did the dishes. For a moment, he contemplated going back up to join them. But what if Rose didn't understand? What if she thought he was a lady's man—just interested in a good time? He didn't think he could bear another disappointment. Should he just leave it again?

He sat on the side of his bed and then finally sank to his knees beside it. Why did Graham have to do this? Was church life just to be one disappointment after the other?

Several hours later, he heard a car drive in. *Say, that must be Blake. I think Jane said he's coming for supper. I wonder why she asked Rose over if Blake is coming. Rose will feel out of place with him here. Maybe I should go up and be with them too. That way it won't be so awkward for her.*

So it was that a few minutes later, the four had settled in the living room together. Rose had been more open with Dale since their game of checkers, but he could see that she felt a little uneasy. All of a sudden, he realized how she was feeling. *She is probably wondering what I have in mind. She does not want to seem too friendly, yet she probably does not want to be standoffish either, in case I am interested. I'll have to let her know how I feel.*

Naturally, the conversation centered on what had happened that morning. "How could Graham decide to go and leave us?" Jane asked, a catch in her voice. "We were just like one large, happy family since the Jacksons left."

Dale's shoulders sagged a little as his mind came back to earth. "I know," he said wearily. "I've been wondering too. Is church life just going to be one disappointment after the other?"

Blake shook his head. “We’ve had a lot of good times together as a congregation,” he said. “We mustn’t forget those. This is just a low point.”

“I suppose Satan just decided it’s time to give us another blow,” Dale said. “But I feel sorry for Graham. I don’t think the old church will accept him any better than they did the Jacksons. I wonder why he felt he had to do that? He could just have resigned and stayed as a member.”

“I wonder if he felt that he couldn’t lead the church well enough to satisfy Henry,” Blake said. “But I don’t believe Henry would make it hard for him if he stayed. Henry really isn’t anyone to be afraid of.”

The conversation died for a moment, and then Jane jumped to her feet. “Let’s go outside for a walk,” she said impulsively. “It’s too nice out to be cooped up in the house all day.”

The others agreed. “Let’s walk back to the canal and see if we can see some deer or antelope,” Dale suggested.

It was a beautiful day. And it became more so for Dale, with Rose as his partner. It came about very naturally, since Blake and Jane walked together. In order not to intrude on their conversation, Dale and Rose ended up lagging behind and starting their own conversation. To his surprise, Rose talked to him almost as easily as she did to Jane, though he noticed again that she was more reserved than the girls he had been used to. But somehow, today it didn’t bother him.

Rose seemed to sense, however, that Dale had something on his mind. Gradually their conversation died down, and they walked quietly for a few moments. Dale knew that this was his chance. He would have to decide right now. *Should I or shouldn't I? It isn't fair to her to keep putting it off. But what if it doesn't work out? Still, I won't find a more sincere girl anywhere, and my parents approve of her. I guess I could write her a letter. But somehow that seems to be the coward's way out.*[2]

He took a deep breath and stopped walking. Rose stopped too and looked up at him curiously; then she caught her breath and dropped her eyes as she saw the look on his face.

"Rose," he said gently, then stopped. She didn't answer or look at him. He took another deep breath and tried again. "Rose, I—I was wondering if you would care to start—to start . . ." He ground helplessly to a halt. Why was it so hard to get his thoughts out? He had never had such a problem when he asked Sheila.

"You see, I—I've been interested in you for quite a while," he said, trying again. "Would you be interested in starting a closer friendship so that we could learn to know each other better?" He breathed a sigh of relief. There, it was finally out.

Rose blushed and pushed a pebble around with her toe. He waited quietly until she looked up at him. "Could I have a week to think and pray about it and to discuss it with my parents?" she asked quietly.

---

2 Proposing courtship to a girl by letter was not nearly as common then as today. Also, young men seldom asked the girl's father first for permission, as is expected in some areas today.

He nodded. "Certainly," he said. "I've had lots of time to do that—it's only fair for you to do the same. I would much rather have a no now than a year from now." He paused and then added, "And even if you decide not to, let's stay friends anyway, okay?"

Rose nodded mutely. "I'll let you know by next Sunday," she said softly.

Henry made a special trip to try to help Graham, but to no avail. He preached to the despondent group on Wednesday evening, at their regular prayer service. "I'm sorry to tell you that I have not been able to persuade Graham to change his mind," he told them. "He feels that he simply can't handle the pressure. He wants to get away completely."

He looked around the room before continuing. "I know that this is a disappointment to all of us. Brother Graham had some weaknesses—we all do—but we all loved him. Let's keep praying for him. I'm sure he will not be happy back in the setting he came from.

"But don't let this discourage you," he finished. "Instead, let it make you more sensitive to notice the needs of those in your midst who might be struggling. We will go on with God's help. Brother Robert will be in charge here for now. Remember him and his wife in your prayers."

23

Roses Bloom in the Springtime

"He hath made every thing beautiful in his time:
also he hath set the world in their heart,
so that no man can find out the work that God maketh
from the beginning to the end."
—Ecclesiastes 3:11

In one sense, it was a long week for Dale, since he was eager for Rose's answer. Yet he felt at rest about it and certain that God was leading. Whichever answer she gave, he would accept it as God's answer. Yet he knew deep in his heart that he would be disappointed if she turned him down.

Friday evening was a leisurely meal. While they were finishing their after-supper coffee, Jane suddenly looked at Dale. "You know what I heard in town today?" she asked. "Sheila is getting married to Andrew Martens—the boy she dated after she broke up with you."

Dale looked blank. "I thought she had broken up with Anne Carter's crowd," he said. "Isn't Andrew part of that group?"

"Apparently not," Jane said. "Anyway, they're getting married in about three months, or so I heard. I hope she'll be happy."

Richard had been listening to this exchange quietly. "So how do you feel about that, Dale?" he asked. "Does it still hurt?"

Dale pondered the question for a moment. "No, not really," he said. "I still feel sorry for her, and sometimes I think of her, but the old flame is gone. I'm not jealous at all. God took me a direction that she wasn't willing to go. I guess she was wiser than I was, and understood that we were going different directions."

His father sighed. "She was a nice girl," he said. "I still think that someone will need to give an account to God someday for her loss. Unfortunately, there are many others like her."

He shook his head. "It's true that every person is responsible for his own choices," he added. "Sheila could have chosen a different course. But I would hate to be in the shoes of the parents and church leaders who helped to lead young people like that astray. So many could have been rescued with the proper guidance and example."

He turned to Dale. "What's happened to Allister?" he asked. "Have you heard about him recently?"

Dale bit his lip. "I haven't heard much," he said. "But it sounds like he has pretty well lost out." He shook his head. "I was afraid of that all along," he added. "If only he could have come with us, I think he would have made it. But he has never had the strength to stand alone."

Jane started to gather up the dirty dishes. "That's too bad," she said. "I always liked Allister. But you know," she added soberly, "we probably wouldn't be much better off if our parents hadn't given us the help we needed."

Dale nodded. "I know," he said. "I've been really grateful for my home. And also for my congregation," he added.

Sunday morning finally came, and Dale felt a little queasy as he drove to church. When would she tell him? Would she say yes? How would her parents react to it?

It seemed like a long morning to him. He could see Rose clearly from where he sat, but he couldn't tell what she was thinking. He had met her father on the way into church, but Gary had just greeted him like normal—cheerful as usual, but without a wink or remark such as Donald would have given him. *Oh well, I'd rather have it this way. Donald actually made a lot of trouble for me.*

After church was over, Dale chatted with Blake for a bit, but he kept his eye on Rose. He noticed that she slipped outside alone after a little. Should he follow her? He didn't want to seem too anxious, but he did have to find out somehow. Finally he decided to go outside and see if he could find her.

Outside, he looked around the parking lot. *Where is*

she? Their car is still here. Did she walk home? The Yoders' house wasn't far away, and the family sometimes walked. Then, just as he was about to give up and go to his car, he noticed her at the side of the building. She must have walked around the church while she was waiting for him.

Quietly he walked over to her. "So how are you this morning?" he asked. Inside he was a little irritated at himself. *Why should I be so nervous? I'm acting stupid! You'd think I was just a teenager.*

Rose's shy smile set him more at ease. "I'm fine," she answered him softly. "It's such a beautiful day," she added. "I just had to come outside and enjoy it."

He looked down at her, and she looked at the ground. "So have you had enough time to make your decision?" he asked her gently. "I don't want to pressure you if you want more time."

She hesitated a moment and then looked up at him. "I would be happy for a friendship to get to know each other better," she said softly. "My parents are really pleased, and I'm glad too."

Dale felt as if a load had rolled off his shoulders. He hadn't realized up to that moment how much he had wanted her to say yes. He smiled. "Did your parents have any particular guidelines they want us to follow?"

She nodded. "A few," she said. "Why don't you come over for supper, and we can talk to them about it. They said I should invite you. We don't have church this evening, and we usually try to make that a family time together. Everyone would be glad for you to come."

Blake and Jane came out of the church at that point, and Dale motioned them over. "We'll tell you the news first!"

Blake's face broke into a big smile.

"Oh, I'm so happy for both of you," Jane said, smiling. She turned to Dale. "I have been praying that this would work out for you."

Dale told his parents as soon as they got home from church. They were just as pleased as Jane had been. "I'm so glad for you," his mother said. "I have been praying for so long that you would find a good girl. I know you've gone through hard times, but all the while the Lord was preparing a wonderful gift for you."

Dale's father nodded. "God bless you, son," he said huskily. "We'll keep on praying."

It seemed almost like old times as Dale crawled into his car that afternoon. Yet, so much had changed as well. He was going to see a different girl. Now he had a Scriptural congregation to back up his courtship, and Rose was solidly in support of his convictions. And her parents would not just tolerate his convictions because they liked him, but they would encourage him because they knew that his convictions were right.

His thoughts refocused as he drove into the Yoders' driveway. In fact, his heart beat a little faster as he walked up the path to the door. Would Rose meet him at the door? Sure enough, there she was—her face lit up in her now-familiar shy smile. "Come in," she invited him. "Supper will soon be ready!"

He followed her into the living room, where the rest of the family was waiting. Gary got to his feet with a big smile of welcome. "I'm glad you're here," he said. "Have a chair."

Rose's mother shook his hand as well and added a few quiet words of welcome; then she and Rose excused themselves to get supper on the table. Dale settled down on a slightly dilapidated couch and relaxed. Somehow he felt at home here. He knew there wouldn't be any surprises or pressure to watch out for.

After supper, the family sat around the dining room table and played some word games. Rose bashfully pulled up a chair beside Dale, and they joined in the game. Dale soon discovered that he had met his match in about every game. "Where do you learn all these words?" he asked in despair when she slipped a word away from under his nose.

She smiled and blushed a little. "I don't know," she said. "I like to read, I guess. And we've played this game ever since I can remember."

Her father smiled. "We've always liked family games," he said. "And this is one of our favorites."

Rose looked at Dale and smiled. "This and Chinese checkers," she added.

Somewhat later, the younger children were sent to bed, and Dale and Rose spent some time chatting with Rose's parents.

Finally, Gary smiled at his wife. "Well, we should let Dale and Rose have some time to themselves," he said cheerfully. He turned to Dale again. "I thought I would share a few guidelines for you to think about," he added.

Dale nodded, and Gary continued. "We trust you and Rose entirely," he said. "And we know that you are both old enough to be making some decisions on your own."

He paused and smiled again. "I don't think I'll tell you exactly how often you can be together," he said. "There are always exceptions to rules like that. My main concern is that you aren't together too much. Give yourselves enough time to be alone, but then also take time to be with others. That way you can have a better perspective of what your courtship is all about."

He hesitated again and looked at Dale. "I don't suppose we have to talk about what kind of courtship standards you should have, do we?" he asked.

Dale smiled. "I've got some pretty firm convictions along that line," he said. "I think that any Christian boy will respect the girl he's courting—or any girl for that matter—enough that he will have a hands-off policy."

He sat back in his chair and looked at Gary directly. "I saw so much otherwise in the old church," he said. "It seemed that poor courtship practices were status things. They made you part of the in crowd. That was one reason I never went for casual dating."

Gary looked relieved. "Well, we'll keep in touch," he said. "I would appreciate it if you would try to end your visits by 11:00, or have them in the afternoon. Like I said, I don't believe in too many hard and fast rules in courtship, because too often circumstances make it awkward. If you're reasonable about it, we will be too."

With that, he got up. Rose's mother did too, but she paused for a moment and looked down fondly at her daughter. "Have a good time," she said softly. "We'll be praying for both of you during this time, that you might find your way in God's will." She rested her hand lightly on Rose's shoulder for a moment and Dale saw the look that passed between them. Then her mother slipped away, and they were alone.

Rose sat quietly for a moment. Dale noticed a look of panic in her eyes as she suddenly realized that it was up to her to entertain him now. *She is still her shy self on the inside. I'll have to make her feel at ease.* He thought a moment. Then he asked, "Do you have a Bible close by? Maybe we could spend a bit of time looking at some verses together."

He saw the look of relief on her face and almost smiled. "That would be nice," she said. "I'll get mine."

Rose relaxed visibly as they read and discussed the first part of the first chapter of John together. The time flew, and the first thing Dale knew, it was almost time for him to leave. He closed the Bible and looked at her. "Shall we pray together?"

She nodded her head. "I think that would be nice," she said softly. "We need God's direction and blessing."

They bowed their heads while Dale prayed.

It was a meaningful way to end a happy evening.

Dale had a lot to think about on the way home. He

parked his car behind the house at home and stood beside it for a few moments, looking at the sky. It was a clear night, without a moon, and the stars were bright and beautiful. He stood there, admiring the stars and thinking back over the evening.

God surely had been good to him! He had been brought up in a home with parents who cared for him. He belonged to a church filled with caring brothers and sisters. Now God had given him a wonderful friend and the expectation of setting up a home with God's blessing.

He bowed his head and whispered, "Thank You, Lord! You have given me so much more than I deserve."

Aunt Rose had stepped out on the porch in time to hear the last part of Uncle Dale's story. He reached over and took her hand. "God has been good to us, hasn't He," he said, a little gruffly. It wasn't a question, but she nodded in agreement.

Postlude

Uncle Dale's Last Words

*"Remember now thy Creator in the days of thy youth,
while the evil days come not, nor the years draw nigh,
when thou shalt say, I have no pleasure in them."*
—Ecclesiastes 12:1

Uncle Dale's story had a profound effect on me. I had almost lived through it with him, and at first I had a hard time realizing that we were actually living forty years later. But I knew for sure now that I would have to write this story for others to read.

First, I had a few questions.

"Uncle Dale," I said hesitantly, "what happened to Sheila? and Allister?"

Uncle Dale and Aunt Rose looked at each other. "Sheila had a pretty hard life," Uncle Dale said soberly. "Andrew was always pushing her into things that she didn't really want to do. He ended up leaving the church, and eventually she went to a community church with him.

"He died about five years ago, and we went to the funeral. I met Sheila there for the first time in years. She had changed a lot." Uncle Dale fingered his cane. "She was heavier than I remembered her, and gray. That is only natural, I guess—she could say the same about me. But it looked like she had let go of life. She had a smile for me, but it wasn't natural—it's haunted me ever since. It was too bright for her husband's funeral, and too bright for meeting me. I think she knew that I knew."

"You knew what?" I was puzzled.

"That I knew how she felt, down inside. None of her children are in any church. Most of them are divorced and remarried. There they stood beside her, and not a godly one among them."

He shook his head, as if to make the thoughts go away. "I almost can't stand it," he said. "She wanted so badly to do what was right, at one point in her life. Yet it seems that she never made that connection with God—probably because she wasn't willing to stand alone and be different from the rest of the crowd."

He cleared his throat before continuing. "As for Allister, he was a pharmacist in town for years. A few years ago, he told me his story. He got all messed up in the university—girls and alcohol mostly. He's been married three times, and had a number of women that he never married. He is in a Lodge now, just living out his life. He told me that he had wanted badly to be part of us when we left, but he was afraid of his mother. He hasn't gone to church for years. He told me right out that he has no hope, but he wasn't interested when I tried to help him back to the Lord. He just didn't seem to care."

I was a little shocked. "Surely not everyone in the old church turned out that way," I said. "I mean, I know some of them, and they're nice people."

Uncle Dale nodded. "That's right," he agreed. "But not one of them is standing for the truths the church taught fifty or sixty years ago. They're just a nominal church group now—with less spiritual zeal than most community churches in town."

He looked at me. "I still think that lots of the young people I went to church with back there would have turned out all right if they had been given the privileges that our young people have today," he said. He shook his head. "But you know," he continued gravely, "too many of our people don't realize the advantages they have. They grumble that the church has rules. Sheila would have been glad for a church that gave her some guidance. I also hear young people grumble that their parents are too strict. In fact, some of our youth would probably be glad for parents like Sheila had. But Sheila would have given much, if only her parents had given her direction like we try to give our children today."

He shook his head again. "The young people in the sixties were offered up on the altar of progress. They had a choice, I guess, but not really much of one. Their parents and church leaders thought they were preparing a better future for them, but instead, they ruined their lives.

A few were salvaged. Thank God I was one of them. But so many weren't. And most of them are lost today."

He rested his chin on his cane and looked out across the back yard. "You know," he said softly, "in another decade or two, we'll all be gone, probably. Some of us will go before that. My generation has paid the price for the church's failure."

I left Uncle Dale and Aunt Rose then.

The next week Aunt Rose called me. She had tears in her voice. "Dale died last night," she said softly. "I wanted to be the first to tell you. He wanted me to say good-bye to you . . ."

I went to Uncle Dale's funeral. All day I was in a daze. But at the viewing before the service, I saw an older woman stop at his coffin and look at him for a few moments, while tears ran down her face. That puzzled me because she was a worldly woman I had never seen before. Why was she crying? I looked at Aunt Rose, who was standing beside me.

She answered my wordless question. "That's Sheila," she said gently.